TORTURED ROYALS

TORTURED ROYALS

GAME OF PSYCHOS
BOOK THREE

MIA HARTSON

ISBN: 978-1-7638148-1-3
First printing edition 2025 in United States
Cover design by Trif Book Design

Mia Hartson
PO BOX 1052, Golden Grove Village, SA 5125
www.miahartson.com

I thought you were here to break me, enchantress.
I didn't realize you would make me whole again.
~ Alaric

~

For the readers who have continued until the end. Thank you for coming on this journey with me. I hope you enjoy reading the conclusion to Blake's story. xx

TRIGGER WARNING

This story includes some dark themes and distressing content, including violence and the death of a family member. Please take care of yourself while reading. For the full list of content warnings, please visit www.miahartson.com/triggerwarnings

~ Princess Blake ~

A circle of red fire burns in the distance, the crimson flames barely visible amidst the plumes of smoke curling up from the piles of rubble. The portal is exactly where the demon soldier, Sebastian, instructed, the gateway nestled between the remnants of two Perstalian buildings that are still smouldering. Or at least, they used to be buildings. Now, they're nothing more than large piles of blackened stone. Flakes of ash rain down around us, collecting on my eyelashes, and I swipe my hand across my eyes.

"Collect the other soldiers," I order Sebastian. "And follow us to Toralyn." I figure Dad left the demon guards here for me, so I may as well make use of them.

The demon soldier slams his fist to his chest and rigidly bows before hurrying off. I don't pause to see where he's headed. I simply stride straight for the gateway, not waiting for my mates.

"You sure this is a good idea, gorgeous?" Nate, my shifter mate, asks from close behind me.

I ignore him, not missing a step.

"*Blake,*" Shade says, and my crow friend's voice is uncertain as she shifts uncomfortably on my shoulder, hopping from one foot to the other. "*Let's hold on a sec. We don't know what's waiting for us in the angel realm.*"

I still don't stop. "*Dad left the portal open for me. He's expecting me to join him.*" I'm sure Shade realizes the demon king isn't the only reason I'm going. When Sebastian told us the witches were attacking Toralyn, the look of panic and fury on Prince Callan's face was enough to spur me into action, desperate to grab my blades and get to work.

The archangel catches up to me in a few strides, and he walks directly beside me, his expression hard. If I hesitate, I know he'll go without me. If I hesitate, I could lose my mate. If I hesitate, the witches might conquer the angels and take the demon king down. And the demon realm could be next.

It's not until I'm close to the gateway that there's a split second when I doubt my decision. I've never been to Toralyn. My angel mother abandoned me soon after birth, and I hadn't wanted anything to do with her kind. I'd purposely let myself ignore everything about the realm of the angels aside from the basics I was forced to learn during my schooling. A foolish mistake that won't serve me well now. Not that the angels ever reached out to connect with me.

Forcing myself to ignore the twisting, churning sensation in my stomach, I draw my daggers and step into the portal.

Magic sizzles against my skin, the colors around me a blur of black and red, and then Shade and I are through. I lift my blades, preparing for an attack, but I'm surprised to find there's no one on the other side. Blackened trees surround me in all directions, their scorched branches, thin and shriveled, and an unsettling silence hangs heavy around us. I suck in a sharp breath as a breeze whistles through the forest, and a chill crawls down my spine.

"Uh, Blake, this isn't exactly how I imagined the realm of the angels," Blake says in my head. *"I thought everything would be gold and shiny, and not..."*

"Dead?" I finish for her.

"Exactly."

My brows knit together as I peer at the delicate blades of grass which are the color of ash beneath my boots. They crumble to dust as I walk forward, moving between the thin, blackened trees.

Prince Callan emerges from the portal behind me, and he lets out a harsh breath as he takes in the scene around us. "No." The word is a cracked whisper as it leaves his lips, and my heart aches for my mate.

Walking over, he stops before a tree branch and reaches up. As his fingers brush against a blackened leaf, the leaf turns to ash and the fine grains are blown away by the wind.

"This is Eresten, the golden forest," he mutters, his expression stone-cold as his gaze sweeps the desolate landscape.

The rest of my mates emerge from the portal, and Nate curses as they step away from the gateway. They all have their weapons out in an instant, and their sharp gazes assess the area.

When it's clear there's no immediate danger, Dante sheaths his sword. My demon mate walks over, and he runs his hand along a tree trunk. Pulling his hand back, he stares at the black dust on his palm. "What happened here?"

Mason clenches his jaw as his expression darkens. "This looks like the work of witches. It seems Perstalia isn't the only place to suffer."

Nate curses again. "So, we're too late?"

Mason moves to my side, and I can tell my winged centaur mate wants to grab me and pull me closer, but he doesn't. Everything feels wrong as we stand there in that section of dead wood.

Prince Callan stalks ahead, weaving through the trees to the edge of a nearby cliff. Rays of sunlight make his golden wings glitter as he stands there overlooking the land below, his body rigid.

"We saw what the witches did in Perstalia," Alaric growls, and my attention goes to my assassin mate. "If this continues, soon all the realms will be suffering."

This time, Mason sheathes his blade and reaches for me, his hand winding around my waist. His fingers send warmth into me, but I can't relax, no matter how good his touch feels.

"Sorry," I say to my centaur, a twinge of guilt going through me when I think of all he's been through. "It looks like I've dragged you into another war."

There's no regret and only resolve in Mason's eyes. "The choice to leave The Haven was mine, my mate. For years, I have not lived but have merely survived, tormented by the past. I am glad to be able to fight by your side."

I give him a small smile as Shade lifts from my shoulder, flapping into the air and flying above the trees.

"Do you think the demon king has returned to Seral?" Alaric asks, crossing his arms.

I shake my head, uncertain. "Maybe. But if he has—"

At that moment, the wind in the forest changes direction, and my words falter as a low growl rumbles from Nate's throat.

My head whips toward the shifter. "What is it?"

"Blood," Nate answers. "It's faint, but I smell them."

"Them?" Dante asks, his brows lifting.

"The witches," Nate replies sharply, his slitted eyes focused on the cliff ahead—at the very spot where Prince Callan had stood moments ago.

"Where's Callan?" I ask, my heart beginning to race.

Nate steps away from us, and in seconds, he's shifting. Fur spreads over his skin as his limbs reform and grow in size, his clothes tearing and falling to the ground as he changes into his jaguar form.

My other mates and I share a look.

"Uh, Blake, you might wanna see this," Shade says in my mind, hovering in the air a short distance from the cliff. *"I don't know if they're using some kind of cloaking spell or what, but it looks like the witches are still here."*

~ Prince Callan ~

The screams and sounds of battle reach me the moment I step through the cloaking barrier that covers the below township and the surrounding area. The illusion I'd been witnessing melts away, and where I'd previously seen desolate wasteland and a silent, ruined town, now I see buildings that are still half standing and a battle raging. Angels fight on the ground and in the air as witches stream between the buildings on the offensive. Chemical weapons soar through the air, glass orbs and missiles filled with neon liquid shattering as they land on houses and collide with angels causing explosions of feathers and blood.

The cold numbness that had spread over me instantly shatters, and I tighten my grip on my swords. A single moment of indecision goes through me as I peer back at where Blake is speaking with the others. Blake—my Ahalian Touizda. *My mate.* She shouldn't be here. I should have told Sebastian, the demon soldier, to take his princess home to Seral. The moment we heard about the witches, I should have insisted I enter the portal alone. But I'm not foolish enough to think she would have left me. I think of the press of her lips against mine, and how she had melted against me back in The Haven. Despite the fact I've proven myself unworthy of being her mate countless times, the demon refuses to forsake me. And once again, I find myself turning from her. Because every second I hesitate, more angels die.

I launch into the air, the wind buffeting my wings as I fly away from the cliff. Using my power, I send up a surge of wind to increase my speed, and my gaze sweeps over the battle scene as I draw closer. There must be at least two hundred witches spread around the township, and half as many angels.

I reach the first layer of angels, and they shout

out my name when they see me, raising their weapons in a salute.

"Support from the queen has finally come!" A female angel with long blond braids calls out with relief as she releases another steel arrow, sending it flying into a witch's chest with enough force that the witch is knocked to the ground.

My lips form a hard line, but I don't have the heart to tell her I came alone. I can only hope I'll be enough. This is my duty.

"My prince," someone else calls out, and I turn at the familiar voice. Theon is in the air not far from me, wielding his own bow and arrow. The healer's face is a welcome sight, but as he stares at me, distracted, a glowing red orb smashes into his left wing. The glass orb shatters on impact and the red acid explodes on him, the chemical quickly burning through his bronze feathers. The rancid smell of scorched flesh finds my nose, and the archangel's face contorts with pain as he cries out. He flaps his ruined wing trying to keep in the air, but as his wing burns, the archangel falls.

Sheathing my swords, I curse and send out a gust of wind that catches Theon and brings him to the ground a few hundred yards from the conflict. An orb soars past my head, and I snarl, turning my attention to the witches. Using my power, I blow back a row of witches directly below us, sending them crashing into nearby buildings, but some of the witches brace against my magic, chanting and deflecting my power.

Theon breathes heavily when I drop to the ground, landing hard beside him. His face is scrunched with pain, and he leans against a large boulder, his injured wing splayed to the side and acid dripping to the ground.

"My prince," he wheezes.

"You shouldn't be fighting," I tell Theon. "You're not a warrior, my friend." Memories of my childhood with Theon flash in my mind. Images of me training with the other archangels for hours until I was bruised and bloody, and of Theon being the only one to help me limp away when the instructor finally declared I'd had enough. Even before he discovered his power of healing, Theon had always been a quiet and peaceful soul who would avoid conflict at all costs. He wasn't one to fly head-first into battle. His duty was to lead one of the largest healing centers in Toralyn.

Theon tries to move his wounded wing and hisses in pain, though I can already see the membrane of his wing starting to regenerate, albeit much slower than usual for a typical wound.

"That is true," Theon rasps, "but I felt I owed a debt."

"A debt?" My brows lower.

He nods once. "There were witches in the Perstalian ruins. We were lucky the demon king arrived to help us fight against them. King Dalton created portals and sent the remaining alphas from the competition to their home realms. I was one of the last to go, but I left him there."

"As you should have. The demons had it under control."

Theon's lips thin. "But when King Dalton arrived in Toralyn not too long after, I had to know why. I followed him to the palace, and through the whispers of servants, I discovered that you and your new mate never made it to the demon realm. The demon king also warned Queen Vespera that the witches planned to attack the angels."

"So, King Dalton saw the queen," I say, thinking of my mother in the royal palace.

"Oh yes, he saw her," Theon confirms, his words labored. "Though, from what I hear she had little interest in listening to him. Not even after the witches attacked Toralyn, appearing in multiple locations at once. Your brothers are already fighting witch assaults at the other cities around the realm."

I peer at the half-destroyed town not far from us. "And I imagine, this township isn't high up on the queen's list of places to protect and preserve." The queen has never cared much for the township of Sailyn. To the angels it's a sacred place of rejuvenation and tranquility. Built beside the golden forest, it's a favored spot angels visit when they wish to escape the city and find peace. The soil in this area is said to contain unique properties that helps cleanse the mind, and angels will come here simply to spend days tending to the land before they return home. Of course, the queen never saw the value in a place like this. Not when the angels could be more useful elsewhere.

"Queen Vespera dismissed the king," Theon goes on. "She refused his offer of help and declared that it's an angel matter. When he left the palace, I followed the demon king's entourage. After Princess Blake helped to free me from the creature in the Perstalian ruins, I felt I owed it to her to see that he left our realm safely."

"You're a good archangel, Theon," I tell him.

Theon shakes his head. "But the demon king didn't leave. While he was in the city, he encountered an angel from this township. They spoke of witches, and the king made this his next destination. I continued to follow him, and by the time we arrived, the township was already under attack. I sent word to the queen, but no help has come. Either she didn't send any soldiers or the forces she sent never made it past the cloaking magic before turning back."

I lean closer to Theon, my mind fixating on something he's just said. "Wait. You're telling me, King Dalton is still here?"

"Yes," Theon replies, and he lifts his hand, pointing weakly to the outskirts on the right side of the town. There, far in the distance, the demon king and a contingent of his guards stand back-to-back. A circle of witches surrounds them, the hooded figures chanting and swaying as power flows from them, encasing the demons. I mutter a curse, thinking of how angry my demon mate will be when she discovers this.

"Stay here," I order Theon. Standing, I ready myself to launch into the air when a blur of yellow and black bolts past me. Nate growls and hisses, his powerful paws kicking up ash and dirt as he sprints toward the closest witches. Moments later, he's pouncing, his powerful muscles rippling as he tears into a witch. The jaguar is onto his third witch when Princess Blake, Mason, and Shade fly overhead. The sound of fluttering fills my ears, and hundreds of white doves soar up behind Princess Blake, following her toward the town.

Alaric and Dante are just behind them on the ground. The males sprint past me, wielding their weapons as their boots kick up the dust.

"Looks like your friends are here," Theon comments with a wry smile.

Without replying, I start forward, catching up with Dante and Alaric. "What are you doing?" I bark out.

Alaric only grunts in response, but Dante's lips curl upward, his pace not slowing. "Killing the witches, of course," he answers like I've asked a ridiculous question. Then he disappears from sight, using his invisibility power.

CHAPTER

TWO

~ Princess Blake ~

"**I**s it just me, or do they look like toasted marshmallows?" Shade asks as we fly toward the battle.

"Are you seriously comparing the burning homes of angels to sweet treats right now?"

"I'm just saying," she defends. *"I mean, they're small white domes with charring on top. Don't tell me you don't see it."*

Of course I do, but I shake my head and instead focus on the images being sent to me by the hundreds of birds I've called from the surrounding forest. While the trees around the portal are completely dead, it seems that death didn't spread too far. When I'd reached out with my magic, I'd sensed a large flock of the small white birds not too far away. Like the Pecos birds in The Haven, the creatures responded when I called, and now they fly up behind me filling the air around us like a giant white cloud.

"Oh, there he is! And that healer guy is there, too," Shade's voice intrudes in my mind.

"Who?"

"Prince Callan is below us and he's with Theon, the archangel we met in the Perstalian ruins. Yeesh, he doesn't look too good right now, though, buuut I'm sure he'll be fine."

Frowning, I peer down only to find Theon now left behind, propped against a rock, and Prince Callan running with Alaric and Dante. The archangel looks annoyed as he stares up at me, and I grin and give him a little wave. He might not realize it yet, but we're about to save this situation.

My attention goes to Nate as the giant cat leaps into the air, pouncing on another witch. His powerful jaws clamp onto the witch's head and tear it off before tossing it away. My lips thin. Truthfully, now that I know the history of King Celzar stealing from the witches, it's hard to look at them in the same way. For a brief moment, I wonder if I should call my shifter mate off. If we could declare a ceasefire, maybe I could talk with the witches. Maybe we could find a way to come to some sort of an agreement. But just as I think about yelling out to Nate, I spot Dad on the opposite side of the town.

The demon king stands with at least a dozen demon guards, the group of them enclosed by a circle of witches who are chanting, their hands outstretched before them. Whatever they're doing, it can't be good, because the king and the soldiers look like they're in pain. Dad tips his head back bellowing in agony as he falls to his knees, and my heart stutters.

"No!" Snarling, I point in the direction of the witches.

Following my internal command, the doves shoot past me, dropping into a dive and streaming through the town houses, attacking the witches.

Before, I had wondered if I should spare the witches, but now all I can think about is spilling their blood and stopping this. When Sebastian had talked about Dad leading the demons to defeat the witches in Perstalia, I'd imagined him as he always was—strong, powerful, and a force to be reckoned with. But now, surrounded by the witches, the demon king looks...weak.

Nate snaps happily at some of the doves as they pass him, like he just can't help himself, but the doves avoid his jaws, and he goes back to tearing through witches.

Dante and Alaric are with him now, moving like harbingers of death, sweeping through the town. I hardly see Alaric's blades move before they're embedded in another witch. Around them, my doves make quick work of the other witches. Multiple birds attack each witch, swarming them until they're covered in white, and it's not long before the dove's feathers turn black with witch blood. Prince Callan lifts into the air, following me, and we all drop down close to Dad.

Mason's face is hard as he lands, his wings flaring wide as he drives his sword into one of the witches standing in the circle. The female screams, already blinded by my birds who are clawing at her face.

A projectile flies at me, but I dodge to the side, and it slams into the building behind me. The explosion throws me forward, and when I look up again, there's a witch before me. Dead birds are littered around her feet, and she lifts her hands, a crooked grin on her face. Cackling, she sends power rushing at me, but before I can even think about deflecting, Nate leaps over my head. She screams as his fangs sink into her flesh, and then she's silent.

I jump to my feet, and my mates form up around me as we attack the remaining witches. Many of them are still chanting, my birds bleeding on the ground around them, and I snarl, anger pulsing through me. A few of the witches try to redirect their power and attack us rather than trapping my Dad and the demons, and the moment their chanting changes, the king and the demons are freed from their magic prison. Dad bellows, lunging for the closest witch, and the demon soldiers help us to disband the rest of the witch circle.

When there's only one witch remaining, she stares in horror at her sisters, and her shrill wail cuts through the air. She draws her hands together and glares at the king, whispering something in a language I can't understand. I expect Dad to take care of her, but he just straightens, his face lined with fatigue as he merely watches the female. Her magic surges toward him, and he doesn't even try to fucking move. I'm caught off guard, and I know I'll be too late to stop what's about to happen. For a moment, time seems to slow, and I watch as Prince Callan's blade cleaves through the witch's abdomen.

It doesn't stop the rippling ball of magic that shoots toward the king, but before it can slam into Dad's chest, Mason is there, grabbing the king. The pair of them tumble to the side, and I shout as the witch's magic flies past, crashing into the building behind them and setting it alight with green flame.

Breathing heavily, my gaze scans the area for more threats, but the witches around us are all dead, and going by the cheering from the angels in the air and on the ground, I'm guessing the witches have all been defeated in the township.

I move to the demon king, but Mason is already up and has his hand out. Dad's dark gaze assesses the winged centaur, but then his lips twist into a smile and he takes Mason's hand, letting him lift him to his feet.

"And you would be?" King Dalton asks casually, as though we weren't just under attack.

"Mason," my mate replies.

"He's from Perstalia," I say, going to stand beside Mason.

Dad stares at my centaur like he's trying to decide if my mate is a friend or foe.

"Turns out, not all of the Perstalians died," I explain. "They were just underground."

King Dalton turns toward me, his gaze softening. "Ah, I was wondering when you'd join me, daughter." His voice is as affectionate as I've ever heard it, and I wonder if it's because the battle has worn him down.

I clear my throat. "I would've been here sooner if it weren't for…" I trail off before saying, "well, we can discuss that another time."

His shrewd gaze sweeps over me and my other mates. "Yes, I heard you had completed your task and left with your mates," he says slyly.

I don't miss his insinuation, but I choose to ignore it. "If by my 'task' you're referring to the competition of survival you threw me into so I could find my mates, then yeah, I guess so." I would be more irritated at Dad for orchestrating the competition if it hadn't in fact led to me discovering Nate and the others, and even Mason.

"But I didn't exactly *leave* with my mates," I mutter, though I don't explain further. "None of that matters right now. Can we please talk about the fact that you shouldn't be fighting? What are you doing here?"

"I'm fine," Dad says with a dismissive wave of his hand, but when he stumbles, I grab his arm to steady him.

"You're not fine," I chastise, staring at his pale face with concern. "Why isn't the angel queen here?"

He pats my hand, but his eyes darken. "Queen Vespera refuses to believe the witches are a real threat. Even though the witches have now attacked numerous cities and townships around Toralyn, the queen believes it's an angel problem that she'll be able to easily manage."

I stare incredulously at the carnage around us, including the mass of dead witches and angels. "Easily manage? Has she forgotten what happened the last time the witches declared war?"

"She's always been stubborn," Prince Callan says, stepping close. "And in all fairness, until recently, we had thought the witches had been eradicated." I'm not sure if it's because of the sunlight glinting on his golden wings, but my archangel looks even more princely than usual. "I've been advised that my brothers and the majority of our forces are busy protecting other more important cities around the realm."

My brows lower even more as I continue staring at the damage around us.

King Dalton grunts as he stretches his body, moving his head from side to side until his neck cracks.

"Queen Vespera should call on the allied realms,"

I say. "Before the angels are overwhelmed. Clearly, there are more witches than any of us would have imagined. Do we know why the witches are in Toralyn?"

"Whatever the reason, Queen Vespera is determined that this is an internal problem they can solve without intervention," Dad replies grimly. "As to the why...I was hoping coming here would shed some light on that, but so far, I've discovered nothing."

I turn my attention to Prince Callan. "Is there something special about this town?"

"Nothing that would be of use to the witches," he replies.

I think on this, but I can feel Dad's eyes on me.

"So, is he one of yours, too?" the king asks with amusement, distracting me as he scrutinizes Prince Callan.

I don't answer, mostly because I'm not sure what to say. Despite everything, Prince Callan still doesn't believe we can be mates.

The prince dips his head, and I wait for his answer, but he ignores Dad's question entirely. "I appreciate your assistance here, King Dalton," he says instead.

Dad merely looks intrigued by his change in subject. "Of course. And I trust you'll pass this on to your queen."

Prince Callan wipes the blood from his swords

and sheathes them. "It will be recorded that you aided in the battle for this township."

Dad hums his approval, and he turns his attention from Prince Callan to where the others have formed up behind me. "Four mates, daughter? I had suspected you may have more than the common number for a demon, but it looks as though you'll have your hands full."

Shade snickers in my mind. *"He means hands, and mouth, and..."*

"It's a surprise for all of us," I say with a tight smile, cutting Shade off. Listening to that while having a conversation with my dad is just plain wrong. I don't correct Dad and explain that I actually have *five* mates. Alaric is nowhere to be seen, but given his hatred for demons, I'm not surprised.

King Dalton nods, looking to where Nate now stands naked, back in his non-shifted form. "Yes, these are some very interesting matches that will undoubtedly lead to...interesting times."

I'm not sure 'interesting' is the word I'd use, but I'm just glad he doesn't seem to disapprove of my mates from the other realms.

"However, I am confused that you have not yet bonded, my daughter. These are trying times, and you need all your power."

And of course he had to ask. I groan internally. "Not bonded? What makes you think that?" I reply casually, hoping Dad will drop it.

The demon king's eyes sparkle with mischief, his

gaze roving over my reddening cheeks. He points a long finger at my archangel. "Because if you were bonded, our princely friend over here wouldn't be standing apart from you like he's not sure what to do with himself. That is not how a bonded mate would act. Not when their female is so close."

Nate stifles his grin, and Prince Callan scowls, looking supremely uncomfortable.

Shade, of course, cackles in my head. *"Oh, I have missed our demon daddy. Why don't you tell him about Alaric? That asshole could use a chewing out, too."*

Despite the fact Prince Callan and Alaric are still my reluctant mates, I suddenly feel the need to defend them. I mean, they did just fight by my side *and* saved my dad. *"Firstly, don't call him that because I don't need that in my head right now,"* I tell Shade, *"and secondly, something tells me now isn't the right time to explain that I also have a Drozac assassin as one of my mates."*

"What's wrong with demon daddy?" Shade counters. *"I've always told you I think King Dalton is—"*

"Nope," I cut her off before she can explain further, and I give Dad a tight smile. "It's complicated. This isn't something any of us expected."

"It never is," King Dalton replies, his eyes getting a faraway look, and I get the feeling he's thinking about mom—his bonded angel mate. The thought makes me squirm. Despite all his talk about how mates are supposed to act toward one another, my parents were mated and mom still dumped me as a baby and left my dad. The idea of any of my mates one day leaving me makes my stomach churn.

"I suppose I should thank you for your efforts," King Dalton says, staring at Mason. "You saved my life, and I'm in your debt."

My centaur mate smiles. "No thanks necessary, your highness. I would do anything to protect my mate." He pauses, wrapping his arm around me. "And of course, her family."

Nate groans and mutters under his breath. "Kiss ass."

I smirk, glad that at least one of my mates won't embarrass me in front of my father.

King Dalton's lips quirk up. "As it should be. Nevertheless, you have my gratitude."

I'm busy thinking about Mason's hand on me when Theon stumbles forward, moving to Prince Callan's side. His wounded wing is now half healed and still slowly regenerating. I'm glad the healer will make it, but seeing his wounds is enough to pull my thoughts back to the witches, because that's what's important right now.

"Do we know what the situation is back in Seral?" I ask Dad, drawing the conversation away from bonding and my mates.

King Dalton frowns. "Peace between the clan leaders has been fragile since I mentioned my retirement, but there had been no more signs of the witches before I left. That was days ago, and I cannot be sure how General Josek has fared in my absence."

My mood sours when I think of the unhinged demon general currently in control of the demon realm. Only Lady Fate knows what the male has been up to while on a witch hunt.

Nate looks over his shoulder, and a moment later, Sebastian and eleven other demons march closer to us. "Our king!" Sebastian barks when he draws close, slamming his fist to his chest and falling to one knee. The other demons do the same, and King Dalton arches a brow at me.

"I told them to follow us here," I explain.

Prince Callan folds his arms across his chest. "What are your plans now, King Dalton?" His expression is hard, and I can tell the prince is keen to keep moving.

Dad lets out a heavy sigh. "Unfortunately, unless Queen Vespera agrees to receive aid, there's not much more we can do here. I will return to Seral before matters get out of hand at home." He fixes me with a stare. "But now that you have the archangel prince as your mate, I must request, daughter, that you travel to the queen and implore her to reconsider. Perhaps, when she learns what transpired here, she will be more receptive to hearing the truth."

Prince Callan stiffens, tucking his wings in tighter. "Your highness, I must insist that Princess Blake returns with you to the demon realm. Queen

Vespera is not known to be the most hospitable to—"

"I will, my king," I blurt, cutting Prince Callan off. Truthfully, I don't care much to see the angel queen, but it's obvious Prince Callan is going there, and the fact that my archangel mate suggested I leave him is pissing me off. Besides, Dad is right. The queen needs a wakeup call.

"Callan might be right in suggesting that Blake should return home," Nate says, looking uneasy.

I cut a glare his way, and Nate lifts his hands in a placating gesture. "I'm just sayin', Queen Vespera is prickly on a good day."

"We're only going there to pass on the message," I say. "We'll keep our stay brief, and then we'll be off to the demon realm."

No one argues with that, but Prince Callan's temple pulses with irritation.

When my archangel stays silent, Dad smiles. "Good. Then it's settled."

CHAPTER

THREE

~ Alaric ~

I wait silently in a crouch, hidden in one of the few town houses that wasn't destroyed. The top window is cracked just enough that if I release my arrow, it could fly free of the building... and into the demon king.

Ordinarily, such a weapon wouldn't be able to kill the demon monarch, but bright orange liquid stains the tip of my arrowhead, the unique poison procured from a witch I'd slain not too long ago.

King Dalton stands with Blake and the others, the group of them engaged in conversation, but while I'm skilled in the art of reading lips, my focus isn't on what is being said. I keep my arrow there, aimed at the king's heart.

During the battle, I had stayed long enough to ensure the witches would fall, and then I'd disappeared into the background, slinking away while the demon princess was distracted. Just the thought of how I'd left my mate has my scowl deepening, but I force the memory from my mind. Keeping my grip on my bow and arrow, I let out a long, steady breath, ignoring the high-pitched ringing in my ears.

After an age of waiting, the chance for retribution is finally here. The demon who murdered my twin brother, West, stands unsuspecting, and my muscles tense as I let my anger flow through me, filling every part of my being. I'd planned to kill the demon king's daughter. To make him feel something akin to the pain I'd felt when West had been taken from me, but it was becoming painfully clear that I wouldn't be able to kill my mate. *My Enchantress.* She was a surprising twist in my fucked-up life, but right now it didn't matter. King Dalton, the murderer himself, was before me, and simply seeing him dead would have to suffice.

I pull the arrow back another inch, tightening the drawstring even more. I shouldn't be hesitating. I'm a member of the Drozac. An elite assassin, bound by a code that's centuries old. The king still stands directly in my line of sight, his broad chest exposed. One arrow, and the vengeance I've sought for so long will finally be mine. One arrow, and I can finally get revenge for my brother's death. One arrow, and my mate will hate me just as I detest the demon king. *Blood for blood.*

My fingers don't move.

Growling under my breath, I close my eyes, trying to ground myself. This is all I've wanted for so long, but it was never meant to feel like this. My hatred wavers as thoughts of my enchantress fill my head. Of her soft skin and fiery spirit. Of the way she feels when my hand is wrapped around her throat, my thigh between her legs as she lets out soft pants.

Growling, I wrench my eyes open, and my heart almost stops. Because it's not the demon king I have targeted now. A female with long dark hair and silky black wings stands in the way of my arrow, and fear spears into me, penetrating so deep it's as though an arrow has punctured my heart rather than the demon king's.

Enchantress. Sweat breaks out over my skin, and I lower my arrow, loosening the bowstring as my heart pounds an erratic beat. A stream of curses whisper from my lips. There was a time when I'd dreamed of having the demon princess in my line of sight. When I'd fantasized about the demon king mourning her twisted and lifeless form.

But now that thought makes me sick.

Because the female is my mate, and no amount of denying it on my part will change that. Her soul calls to mine, and that...terrifies me.

I stare at my trembling fingers. My hands have

always remained steady in the past, and yet here I am, my fingers shaking.

The she-demon is changing me, and I'm hopeless as I fight against the pull of fate, and the threads that bind us.

I don't lift my arrow again.

Instead, I remain crouched, watching in grim silence as the king creates a new portal thick with red flames, and he disappears with the remainder of the demon guards.

~

~ Princess Blake ~

Alaric reappears soon after Dad departs through a portal, and I get the feeling it's not a coincidence, though the assassin refuses to admit where he's been. A scowl remains on his face for the rest of the day, but he stays close to me as we work. My mates and I hardly speak as we spend hours tending to the wounded and helping to gather the bodies. Theon isn't the only healer, and thankfully, many of the wounded angels will recover. The damage to the township is severe, but the angels are determined as they clear away the debris and start devising plans to rebuild. No one mentions that the fight with the witches is likely far from over.

I'm busy carrying a long, splintered beam from one of the destroyed townhouses, when Dante plucks it from my hands. He carries it over to a pile of torched wood and drops it, dusting off his hands as a cloud of ash puffs into the air.

"I had it," I tell him, though I can't help but grin when he gives me a devastating smile.

"So, you did," he drawls, his tail hovering in the air behind him, "but I think it's time we went on our way, don't you, princess? We have a queen to visit."

I frown at his words, because he's not wrong. Lifting my chin, I squint up at where the sun is still high in the sky. Streams of golden light shine down on us, and if I were back in Seral, I would have guessed it was only midday. "How long is it until nightfall?" My question isn't directed at anyone in particular, but it's Theon who answers, his silky bronze wings now fully healed.

"A few months, your highness," the archangel replies.

I jerk my head, blinking at him in surprise. "Months?"

"This is the season of summer light," Theon explains. "We will not experience night again for many days."

"*Okay, just hearing that is making me sweaty,*" Shade complains from my shoulder. "*Any chance they can include a birdbath in their designs? I mean, look at me, I'm a creature of the night.*" She stretches out her black wings dramatically like she's trying to prove her point.

I shake my head at her, my lips twitching. "*Crows

normally sleep at night, Shade. And besides, you don't sweat."

"Maybe normal crows sleep at night," she defends. *"But the royal bestie of the demon princess has been trained to sleep when the sun is up. You can't blame me for your conditioning."*

"Royal bestie?" A grin breaks out on my face, though she's not wrong at her being conditioned differently. In the demon realm everyone generally sleeps when the sun is up, and at some point, Shade started doing that, too, to keep on the same schedule as me.

"And you know what I mean," Shade continues. *"I feel like I'm roasting in this heat."*

It shouldn't have happened, but at the thought of roast and the idea of food, a low rumble starts up in my stomach.

Shade squawks, hopping up and down on my shoulder. *"Girl, please tell me your stomach did not just growl at the thought of me being roasted?!"*

"What?" I say innocently. *"Battling witches takes a lot out of a demon. You can't tell me you're not hungry."*

Shade huffs in my mind, though I know she's not as mortified as she pretends. For some reason, she has always been surprisingly understanding when it comes to my eating habits, though it probably helps that I haven't eaten any bird, chicken or otherwise, in years. Still, she turns on my shoulder, showing me her tail feathers.

"What's wrong with her?" Nate comments,

coming up beside me. He's wearing the clothing of a deceased angel, and it fits him surprisingly well, though the material is tight across his chest.

"Oh nothing, she's just upset that my stomach growled at the thought of roasted bird," I explain.

It takes the shifter a moment to realize what I've said, but then he lets out a hearty laugh.

"And no, that wasn't an indication that you can eat her," I add, narrowing my eyes on Nate. I might be able to handle the joke, but I still remember how he'd snapped at the doves flying past him not too long ago.

"Don't worry, gorgeous," he chuckles. "I'm always craving demon these days." He pulls me close, his hand resting brazenly on my ass, and my face heats as need makes me press my thighs together.

"Good lord, someone at least get me a bucket to bathe in," Shade says, a smirk in her voice as she turns back around, our little tiff instantly forgotten now that she's distracted by Nate's dirty mouth.

I lean in to my shifter. Memories of his barbs inside me make my core clench, and I swallow hard thinking about how good he'd made me feel.

His nostrils flare as he scents my arousal, and he gives me a shit-eating grin as he squeezes my ass harder. *Stupid shifter senses.* It's then that I notice my other mates are all looking at me intently, appearing just as bothered as I am.

Theon clears his throat as he shifts

uncomfortably, no doubt sensing the tension. "Uh yes, so there won't be any nightfall any time soon, but if you need somewhere to rest before you set off, there are a few buildings that are still standing and structurally sound."

I'm about to thank him, when Prince Callan speaks up, his voice clipped. "We'll rest at the springs. Gather some supplies and lead them there. I need to discuss a few matters with the other angels before I depart."

Theon dips his head. "Of course, my prince," he answers primly.

I open my mouth, about to question Prince Callan about these springs, but a male angel with teal hair appears around the side of a building. A long scroll of parchment is in his hands, and when he calls out, Prince Callan barely spares the rest of us a glance before striding toward him.

"Okay, then," I mutter under my breath.

The rest of us turn to Theon expectantly, and he gives us a nervous smile. "Excuse me for the moment. I will gather some supplies and return shortly."

The healer hurries out of sight, and the rest of us stand around idly. I move to the shade of one of the nearby buildings, and Nate, Dante, and Alaric follow me, leaning on the white stone. Mason takes a step toward us, but then he stops abruptly, his gaze fixed to something on the ground.

I notice the severed finger in the dirt, not far

from his position. Going by the dark ink patterned onto the wrinkled skin, and the ruby ring that's still attached, I'm guessing it's from one of the witches. Mason reaches down, and I wince, already knowing where this is going.

"When will they learn that severed limbs aren't my favorite?" I mumble to Shade.

The crow laughs in my head. *"Well, you are a demon. I can see why they're confused."*

Nate shoots me a grin, and it's obvious he's eager to see how this plays out.

I open my mouth, about to explain to Mason the same thing I had to explain to Prince Callan and Nate when they'd brought me severed heads as gifts, but my eyes widen when my mate turns and there's a single flower in his grasp. It's a wildflower that has been growing between the flat stones of the street, a small golden flower with six delicate petals and a splash of violet in its center. Somehow, it was completely spared from the violence, and there's not a single drop of blood on it.

"For you, my mate," Mason says as he moves in front of me. "Because at all times we must treasure those most precious to us." He leans over, tucking it above my ear, and my skin flushes with heat.

"Swooooon," Shade gushes, gazing appreciatively at Mason.

Nate blows out a breath and runs a hand through his hair. "Fuck me, he's good," he grumbles.

I smile, completely ignoring Nate's defeated

expression, and the way Alaric is glowering as if my centaur mate has personally offended him. Dante merely looks amused, and entirely ready to join in on the action at a moment's notice.

"Mason is definitely my current favorite," Shade muses, and my smile grows bigger, because right now, I have to agree.

~ Princess Blake ~

Theon leads us through the dead forest until the ashen trees abruptly end, and the forest is teeming with life again in the span of a single step. The trees are lush with heart-shaped golden leaves that glisten in the sun, and bees and other insects fly through the air, visiting the flowers nestled amongst the weeds and grasses.

It feels like not much time has passed when we reach a small valley filled with thousands of golden and violet wildflowers that scent the air with a rich, sweet aroma. We climb down a slope, and nestled in the middle of the valley, we find three large pools of water. Steam rises in wispy curls from the water's surface, making the air thick and humid, and magic makes my skin prickle with awareness. Carefully, I assess my surroundings.

"Whoa, so I guess these are the hot springs," Shade comments, perking up on my shoulder. *"Have you ever seen water so blue?"*

"Only once when I visited Norso," I reply, eyeing the crystal water and recalling a time when I'd had to attend a royal celebration in the realm of the water monsters. It had been a strange event that involved a lot of nudity from the citizens, but the water surrounding the island we were on had been an incredible vibrant blue that glittered like sapphires, sparkles dancing on the water like we were staring at an ocean filled with glitter.

Theon places down the large golden basket he's been carrying this entire time, and he walks over to the closest pool. Crouching, he dips one of his hands into the water, and he closes his eyes as he scoops water onto his head. Droplets trail down his face, clinging to his lashes, and he smiles as he lets out a long breath. It's a wide, relaxed, unnatural smile, and I watch the male suspiciously as he opens his eyes and stands, still beaming like he's just heard the best news of his entire life. He looks nothing like the solemn archangel who'd been leading us through the forest not long ago.

"Okay, I don't know what just happened, but I'll have whatever he's had," Shade comments, hopping excitedly on my shoulder.

Frowning, I study the archangel's face and watch him for any more strange behavior.

"What is this place?" Alaric growls, clearly having picked up on Theon's odd change in mood as well. I can still feel the foreign magic in the air, and though my senses aren't telling me it's dangerous, I remain wary.

Theon's eyes sparkle, and he indicates to the three pools with his hand. "These waters have unique properties. Angels come here when they need a little...reminder of how life is to be cherished. Individuals are affected in different ways, but the result is always the same."

"*Unique properties?*" I repeat to Shade.

"*I knew it! He totally just got high off that stuff.*" She opens her wings like she's about to fly into one of the pools, but I lift my hand, stroking her feathers as I try to calm her.

"*We don't even know what it does, let alone how it will affect a bird,*" I try to rationalize with her.

"*True,*" she admits. "*But he said the result is always the same, and if that result is a buzz that lasts as long as their eternal summer, I'm down.*"

I shake my head, and I keep stroking her, mostly to make sure she doesn't dive into the pool. Not until we have more information.

"What unique properties?" Dante asks, looking just as eager as Shade to go for a dip.

Theon stares at us, that giddy smile still on his face. "The water has been blessed by one of Toralyn's most gifted archangels. The magic within it temporarily washes away any negative thoughts and allows you to focus on positivity."

Positivity? I think of how grumpy Prince Callan has been for the majority of the time that I've known him. *"Okay, so clearly Prince Callan never visits this place,"* I tell Shade, and she cackles in my head.

"Why did Prince Callan order you to bring us here?" I ask Theon.

"These springs are a treasured landmark of this forest," he explains. "It might not seem like it, but this location is guarded by a strong protection spell that repels any being with ill intentions."

"So, if there are any witches remaining in the area, they won't be able to find us here," I say as understanding filters through me.

"That is correct, your highness. You can rest here for a while knowing there is no threat to you." The archangel indicates to the basket on the ground. "Please use these supplies I have gathered for you all. I am sure Prince Callan will not keep you waiting for long."

"So, this water," Nate says, pushing for more information. "It's safe?"

Theon's gaze slides to the shifter, and I swear there's an amused glint in the healer's eyes before he says, "Quite safe, I assure you. You are welcome to freshen up before you leave to meet the queen." He pauses as if he's only just taking in our appearance. "Something I would highly recommend given your current state. Queen Vespera may not take kindly to you should you arrive to her halls like this."

I get the distinct feeling there's something the archangel isn't telling us, but he merely bids us farewell and spreads his wings, lifting into the air and leaving us behind.

The moment he's out of sight, Nate stretches in a way that's entirely feline. "Well, now that he's gone let's check out what he's left us, shall we?" He strides to the basket and rifles through the contents. Before long, he's pulling out a golden wine bottle and holding it up triumphantly. "Thank you, Lady," he mutters to the sky. He kisses the glass bottle, removing the cork with his teeth before guzzling some of the liquid down.

Dante moves past him, going to the basket next, and Mason helps the demon spread a golden rug on the ground. They arrange an assortment of food on it, from lush golden apples to a range of glittering cheeses and breads that look so good my mouth waters.

"Princess," Dante says to me, flourishing his hand toward the blanket dramatically when he's finished.

I grin, settling down and stretching out my legs.

Mason and Dante make themselves comfortable on either side of me, and we spend the next while relaxing and devouring the food. There is fruit and seeds for Shade, and even Alaric eats his fill, though he watches me with intensity, staring at my mouth as I eat.

When I can't fit in another bite, I lean back against Dante's hard chest, entirely ready for a nap. Yawning, I close my eyes as the sun beats down on us.

Dante's tail curls around my thigh as his fingers trace lazy circles on my arm, and the idea of sleep quickly vanishes as I focus on his touch.

"Feel better?" he murmurs in my ear.

"Mhmm," I mutter, mentally willing him to move his hand lower. My stomach might be satisfied, but liquid heat pools between my thighs as my mates' scents swirl around me.

Opening my eyes, I find Alaric, Mason, and Nate are all watching me with interest, their bodies tense. Nate's stare is predatory as he finishes another bottle of wine, and I get the feeling he's looking for any excuse to pounce. Blood pounds in my ears, desire making my body tighten.

"You do realize you're all still filthy, right?" Shade's words cut into my head, and I blink. I'd almost forgotten she was there, eating on the grass.

I take note of the mottled blood and gore still covering me and my mates. Blood doesn't usually bother me, but there's something about the battle with the witches that still has me feeling unsettled.

"What did Theon say?" Shade goes on. *"That you should clean up before seeing the angel queen? Hmmm,"*

she muses. *"If only there was water nearby that you could use."*

I give her a deadpan look. *"You just want to go into one of the pools."*

"Can you blame me?" she says, staring back at me with beady eyes. *"Don't tell me you're not curious."*

Lifting my head, I stare over at the crystal blue water. Curls of steam rise into the air like small puffs of smoke, and the light breeze is pleasant against my skin. Going in there *does* sound amazing, and surely Prince Callan wouldn't send us here if it was unsafe. Right? Then again, who knows what goes through that archangel's head. At the thought of my missing mate, irritation sparks through me, and I sit up.

Dante raises a brow, his hand falling from my arm. "Something wrong?"

"We should be on our way to the palace," I answer. "Not stuffing our faces and lazing in the sun."

"Speak for yourself, gorgeous," Nate replies, tipping up the bottle to get the last drops of wine out. "We earned this."

"We should wait for Prince Callan," Mason adds. "This is his land, after all."

His words sting a little, but only because I'm once again reminded of my mother. Of the fact, that in a way, this is my land, too, even if the place feels foreign to me.

Standing, I walk to the closest pool, remembering how happy Theon had been after he'd doused himself with water. The water is so clear the smooth stone at the bottom of the pool is easily visible, and if I'm seeing correctly, it's not that deep. *At least I know this isn't like the bath in Perstalia.* Not that I would expect any ancient water demons in Toralyn, but Dad has taught me not to underestimate any situation.

"*Yesss,*" Shade hisses in my head. "*You go in there and if you don't die, I'll follow you.*"

I grin at her. "*You really are keen for this, aren't you?*"

"*I'm dying of heat exhaustion,*" she squawks dramatically. "*If you're not going to let me go first, you can at least take one for the team.*"

My lips stretch wider. I'm still pretty certain there's something about these hot springs that Theon didn't tell us, but if we're going to get ourselves cleaned up to meet the queen, there's no point wasting more time. Without hesitating any longer, I start peeling off my shirt.

I barely have the garment over my head when a large body is behind me, taking over, and gently pulling my shirt off. I don't even need to look to know who it is. Mason's rich amber and leather scent fills my nose, and awareness prickles through me.

"I can undress myself," I grouse.

"If you couldn't, I would be worried," my centaur replies, a hint of humor in his voice as he kisses my neck, his hands sliding up my arms.

My hands are still in the air when Dante moves in front of me. He crouches down, removing my weapons belt before he works on unfastening my pants. Slowly, he pulls my pants to my ankles before sliding them off entirely.

"No one is doubting your capability, princess," my demon drawls, "but why should you have to when you have us?" I'm completely exposed now, and my legs tremble at the thought of having Dante's face between my thighs. He smirks up at me, his midnight blue eyes framed by thick black lashes, and my breathing starts to quicken.

"Soooo, I'm guessin' it's bath time?" Nate says, cracking his neck and coming over to strip beside me. In a matter of seconds, he's naked, and he leaves his clothes in a pile next to the pool. "See you in there, gorgeous," he says with a wink, and he dips his fingers into the water before striding into the pool. The water reaches to just under his muscled butt, but he sinks down until he's submerged up to his chest. My shifter mate becomes preternaturally still, and for a moment, my heart skitters.

Shade squawks in my head. *"Please tell me your sexy shifter is still alive."*

My heart pounds, and I watch intently, the seconds clawing by as Nate keeps his back to me, but then he turns toward us. The predatory gaze on his face is purely carnal, and his slitted eyes never leave me, the tips of fangs showing from between his lips.

"Oh goodie, he didn't die," Shade comments, and

she pauses before adding. *"But damn, when is it my turn to have a guy looking at me like that?"*

I swallow thickly. "We're just bathing and washing our clothes," I say aloud, my voice annoyingly breathless. "Prince Callan will be here soon, and we'd better get to the queen."

"Of course, my mate," Mason agrees, still kissing my neck, and Dante gives me a sensual smile, his dark gaze promising pleasure.

"Don't forget to tell me how the water is," Shade sing-songs in my mind as my demon leads me into the pool.

CHAPTER
FIVE

~ Princess Blake ~

Tingles race up my body from where the water has touched my skin, and euphoria spreads through me. All of my worries about the witches, about Seral, and even about the fact that Prince Callan still isn't here, they all melt away, and for the first time in a long while I feel simply...happy.

It allows you to focus on positivity. That's what Theon had said about the water, and I finally understand what he meant. It's like light is traveling through my veins, warming my insides, and for once there's no self-doubt. The negative thoughts vanish from my mind, and a giddy smile forms on my face.

Shade flutters her feathers from her position

back on the grass. *"Whoa, girl, you have the same smile Theon had. That's it, I'm going in."* She flies over, stopping at the edge of the pool. Cocking her head, she peers into the water. *"Do you think we could bottle this stuff for the times when we're having a really shitty day?"*

When I don't answer, she lifts her head and chuckles in my mind. Nate, Dante, and Mason are all naked and in the water now. They surround me, their hands moving to my body, and their lips pressing to my skin as I struggle to hold on to a coherent thought. "Merciful Lady," I gasp when Dante's mouth finds one of my nipples, his tongue flicking over the sensitive tip.

I'm vaguely aware of Shade mumbling something about not wanting to intrude on my fun, and the next time I open my eyes, my crow friend is no longer there. There's only Alaric standing before the pool with his arms crossed and a stern expression on his face. He watches me intently, his muscles taut.

"Get out of the pool," my assassin growls. "The water is affecting you."

He's right. Obviously. But I don't even care. Is it so bad to forget about my worries for a while? A hint of something brushes the edges of my mind—a reminder of something I'm meant to do—but it vanishes as quickly as it came.

I want to tell Alaric to join us. To pull him into the water with me, but Mason grips my face, and his lips slam to mine. The male devours my mouth, his tongue stroking and demanding all my attention.

Nate's hands press harder on my hips, his cock prodding at my back as he kisses and sucks at my neck. He traces his lips lower, his teeth clamping onto my shoulder hard enough to draw blood. I gasp as he licks the wound, the brief sting of pain morphing into pleasure.

Dante squeezes my breast, and he grazes my other nipple with his teeth as his tail flicks around my hips, sliding between my legs.

Fuck. I curse as his tail slides up and down my center, making me writhe in their hold.

Before us, Alaric continues to watch, his eyes blazing as he takes note of everywhere the others are touching me. Every kiss. Every bite.

"We don't have time for this," the assassin growls, but he doesn't move from his position, his nostrils flaring as he watches us.

"Do you wish us to stop, princess?" Dante asks, lifting his mouth from my breast to my ear. I can feel the curve of his lips against my skin, and I shiver.

Stop? The thought hadn't even crossed my mind. I've tasted my mates, and I want more. I will *always* want more.

"Now, why would I want that?" I reply, a whimper slipping from me as Dante's tail flicks my clit. There's no risk of me killing my mates anymore, and I'll be damned if I'm not going to enjoy them. I only wish Alaric would get into the water and stop being such a stubborn ass about everything.

Nate's chest starts to rumble, and the shifter presses closer, his hard cock a constant reminder of what I want. His hand moves around my hip and between my legs, and he pushes a finger inside me as Dante's tail continues to tease my clit.

I hiss as Nate's teeth clamp hard onto my shoulder again. He licks at the wound, and when he lifts his head, I kiss him, enjoying the taste of my blood in his mouth. I bite his bottom lip, my teeth making him bleed as well, and he growls, his lips forming a feral smile. "My queen," he purrs, and the sound is like liquid honey as it vibrates in my core.

His lips move to my jawline as he pumps the finger inside me and adds another one, sliding them in deeper. I moan, my breasts full and aching as I arch my back, leaning harder against him.

"You're such a good girl, my mate," Mason murmurs from by my side, and the words make my stomach flutter.

I squirm, trying to make Nate move his fingers faster, and the thought of his barbs inside me makes me pant. "Good?" I ask with a smirk, because even in my euphoric state, the word doesn't seem quite right.

"You're fuckin' perfect," Nate rumbles, and he lowers himself, his cock prodding at my ass.

He pulls his fingers from my pussy, and I spin, facing the shifter. I rub my nipples against his hard chest, desperate for more friction, and Nate utters a curse. Lifting me, he grips my ass hard. I wrap my legs around the shifter's waist, and he bares his fangs as his cock sinks into me. He buries his cock in so deep I hiss at the sharp sting of pain, and then moan as that pain turns to pleasure. I'm entirely consumed by the delicious feel of him filling me. Stretching me. And as his barbs explode, pressing against my walls, *ruining me,* I cry out.

Dante chuckles darkly from behind me as he presses closer, and my breaths come in shallow pants as Nate fucks me. "Breathe, princess," my demon drawls in my ear. "You're too tense."

I don't understand what he's getting at. Not until Nate's thrusts slow, and his grip loosens a little. He helps position my ass for the demon to enjoy me as well, and then I feel Dante's finger at my ass. He pushes it inside me, and my mouth falls open as Nate continues to glide his cock in and out of my pussy.

Merciful Fates, it's too much, and I can't stop myself. I fall over the edge, crying out as I come, my golden tattoos lighting up on my skin. Dante's finger pumps into me, and Nate continues thrusting into me as I shatter in his hold.

"Fuck," Nate groans, and then he's coming as well, his cock pulsing as his body seizes, and he spills inside me.

He holds me like that for a while, but anticipation rises in me again when Dante steps to the edge of the pool. He pulls himself out of the water, laying with his back on the bank, and his knees still over the edge in the water. I wade over and climb up and onto him, not wasting time in jumping onto his cock.

"So eager, my princess," Dante says with approval, his face flush and his eyes hooded.

Mason moves close, coming up right to the edge of the pool, and his hard cock presses against my ass. "May I, my mate?" he asks. "Shall we both enjoy you this time?"

Biting my lip, I smile at how tentative he is. I've taken two males before, but my centaur mate is too sweet. "If you think you can handle it," I tell him coyly, and when I twist my head back, Mason's expression is heated as he stares down at my ass.

I remain still as he lubricates himself and works the head of his cock in slowly before stopping. I gasp at the feeling of him stretching me even more, only a thin wall separating his cock and Dante's. His callused hands hold my hips firmly, and then Mason pushes his cock the rest of the way in. I groan, my head hanging as I keep my hands on Dante's chest.

"You, my mate, are truly a wonder," Mason breathes, leaning fortward to kiss the sensitive edge of my right wing. I start moving on Dante, and Mason matches my rhythm, the three of us moving in tandem.

"Our princess," Dante grits out, his face strained. "Feel how fucking deep we are inside you."

I moan, my breathing ragged. Nate watches nearby, stroking his cock that's already hard again though currently without his barbs, and I try to search out Alaric.

He stands some distance away from us now, still watching, though instead of having his hands folded, they're by his sides, his fists clenched so tightly his knuckles are white. Hatred swirls in his eyes, mixing with the heated desire there, and pain is etched into the hard lines of his face.

I want to yell at him. To tell him to get his stubborn ass in the pool and fuck me like it's clear he wants to, but at that moment, Dante reaches up, grabbing my breasts. The demon rubs his thumbs over my sensitive nipples, massaging them.

"Come for us, our mate," Mason says, and when Dante's tail slides between my legs, teasing my clit as Mason kisses my back, the pleasure that had been building in me becomes too much. I cry out as I fall over the edge, my wings flaring out as tingles race over my body and light flashes behind my eyes.

Mason and Dante find their release as well, both of them groaning as they tense and spill inside me, their hands gripping me tightly.

When we're no longer a shuddering mess, Mason kisses me again and pulls out. I climb off Dante, and Mason helps me slide into the water, exhaustion dragging at me. I don't even complain as my three mates spend the next while fussing over me and getting me cleaned up. It's strange being treated this way, but oddly comforting.

Lifting from the water, I go to grab my clothes, but Dante wraps his arms around me, not letting me go. "And where do you think you're going?" he drawls.

My lips twist. "I need to wash my clothes. There's no point bathing if our clothes are still covered in blood."

"And what makes you think you have to do that?" Dante asks.

I frown, wondering if my demon is confused, but as Mason reaches my clothes and sets about the task of washing them, I realize what my demon is getting at.

"Rest, my mate. It is our duty to take care of you," my centaur shifter says with a smile as I gape at him.

"See," Dante says smugly. "He wants to do it."

I smirk, knowing full well Dante wasn't going to. "And what about *your* clothes," I point out, indicating to where his bloodied clothes are in a heap on the bank.

"All in good time," he murmurs by the side of my head. "For now, just let me enjoy you."

~ Princess Blake ~

A short while later, all our clothes are hanging from the nearby branches to dry, and Nate, Mason, Dante, Shade, and I are lazing in the sun. Alaric hasn't spoken a word since watching us in the pool, and he rests with his back against a tree, using one of his blades to whittle down a piece of wood he's collected. He carves the end into a tip, and I guess he's creating a wooden arrowhead. I ask him about it twice, but each time he only responds with a grunt.

"Yep, he's definitely making you a wooden butt plug," Shade comments as we theorize what it could be.

I cough, choking on my own spit. *"Excuse me?"*

When she'd returned to the hot springs after my time with the guys, she'd squeezed details out of me, and I'd admitted how I'd been with Mason and Dante at the same time.

Reaching across, Mason rubs my back soothingly. "Are you okay, my mate?" he asks with concern.

Clearing my throat, I pat my chest with my hand. "Never better."

"It's probably so that next time you can take his giant cock," Shade adds, ignoring Mason.

I narrow my eyes at where the crow is crouched in the shade. She stretches out her wings before folding them again. *"And to think, I used to believe all birds were innocent creatures."*

"What can I say," Shade replies. *"The humans corrupted me."*

I frown, but I don't comment on that. I've tried to ask Shade about her past on multiple occasions, but for the most part, she tells me she doesn't remember much. Just her cage. Her other memories come in snippets, but she struggles to piece them together.

"What's with the giant, anyway?" Shade asks, pulling me from my musings. *"I swear after the battle in town, he's gotten grumpier. I didn't even think that was possible."*

I shake my head. *"Who knows what goes on in his mind."*

I'm about to ask Alaric what he's carving for a

third time, when Prince Callan finally makes an appearance. He strides toward us, his expression weary as he stops close to where we're relaxing.

Like Alaric, his clothes are still splattered with blood and grime.

"Nice of you to join us, brother," Mason says, resting his arm on my side.

Prince Callan's eyes lower, and his gaze goes to Mason's hand before tracing over my naked body. His attention goes to the pools of water, and then to where our clothes are hanging in the trees.

"How is everything back at the township?" I ask the archangel, and he blinks, his gaze snapping to my face.

"Construction is well underway," he replies coldly. "The town will be whole again before long."

"Well, that's good news, so why does he still look like he's about to be sick?" Shade comments. *"Maybe you should encourage him to have a dip. Something tells me he'd feel a whole lot better if he did."*

She's not wrong. Now that I'm out of the water and dry, all those worries and concerns are on my shoulders again, weighing me down. The archangel could use a break, but something tells me that bathing is the last thing on his mind.

"And what are our plans from here?" Mason asks, pulling my thoughts back to our conversation. "When are we to depart for your queen?"

Nate, who had looked like he was snoozing a moment ago, stretches and props himself up on his elbows. "Yeah, 'bout that, we sure that's a good idea?"

My brow creases, and I whirl on him. "We've talked about this. I need to see Queen Vespera and try to convince her to call for aid from the allied realms. If Toralyn falls, who knows which realm will be next."

"For all we know, attacking Toralyn could be a diversion," Nate counters.

"Toralyn is one of the strongest realms," Dante says. "If the witches conquer this land, it will not look good. Nor will it bode well for the rest of us."

"Whatever the reason, Nine Lives is right," Prince Callan says harshly. "You should all go to Seral. This is my home and my problem. I can handle it."

I gape at the archangel. "You can't be serious. This affects all of us."

Prince Callan clenches his jaw. "At least, if you won't return home just yet, then all of you wait here while I go ahead to speak with the queen." His gaze flicks to the water, and I suddenly wonder if the choice for us to be here wasn't just about finding a safe place for us to rest. *He was hoping we'd be tempted to stay here.* I narrow my eyes at the archangel, irritation prickling at my temple.

"I could be wrong," Dante muses. "But I get the feeling you don't wish for Blake to meet your family."

I blink rapidly. "Is that true?" I search Prince

Callan's face, but his expression is unreadable. "Is it because I'm half angel?" My walls fly up, anger simmering in my veins. There had been times when I'd wondered why the angels never tried to reach out to me. I was heir to the demon throne, after all, and a half angel.

As a child I was ridiculed for being a half-breed demon, and now I wonder if the angels feel something similar for me. Mason's hand rests on my shoulder, and he massages my tensed muscles.

Regret flashes on Prince Callan's face as he holds my gaze, and he blows out a breath. "It's not that," he says, and I visibly relax, not realizing how much the thought had bothered me until that moment.

"Then what is it?" Mason asks, his voice hard like he's about to make Prince Callan hurt if the archangel says the wrong thing.

Prince Callan runs a hand through his golden hair, and I note how different he looks in comparison to the archangel I'd first witnessed in the ballroom. Instead of oozing confidence and arrogance, right now the male just seems...tired.

"And this is why I'll never have to worry about bein' the biggest dick of the group," Nate comments with a lopsided grin.

Prince Callan glares at him.

"We're not staying here," I tell Prince Callan bluntly. "If you're embarrassed of me, you're just going to have to deal with it. Visiting the queen isn't about you or any of us."

"Embarrassed?" Prince Callan says incredulously. "You don't get it. I want you to stay out here for your own safety. All of you."

My brows lift. "Nowhere is safe. Not anymore." Okay sure, there was some kind of barrier around the valley, but who knew whether the witches would be able to break through it if they really tried.

I'm surprised then, when Prince Callan's gaze goes to Nate, like he's imploring the shifter to side with him. For the entire time I've known these two, they've been at each other's throats, and now I get the undeniable feeling that I'm missing something.

"I would have thought of all beings, you would know to stay away, Nine Lives," Prince Callan says bitterly to my shifter.

Nate shrugs. "I was proven innocent, and I can't stop Blake if she's determined to meet your queen. I plan to go where our mate goes. Besides, times have changed, prince."

The archangel's face tightens, and he runs another hand through his hair.

"Wait, what do you mean by innocent?" I ask Nate. I think about the shifter's reputation. Nine Lives is the name he's called throughout the realms, in reference to the nine times he's escaped an execution sentence, due to his thieving exploits. "Let me guess, you took something from Queen Vespera in the past?"

Nate grins broadly. "Hey, I wasn't about to

exclude kingdoms and deny them the joy of my presence."

I groan. "What did you steal?"

"I never *stole* anything," he defends, mocking a hurt expression like he's offended I would imply such a thing. "Whoever took the jewel from the treasury merely made it look like it was my fault. Some kind of annoying copycat. Timed it perfectly when they knew I would be in the realm and everythin'. The angels only figured out the truth in the weeks after they had condemned me to death. It's lucky for them that I escaped, or they'd have my innocent death on their conscience."

"Yes, innocent," Prince Callan says dryly.

"Innocent in regards to that crime," Nate says. "And anyway, the queen wouldn't kill me now that she knows she was wrong. Besides, I'm bonded with you, gorgeous." He winks at me. "I'm sure you wouldn't let her take your favorite mate from you."

"Favorite? Is that right?" Dante drawls.

I roll my eyes, but Nate's right about one thing. There's no way I'd let the queen take one of my mates. Still, I feel a little uneasy about letting Nate come along if he has a history with the queen.

"Is it true?" I ask Prince Callan. "Does Queen Vespera know Nate wasn't the one who stole the jewel?"

There's a flicker of something in Prince Callan's eyes, but before I can question it, it's gone.

"Yes," the archangel replies. "She knows the shifter is innocent of that crime."

I stare at the prince for a moment, convinced that I'm still missing something. When he doesn't say anything more, I nod slowly. "All right. Then I guess we'll be joining you."

Prince Callan's nostrils flare. "I must insist you all stay here."

But it's too late. I lift to my feet, plucking my clothes from the tree and pulling them on before grabbing my weapons belt. "I think we've waited long enough. I'm not staying in this valley when your realm is at war, and Seral could be next. Now, are you coming or not?"

Prince Callan still looks like he wants to argue, but he doesn't.

Shade flaps her wings, flying over and landing on my shoulder, her claws cutting through my flimsy shirt and scratching against my shoulder. *"Uh, Blake, what do you even know about the angel queen? Because for once, I get the feeling Prince Callan isn't just trying to be an ass. What if this is a bad idea?"*

"Then it wouldn't be my first one," I reply. *"We can't stay here, Shade."*

Realizing that I'm going whether he wants me to or not, Prince Callan waits while everyone dresses, and then he begins leading us from the valley, his long strides taking us away from the hot springs.

Shade's last question circles in my mind, and as we walk, I wrack my brain trying to recall all that I know about the angel monarch. Unfortunately, it isn't much. *"I've heard Queen Vespera is a cunning and ruthless ruler,"* I say to Shade. *"It's said she has a weapon that keeps everyone in line. A powerful angel who follows her every command without question."*

"A powerful angel?" Shade asks. *"What can they do?"*

"I have no idea. It's a secret known only to angelkind." And that doesn't include me.

"Then maybe you should ask your archangel mate?" she suggests.

I purse my lips, eyeing Prince Callan's back as he stalks at the head of our group. He doesn't look like he's in a talkative mood. *"I'll ask as we get closer,"* I tell her.

"Okay, so do you know anything else about her?"

I step over a fallen log. *"Only that the queen is also known for her elaborate parties and has a deep love of intricate performances."* I shrug. *"That's about all I've got."*

"Performances? You mean, like she enjoys the theatre?"

"I'm not exactly sure. Queen Vespera doesn't visit Seral frequently, and whenever she has visited, I've been busy elsewhere. But I do remember a time when a group of hand-selected demons practiced tirelessly for months in preparation for a performance directed for the angel queen."

"Well, that doesn't sound so bad," Shade muses, perking up a little.

Nate comes closer on my left side, moving a branch that's at my height level so I don't have to duck under it.

"He might be a prick, but Queen Vespera is a real piece of work," the shifter says, indicating with his head to Prince Callan. "We'll need to keep our wits about us when we're around her."

"We will, or you will?" I ask, recalling what he'd said about being sentenced to death.

"We will," he confirms. "She had me imprisoned for days, and it was the first time in my life that I wondered whether I might not be able to find a way out."

Turning my head to the side, I eye my shifter. "And how *did* you escape? They say she has a weapon. An angel under her control who wields immense power."

Nate frowns, and his gaze focuses on Prince Callan again. "You'd better ask him that one. I might steal treasures, but I don't share secrets. Not unless they're mine to tell."

Facing forward again, I think about this and continue following my archangel.

CHAPTER
SEVEN

~ Princess Blake ~

We exit the forest, walking out onto farmlands, and Prince Callan leads us down a hill to a narrow dirt road. From the lack of footprints and markings, it's been some time since it's been traveled. Not that I'm surprised. In a land of angels, I doubt walking is common. We pass farms with trees bursting with golden fruit, and herds of braying four-legged animals that remind me of the cows I've seen in the human realm.

Over the following hours, on two occasions the road seems to disappear entirely until Prince Callan finds it again. My wings are heavy as I follow the prince, streams of sunlight beating down on us.

Mason comes up beside me, sweat coating his brown skin. "Will you remind me why we aren't using my portal ring right now, my mate?"

I stop where I am, my gaze sliding from the golden fields around us and settling on his face.

Nate groans. "Fuck, I forgot about that thing."

I wipe the sweat from my forehead.

"And you couldn't have reminded us about it sooner?" Dante asks.

Mason fiddles with the ring on his finger. "I can't use it as I wouldn't be able to visualize our end destination. When no one asked, I figured there must be a reason." He turns to Prince Callan. "But you know where we're going. You could use it."

I glare at Prince Callan, who looks more annoyed than relieved at Mason's reminder.

"I had hoped with time you would all come to your senses," the archangel says simply.

"*Unbelievable,*" Shade gripes. "*Are you telling me we didn't need to walk all that way in this heat?*"

"*To be fair, I think it's only been a few hours, and you haven't walked a single step,*" I reply.

"*That's not the point.*"

Sighing, I pinch the bridge of my nose. "We're seeing your queen," I tell Prince Callan. "Now, are you going to use the portal ring or not?"

The prince strides close to me. So close that his chest almost presses against mine. "You're not taking this seriously."

"I am," I say, gritting my teeth. "But you're not

taking *me* seriously." I want to be angry, but his gaze dips to my lips, and his scent makes my head light. I swallow hard. "I've told you already. We're seeing your queen. Once she's heard us, we'll be on our way."

Worry shines in Prince Callan's eyes, but it's gone a second later.

He stares at me for a moment longer, and then he steps back, holding his hand out to Mason. "Pass it to me."

The centaur places the ring on Prince Callan's palm. As the archangel encloses the ring with his fingers, I blurt, "The weapon. The angel your mother has under her control. What can they do?"

Prince Callan stiffens, his expression darkening, but he doesn't reply and steps away from the group. Turning to the stretch of road before him, he closes his eyes, muttering something under his breath. A moment later, a portal appears, a circle of flames flickering in the light breeze carrying over the fields.

"Where does it go?" Alaric growls.

Prince Callan keeps his focus on the portal. "To the front gates of the palace."

"*Oh, thank god,*" Shade mutters, stretching out her wings from her position on my shoulder. "*I wasn't sure how much longer I could last in this heat.*"

I grin. "*You know, you could have gone back to Seral with Dad.*"

She squawks in my head. "*And miss out on all the fun? I don't think so.*"

When I look up, Prince Callan pins me with a stare. "Keep close to me, and when we meet the queen, let me do the talking."

I open my mouth to protest, but he turns, stepping into the portal.

Cursing, I share a look with the others before I follow him.

I emerge from the portal onto a white stone bridge, and my hands immediately fly to my weapons. At least half a dozen armored guards circle the gateway, but before I can draw my blades, Prince Callan is by my side.

"It's all right," he tells me.

It's then that I notice the guards are standing at attention, their spears positioned by their sides. They're alert and watchful, but it's obvious they're waiting for Prince Callan's next order.

"Word of your arrival is on its way to the queen, my prince," a guard barks. "It is good to see you home."

"You as well, Tyros," Prince Callan says with a thin smile.

The guards watch intently as the rest of my mates step from the portal, but none of the guards move into offensive positions.

I stare up at the huge dome structure before us. The palace is made of white stone with intricate patterns of gold painted over its entire surface. The small windows situated at intervals, spiral up the structure, looking like a pathway of stars climbing the glittering stone, and armored guards line the entire bridge and the circular perimeter of the palace.

"*Whoa,*" Shade gasps, clearly as awed as I am. Back home, the demon castle is a fortress, all sharp edges and dark stone, but this palace is like a work of art.

"It's somethin' isn't it?" Nate says, stopping beside me and planting his hands on his hips as he peers up.

Turning my head, I stare out at the city where hundreds of angels follow flight paths above marshmellow houses, moving quickly in neat, efficient lines. "You've got that right," I mutter.

"We should go," Prince Callan prompts, and he shouts an order to the guards. They step back, moving to their places along the bridge, and we stride down the stone path toward the front of the palace. The wind whistles in my ears, tugging at my wings, but Prince Callan lifts his hand, sending out a burst of power. Instantly the air calms, and we walk the rest of the way in silence.

When we reach the front entrance, the guards stationed there salute the prince and move to the side, opening the doors for us. We walk into a gilded entrance hallway that's just as grand as the outside of the palace, and I gape at the portraits of the angels on the walls. There are hundreds of them, each painting kept in a large golden frame, with an inscription underneath. Before I can read any of the words, Prince Callan leads us forward, into the heart of the palace.

"Your highness," a maid with flowing silver hair approaches quickly, bowing low. "Is there anything I can get you?"

"Not this time, thank you, Ivy," Prince Callan says, passing her without a glance. He takes us to the bottom of a flight of steps, and I peer up at the spiraling staircase, which reaches as high as I can see. It curves around, leaving open space in the center of the building where other angels follow orderly flight paths to get to different sections of the palace.

"We should walk," Prince Callan says, taking the first step.

"Or we could fly. Surely between us we can carry everyone," I suggest.

Prince Callan's gaze darts to the closest angels, then he focuses his attention back on me. "I think it would be better if the shifters remain in human form for now."

I frown, wondering if he's referring to Nate's cat form, but then his gaze flicks to Mason, and I understand his meaning. Parading a winged centaur in the middle of the palace, a creature unknown to the angels, would likely draw unwanted attention.

"Walking it is," I say.

Prince Callan takes us up the stairs, and it doesn't escape my attention that we're the only ones on the narrow staircase. Every angel, including the servants, distinguished by their pale blue robes, fly to the different floors. Considering the lack of a handrail, and the nearly perilous narrow stairway, I get the feeling that the golden stairs were merely an afterthought when the building was constructed.

"Well, now we know where Prince Callan gets it from," Shade comments as angels fly past us in almost perfect synchronization, each with intense gazes like their minds are solely focused on whatever task they intend to carry out.

I think of how cold Prince Callan has been toward me, and I twist my head back to ask Nate a question. The shifter is staring at my ass, and he grins like he's been caught out. "What? Can't blame me for lookin'."

I roll my eyes, grinning, before asking him seriously, "Are all the angels like this?"

"Like what?"

I gesture with my head to the angels soaring past us. "So...focused."

He chuckles. "Oh, that. Yeah, the queen runs a tight operation."

"Operation? He makes it sound like a military camp," Shade chimes in.

"This isn't what I expected the palace to look like," I admit. "I thought the queen likes to party?"

"Oh, she does," Nate confirms. "It's just her idea

of a party involves torturin' her prisoners in front of the angel population to showcase her strength."

My brows rise. "Torture?"

"Can't say I made it to the party where I was gonna be the guest of honor, but I hear there's drinkin' and singin' involved, too."

Right... I think of Nate being in the queen's clutches, and my mood sours. *Maybe it wasn't such a good idea to bring him back here.*

"*Why can't a party ever just mean drinking, dancing, and stuffing yourself with food?*" Shade grumbles. "*Or you know, fucking. I mean, everyone loves a good orgy. But no, this Queen Vespera lady sounds like another psycho.*"

Prince Callan's warnings to stay away are slowly starting to make more sense, and I keep my gaze alert, watching the angels around us. In the past, I've always pictured my mother as this innocent female who fell for my dark, depraved father, but now I'm wondering whether she was just as crazy as him because clearly angels aren't the pure souls I thought they were. Maybe it never was an opposites attract relationship, but kindred spirits?

Clenching my jaw, I force the thought of her from my mind and focus on the present.

It takes a long while before we reach the very top floor and the stairs end, leading out into a short corridor where there's a single golden door. We gather as a group, and I'm surprised when Prince Callan pulls me to the side, his hand brushing my arm before he jerks back, his gaze darting to the angel guards stationed outside the door. "Let me do the talking, Blake. The queen isn't someone you want to cross, and she has a way of twisting your words in her favor."

"Ah, so she is like your dad then," Shade comments nervously in my head.

Lines of worry cross Prince Callan's face, but I can't give him the answer he wants. "I'm not simply here because I'm your mate," I say slowly, though it was one of the big reasons why I stepped through the portal to Toralyn. "I'm here because I'm the princess of Seral, and I've been given an order to converse with the queen about the war with the witches. So, I'm sorry, but I can't promise that."

His temple pulses, but his expression is severe. "Then just...be careful and promise me you won't touch anything."

"Now that I can do," I reply. "And are you finally going to tell us about this weapon she has?"

His gaze shutters, his face closing off completely as the vulnerability is replaced with the cold, hard expression I'm accustomed to. "No." He spares a glance to the others, and then he turns, marching toward the door.

"Tell her we've arrived," he barks, and one of the guards dips his head, disappearing inside the room. A moment later, the door swings wide open, and the guard strides out, moving to the side of the doorway.

"Enter!" A husky voice calls out to us, and Prince

Callan glances at me one last time before striding inside. We file into the room after him, and Nate, Mason, and Dante keep close to me. Alaric scowls as he takes up the rear.

"Uh, Blake, what the heck are those?"

"I don't know..." I trail off, trying not to show my surprise.

We're in a large, dome-shaped room, and light filters in from the glass panels above us. Along the walls there are rows of shelving that curve the whole way around. Above the shelves, small storm clouds hover on each ledge, separated from one another. *Or are they clouds of smoke?* Whatever they are, the hairs rise on my arms as I get a horrible feeling.

With my senses on alert, I turn my attention to where a seemingly middle-aged female sits behind a massive glossy stone desk. A jeweled crown rests atop the female's cropped golden hair which is a shade darker than Prince Callan's, and golden piercings run down her right ear. She continues writing on a piece of parchment, and it's not until Prince Callan clears his throat loudly that she finishes whatever she's inking and looks up.

I expect her to be glad to see her son, but irritation flashes on her face as her shrewd gaze sweeps over Prince Callan and the rest of us. Prince Callan's body hardens, his expression devoid of emotion.

"Yes?" she barks, her voice loud in the otherwise silent room.

"Your highness," Prince Callan says coldly, bowing before straightening again. "We come from Sailyn. The witches attacked with force and a large portion of the township has been destroyed. There is some loss of life."

Queen Vespera doesn't look the least bit bothered or surprised by the news. Nor does she comment on the fact that her son has returned after being away for some time. "And has the threat been neutralized?" she asks, her voice even icier than Prince Callan's.

"We've beaten back their forces for now," Prince Callan reports. "But we should acknowledge the aid we received from the demon—"

"Then I suppose you're good for something," the queen says, not letting him finish. She smiles, but there's no warmth in her eyes. "See to it that the rebuild is completed." She waves her hand dismissively and turns her attention back to the parchment in front of her.

Shade whistles in my head. *"Well damn, did it just get colder in here or what?"*

Anger simmers inside me as I stare at the queen. The demon king has always been hard on me, and the challenges he's put me through have nearly killed me on multiple occasions, but in his twisted way, I've always known he did it because he thought it would make me stronger. He's never spoken to me with such disrespect, and I bristle at the way the queen is speaking to her own son.

"You need to do more than oversee the rebuild," I say before Prince Callan can speak again. "The witches are organized and dangerous. Who knows how long they've been planning their attacks. You must call for aid from the allied realms."

The queen places down her quill pen, and her ice blue eyes lock onto me. "Ah, the demon princess decides to speak even when her voice is unwelcome. I had wondered if you'd be bright enough to keep quiet. Though, I guess I shouldn't be surprised your father has sent you. Even if I had made it painfully clear to him that there is no need for a call to aid. The angels have it in hand. Perhaps, you should worry more about your own king. He doesn't seem quite as...spirited as he once did."

I grind my teeth, wondering just what happened when Dad visited the queen. "If you ignore this, it's not only your kind who will suffer." I'm vaguely aware of Shade moving from my shoulder, but I'm too distracted to take note of where she's going.

"Ignore it?" Queen Vespera's eyes narrow on me. "My forces have been directed to where they are required, and should the need arise, I will reassess the situation. In any case, according to your father, the witches were all but eradicated all those years ago. Now, I'm expected to believe that they've amassed enough forces to bring down the realm of angels?" She laughs cruelly. "I understand the need for excitement, but I don't have time to entertain such a ridiculous notion as a false war. Now, if that's all."

"They should not be underestimated," Prince Callan adds.

Queen Vespera bares her teeth. "And neither should I. When my mother agreed to unite with the other realms all those years ago, we were left with no choice. The realms were all suffering, and the witches had created a force that could not be ignored. But now they are but shadows of a defeated race. If the time ever comes for us to see them as a real threat we will, but for now, there are much more pressing matters at hand." She turns to the doorway and calls out. "Guards!"

The archangel guards stationed outside the room, march inside, standing on either side of the open door.

I let out a noise of frustration. "With all due respect, you're not seeing sense, your highness. Now *is* the time to call for aid. You need to think of the lives at stake."

Queen Vespera's lips thin. "And you would do well to remember your place, half-breed."

The slur stings, but I'm careful not to let any emotion show on my face. My mates shift around me, tension emanating from them, but I shake my head subtly. The last thing I want is for my mates to start a war simply because the angel queen stated the truth.

"The demon princess is right to be concerned,"

Prince Callan says, his eyes shining with hate as he stares at his mother. "It can't be a coincidence that the witches are targeting Toralyn after all this time."

Queen Vespera's gaze drifts from me, settling briefly on my other mates before finally landing on her son. Her lips twist into a humorless smile. "And you, turning up here with these..." She wrinkles her nose. "Visitors. You never were any good at following our laws." Her dark gaze goes to Nate, lingering on my shifter mate. I step to the side, shielding him, and drawing her attention back to me.

The queen opens her mouth to say more, but she presses her lips together when moaning fills the air. The sound is quiet at first, but it grows louder, and there's a slight static buzz as if we're listening to a recording.

"Oh, my magnificent Kalea," a masculine voice groans, blaring out across the room, the male sounding as if he's in the throes of passion. **"Now the two become one. Yes, let me bury inside you and feel your soft walls."** There's grunting, and then that voice again, **"I love it when you milk my cock like that. Mmm, just like that my precious."**

This is followed by feminine whimpers and pants, and a female cries out in an overly exaggerated voice. **"Uriel, faster. Faster!"**

"Oh gods, it's like listening to the worst porno ever! Crap! How do I turn this thing off? Please. Please!"

All of our gazes dart around the room, and as the

dialogue keeps going, I spot Shade perched on one of the lower shelves, standing right next to a dark cloud. She's hidden by Alaric's leg, but it won't be long before the queen spots her.

"What did you do?" I hiss at her.

She frantically pecks at the cloud puff like a possessed bird. *"Ohhhh, it's like I'm living every bookworm's nightmare, except the book porn isn't even good!"* she wails.

"Shade!" I hiss again as Queen Vespera steps to the side, and her gaze locks onto my crow. *"We don't have time for your rambling right now!"*

"I didn't mean to, I swear," she replies, panicked. *"How was I supposed to know the queen has porn recordings on display, and all you have to do is brush by them to turn them on?"*

"Porn recordings?" I frown, not sure why the queen would have them either. Then I remember Prince Callan's warning not to touch anything. *Great. So much for that.*

"Yes, let me fill you with my seed, my precious flower," the masculine voice goes on, and there's a noise as if an animal is dying.

"Guess he just found his release," I say to Shade, wincing at the sound.

She makes a gagging noise in my head, and behind me, Nate and Dante struggle to hold back their laughter. Prince Callan's face is pale, as if he's going to be sick, and the queen's temples pulse, fury burning in her gaze.

For a while there's only heavy breathing until the male speaks up again.

"If I could but stay here with you always," the male replies.

"What's stopping you?" the female says softly. **"Help me keep my bed warm."**

There's more heavy breathing. **"You know I would love that my precious, but I can't. Not tonight."**

"And what could be so important that you need to leave right now?" the female asks, her tone a little too interested.

"This isn't porn," I tell Shade. *"I'm guessing we're about to hear a confession."*

Just as the male starts speaking again, the cloud flies across the room, stopping above Queen Vespera's outstretched hand. The instant she closes her fist, the recording cuts off and silence fills the room.

Shade squawks in surprise, and she flaps her wings, flying to my shoulder.

Queen Vespera lets a slow, sinister smile spread across her face. "I'll tell you what," she says to me, moving her fingers like she's stroking the gray cloud above her hand. "I can tell that the matter with the witches is of great importance to you, and if the rumors are correct, it's said that my son is one of your fated mates."

Prince Callan's jaw tenses, but he doesn't deny the claim.

"So why don't you all stay and join us for a little party to celebrate the victory in Sailyn and the discovery of your mates. Once the celebration is over, I promise to check on the other battles around Toralyn. If it so happens that the witches are not yet defeated, I will call for aid from the allied realms." Her gaze stays on me, like the question is mine to answer.

"I don't think that will be necessary," Prince Callan growls, and concern flashes on his face before it's gone again.

Queen Vespera lifts her hand to silence him, her gaze not leaving me. "What say you, princess? How badly do you want to ensure Toralyn does not fall?"

It's a little fucked up that she's asking if I care for the angel realm more than she does, and I hesitate.

"Don't you even think it, girl. Remember what Nate said about her parties."

But I've never let the demon king down, and I refuse to let the witches end us all. My lips stretch into a dark smile to match the queen's. "Sounds great."

CHAPTER

EIGHT

~ Princess Blake ~

"*Tell me I'm not the only one who has a bad feeling about this,*" Shade says as she stands on my shoulder.

"*It's not just you,*" I reply with a tight smile. Reaching up, I adjust one of the straps of my black gossamer gown. After our discussion with Queen Vespera, we'd been escorted to a bedchamber where we could freshen up and prepare for the party. Prince Callan had disappeared, saying something about having errands to attend to, and the garments had been promptly delivered to us with a message that guards would escort us to the ballroom in a few hours.

Prince Callan arrived in time to join our escort,

and unlike the rest of my mates who are wearing black suits that match my dress, he's wearing a pristine, white suit trimmed with gold. It shouldn't bother me, but I can't help but feel like his clothing choice is some kind of statement.

Blowing out a breath, I try not to think about it as we turn down a long corridor that's completely bare besides the decorative golden cornices and patterned cream wallpaper.

"Well, it's still not too late to turn back," Shade says. *"We could use Mason's portal ring and hightail it back to Seral."*

"We need to get through to Queen Vespera. If this is what it takes to get her to agree to call for aid, then we'll attend her party. How bad can it be?" I say the last part sarcastically, but Shade answers anyway.

"Uh, have you forgotten about the torture and death part?"

"I haven't forgotten."

"Well, you could have fooled me, because for someone who still hasn't bonded with her mates, this feels a little risky."

She's right, but it still doesn't change anything. I tell myself the only reason I'm going is to ensure the queen seeks help in Toralyn, but I know that's not the full truth. I saw how Queen Vespera treated Prince Callan, and it bugs me. I want to know more about him, and more about her. More about this whole damn place where my mother came from.

Shade adjusts her perch on my shoulder,

balancing on a small patch of leather that's strapped there.

"And what if the queen is right, and the witches don't pose as big a threat as you think?"

"Then everyone goes home again after we've squashed whatever resurgence this is. It's better to be overprepared."

Before we reach the guarded double doors at the end of the corridor, Prince Callan stops and turns to face our group. Lines of worry crease his handsome face. "Once we enter those doors, there's no going back. The queen has different wards around specific areas of the palace, and portal magic won't work in there. If you wish to return to Seral, this is your last chance." There's the faintest slice of hope in his eyes.

I hold his gaze. "Would you be coming with us?"

His brows lower. "I—No, not today."

I shrug. "Then we're staying. Besides, you know I can't go. Not until the queen calls on the allied realms."

"And you know we're not leaving without our mate," Mason adds. "A lesson you would do well to learn."

Prince Callan's gaze hardens. "Then so be it. But don't say I didn't warn you."

"Yeah, like he warned us about those porn clouds? Great job, buddy. Great job," Shade snarks. *"Wait, you don't think the queen will have them in there, do you?"*

"What?"

"The porn clouds."

"I wish you would stop calling them that."

She continues rambling, but I don't hear a word she says. I'm busy staring at Prince Callan as his expression closes off, and his muscles harden like he's preparing for battle. He turns from us and strides the rest of the way to the double doors.

Dante's hand rests on the small of my back. "He may be right," the demon says quietly against my ear. "We could return home knowing that we'd tried to convince the angel queen. King Dalton himself didn't succeed. He'll understand."

I roll my shoulders back and stare into Dante's midnight-blue eyes. "We can't leave him."

~

~ Prince Callan ~

Whenever Queen Vespera peers at Blake, I want to gouge the queen's eyes out. I hate my mother's attention on my *Ahalian Touizda*. My mate. I can see the queen's mind working as she assesses Blake, no doubt trying to determine the best way to break the demon, and how to use the princess to her advantage.

The invitation to attend the party was more of a command than it was a request, but I'd still hoped Blake would refuse. I'd hoped she would see the queen for what she was and know that the words spilling from the queen's lips were simply lies spun to ensnare her.

But Blake had agreed.

My promise to my younger sister, Mirelle, surfaces to the forefront of my mind, and with every step I take toward the ballroom, I can feel everything inside me unraveling.

For years, I've endured the queen, caught in her trap like so many others. Everything the queen has asked of me, I've given, but now Blake is shaking the foundation of all that I've worked toward.

The walls are closing in, and I feel that vice around my neck closing. Because I won't lose my sister, but I won't lose my mate either.

The others don't realize it, but blood will spill tonight. And I'll make sure it's by my blade.

~

~ Princess Blake ~

"Holy moly, this place is gorgeous," Shade says in my head, her beady eyes taking in the giant ballroom.

There must be hundreds of angels in attendance, all dressed in sparkling garments with an array of piercings and jewellery. A giant harp sits to one side of the room, the strings being plucked by invisible fingers to create an intricate melody, and puffs of wispy white clouds blanket the floor, making it feel as though we're in the sky.

Across the room, Queen Vespera sits on a golden throne, and her gaze finds us when we walk forward, the clouds stirring around our feet as we move. Thankfully, unlike the clouds in her office, nothing bad happens when we walk through these ones, but the queen smiles as she watches us.

A server walks by with a golden tray of drinks, and I take a glass and raise it into the air, smiling at the queen.

Queen Vespera lifts her own glass, returning the gesture, and Prince Callan glares at me.

"Don't drink that," Alaric growls, no doubt saying what Prince Callan is thinking.

My smile doesn't falter, and I keep my eyes on the queen as I reply carefully. "Relax, I wasn't planning to."

"Wait, why can't we drink it?" Nate says, pulling his mouth back from his own goblet. A droplet of liquid hangs from the side of his lips, and he peers at us sheepishly. "I'm not goin' to die, right?"

"How the fuck you got your nickname is beyond me," Alaric growls.

We all stare at Nate, but moments pass, and nothing happens. The shifter licks his lips. "Not quite as good as that stuff you brought me last time we were here, Callan, but it's not bad. Not bad at all."

Prince Callan glowers at the shifter.

"Is it poisoned?" I ask the archangel, knowing full well that not all ingested poisons show symptoms straight away.

Alaric snatches the goblet from Nate, and he dips his head, ducking behind Mason as he sniffs the remnants in the cup. "Not poisoned," he growls.

My shoulders loosen, and I slap Nate on the chest. "Can you *try* to stay alive tonight?"

"What? I figure she wouldn't have coaxed us here simply to poison us," Nate defends. "The queen likes a spectacle when it comes to her enemies."

"Enemies? I thought we were supposed to be her guests," Mason comments.

Prince Callan straightens the collar of his shirt. "The shifter is right. Using poison isn't the queen's style. But I don't suggest you drink the wine. It's strong, and we'll need our wits about us."

Nate gives us a lop-sided smile. "Yeah, I'm feelin' it. And I don't have a single regret."

Prince Callan let's out a frustrated noise, and he leads us further into the ballroom. We stop beside a giant stone pillar, sheltered from the queen's view.

"So what now?" I ask the prince. "I'm guessing Queen Vespera doesn't really intend to keep her promise once this party is over."

Prince Callan stares at me. "If you realize that, then why are you here?"

"Why are *you* here?" I counter. "It's obvious you hold no love for your queen." *Or the other way around.*

"Love?" The archangel's top lip curls. "I'm here because I don't have a choice."

I frown. "Then help me understand."

His gaze connects with mine, and the golden

flecks in his eyes brighten. For a moment, I think he's going to explain. For a moment, I think I'll finally get an answer to his strange behavior, but then the music of the harp grows louder, and he turns his head, distracted. A trio of singers step up to the side of the harp, and the music changes, the tone darkening as they harmonise an eerie tune. The angels around the room start to move, forming a circle around the mass of white cloud in the middle of the space. They dance and sway in time to the music, and the white cloud grows bigger, doubling in size like it's a living being.

Prince Callan's expression flattens.

"What is it?" I ask.

"A demonstration," he replies coldly.

Nate curses.

I look between them, an uneasy feeling spreading through me. "What kind of demonstration?"

The music stops abruptly, and we all move to peer around the pillar as the queen lifts to her feet, the fabric of her long white gown pooling on the floor. Her face is hard set as she looks across the ballroom, weapons strapped to her like she's about to walk onto a battlefield rather than attend a party.

She lifts her hands into the air. "Gather, my angels," she calls out, "for tonight, we celebrate a victory at the town of Sailyn! Once again, we have shown the witches that angels do not fall, and we shall remain victorious, uncowed by them!"

The crowd erupts into applause, and Queen Vespera beams at them, her pearly teeth reflecting the light. "And what better way to celebrate than by enacting justice on another who has wronged us?"

There's more applause, but when I peer around the room, none of the angels are smiling.

"*Did I not say I had a bad feeling?*" Shade grumbles. "*It's still not too late to leave, right?*"

"*We knew this might happen,*" I say grimly. "*The queen is known for torturing her enemies at her parties. We just need to keep our heads down.*"

Mason moves closer to me and glares at Prince Callan. "What is this?"

I grind my teeth, wishing I had my weapons, and my mates all tense.

Prince Callan steps to the side, and it takes me a moment to realize why. *He's shielding me from the queen's view.*

It's a noble thought, but I'm not prepared to hide from this.

"Keep quiet," Prince Callan orders us quietly. "We'll watch her have her fun, and we'll only stay at the party long enough to fulfill our obligation."

The cloud in the middle of the room continues to swell, and then the queen flicks her hands, and the mass stops growing. The music stops, and moaning fills the air. It's the same couple we were listening to earlier when we were in the queen's office, except when it gets to the same place where the recording was cut off, this time it continues.

"And what could be so important that you need to leave right now?" the female implores again, and a feeling of dread winds through me as the conversation continues.

"Oh crap, it's the bad porno recording again," Shade squawks in my head, but I quiet her so I can listen.

"I-It's nothing," the male replies, uncertain.

"Nothing?" the female replies, and I can practically imagine her pouting from the tone of her voice.

Everyone in the ballroom remains silent, all of us listening as the recording continues.

There's more moaning, and it's obvious things are starting to heat up again. **"I'm simply trying to understand you,"** the female says between kisses. **"I'm going to miss you. Are you sure you must leave?"**

The guy groans and there are more wet kissing sounds. **"If I had a choice, I'd stay here forever,"** he says.

"Then stay," the female pleads. **"I love you. You're my... my Ahalian Touizda."**

Prince Callan mutters a curse. "Stop," he growls under his breath.

"What did you just say, my precious?" the male in the recording continues.

"I've never felt for another, what I feel for you," the female replies, and even I can hear the waver in her voice. The *lie*. But the male in the recording doesn't detect it.

There's the sound of more kissing, and then the male says, **"I promise this will be the last time my love. But I must go to Rostof tonight. When I return, we can start to build our family. We can go into the country like you've always wanted. We can get away from all of this and find a place that's secluded before they even get here."**

There's a sharp intake of breath. **"Before who gets here?"**

"Don't worry, my love, they will not harm you. They're only after the queen. And when I give them the plans which detail the layout of the palace, my part will be over."

"Oh, Uriel," the female's voice cracks, and despite earlier when I felt like I could tell she was acting, true sadness coats her words.

The recording ends, and the massive cloud in the center of the room starts to dissipate, the whisps of white smoke simply evaporating until a naked male is revealed. His back is arched, and he remains crouched, his hands and ankles bound in thick chains that shackle him to the floor. Wounds cover his entire body, and his broken wings hang to either side of him, his feathers covered in blood.

Something tells me I know exactly who the male is. *Uriel.*

"Please," Uriel begs, barely able to see through two swollen eyes. "I-I won't take the plans anywhere. I was a fool, brainwashed by the enemy.

P-please. I didn't realize what would happen. I didn't know what they would do."

Queen Vespera sneers before her lips twist into a cruel smile. "Oh, I know you won't take them anywhere, traitor. My daughter has seen to that."

Daughter? I look to where a figure stands not far from the queen. Soft golden curls hang down to her waist, and golden sparks shine in her pale blue eyes. Strange golden markings cover her entire body, including her face, and she stands tall, her shoulders pulled back.

"Hang on, that would make her Prince Callan's sister, right?" Shade comments.

The beautiful girl looks young, maybe only eighteen, and her gaze fixes on Prince Callan.

My brows lower. *"Yes, it would."*

Prince Callan doesn't say anything, but he stares back at her, not taking his gaze from her face.

"Wait. Do you think she's the female from the recording?" Shade says uneasily.

Queen Vespera glares down at the prisoner. "Uriel, for high treason against your queen, you are hereby sentenced to a true death. May your last moments be long and full of agony, and may your memory be forever tarnished."

~ Princess Blake ~

"*W*ell, *that was dramatic,*" Shade comments, and she lifts one wing, shielding her face. "*Tell me when it's over, because I'd rather not see skewered angel right now.*"

"*Queen Vespera might be cruel to use her daughter to extract the truth from him in that way, but she's not wrong to punish him. He was plotting against her. If it were one of the demons, I'd have to use them to send a message as well.*"

"*Yes, but you heard her, right? May your last moments be long and full of agony? I'm not sure I want to know what an angel torture and execution looks like.*"

Queen Vespera turns to her daughter, and there

aren't any words exchanged. The queen simply stares at her expectantly, and her daughter steps to the end of the dais, her face expressionless.

"No, Mirelle, don't," Prince Callan mutters under his breath, his hands clenched tightly into fists.

I figure that must be his sister's name. *Mirelle.* I try to recall the lessons I received regarding angel royalty, but I can only remember being schooled about Queen Vespera's sons. There was never any mention of a daughter.

Uriel stares up at Mirelle, tears streaming from his eyes. "My precious, my love," he cries, sobbing so hard his back shakes. Mirelle keeps her gaze fixed on something high above him, not peering at the male, and a flicker of pain shines in her eyes before it's gone again.

"My A-Ahalian Touizda, w-why would you do this?" Uriel stammers. "You must know I didn't mean what I said. If I had known who you truly are, I wouldn't—"

"S-i-l-e-n-c-e!" Queen Vespera booms, her voice ringing throughout the cavernous room. "If you had known you were bedding my daughter, rather than the female she was disguised as, you wouldn't have shown your truth. Now, daughter, let him see what we do to those who defy us."

Mirelle's jaw tightens, her gaze darkening as she lifts her hands, and Prince Callan curses again. He tenses like he intends to go to his sister, to stop what's happening, but he doesn't, and something tells me this isn't the first time he's witnessed a similar display.

I'm not sure what I expect next, and I gasp when white hot flames erupt over Mirelle's entire body, swallowing her and leaving only a humanoid shape in her place. Her flames lick at the air, crackling and sizzling, and the light is so bright I wince. When she lifts her hand, flames shoot out toward Uriel. He screams the moment they touch him, the flames engulfing him in a matter of seconds. The white hot fire dances as his feathers burn, and the sound of Uriel's cries fill the space, a seemingly endless song of torment that has my stomach twisting. It's over sooner than I expect, and Uriel's cries are silenced, the angel now nothing more than ash on the floor. Going by the queen's glare, I'm guessing she'd instructed her daughter to keep the traitor alive for longer, but Mirelle ignores her mother's gaze, stepping back from the front of the dais.

Queen Vespera's smile falters only for a moment, and then she's beaming out at us all again.

An angel at the back of the room throws up, but everyone else stays silent.

Annoyance fills Queen Vespera's expression. "Well?" she prompts the crowd, and slowly, one by one, the angels start clapping. Soon the applause is like thunder in my ears, and the queen's smile grows wider as she revels in it.

"I think I'm going to be sick," Shade moans, and I reach up, stroking her feathers.

The queen leans back on her throne, her lips curving into a smug smile. "And now that's out of the way, let us attend to our other party guests!" Queen Vespera calls out gleefully.

It's not until Mirelle's gaze lands on me that I realize she's talking about us. Before I can act, white flames shoot from the princess's hand, racing across the room and encircling me and my mates in seconds.

Mason, Nate, Alaric, and Dante form up with me, the five of us with our backs to one another. Prince Callan stands a couple paces away, his face a mask of stone.

"We've attended your party as you requested," I say loudly. "What is this?"

Queen Vespera crosses one leg over the other and traces slow circles on one thigh with her long nails. "You have attended my party," Queen Vespera says, "And should the need ever arrive to call on the allied realms for aid, I shall. But when you all walked into my office, I had no choice but to act."

"Why?" Mason asks, squaring his broad shoulders.

Instead of answering, she flicks her hand, and a small dark cloud appears from somewhere behind her. There's a buzzing sound, and then a recording starts to play. An anguished cry fills the air, and unlike when I heard Uriel, this cry has bile climbing up my throat. It's not until I see the pain on Prince

Callan's face that I realize why. It's because I'm listening to a recording of *him*.

His cry ends, morphing into a choked retching and coughing noise.

"Tell me again," a cold and clinical voice demands. Instantly, I recognize Queen Vespera's voice. **"No one takes what's mine, boy."**

There's the crackling of flames, and Prince Callan's scream rings out again, the sound filled with such pain that my body shakes with fury for my mate. Stepping forward, I place my hand on Prince Callan's shoulder, and he flinches.

"Tell me again, what happened," Queen Vespera insists.

There's heavy breathing, before more screams.

"Tell her," a different feminine voice says, and it's more of a desperate plea than a command. Prince Callan's gaze flicks to his sister, and I guess it's her speaking in the recording. **"Please Callan,"** she says. **"It's been days. Why are you protecting him?"**

Protecting him? My brows lower as I wonder who they're speaking of.

There's a long moment of silence, and when Prince Callan finally speaks his voice is a quiet rasp. **"Nine Lives wormed his way into my mind."**

My heart stutters, my blood going cold as my gaze slides to my shifter. He looks just as shocked, his brows practically lifting to his hairline.

"The thief manipulated me so he could get to her," the Prince Callan in the recording goes on.

Queen Vespera seethes. **"You always were my greatest disappointment. To let a traitor infiltrate your mind is unforgivable."** There's the sound of shuffling feet. **"And to let him get to your sister."** She growls. **"Take him!"**

There's the sound of something scraping along stone and the recording cuts off.

My chest heaves like I've just run up the stairs to get here, and my head is a mess of questions and fury. Nate's face is deathly pale, and Prince Callan won't look at me. He just keeps staring at his sister who's bright with white flames.

"She tortured her own son," Shade's horrified words fill my head, and the fury burns hotter inside me. I can't be sure whether Nate did what he's being accused of. All I know is that this woman, this monster, had Prince Callan in her clutches, and she hurt him. *Badly.*

Queen Vespera's smile is a wicked slash across her face. "So, you see, the confession is plain, and there is yet more justice to be dispensed this night."

"Lies," Nate says, a low growl ripping from his throat, but the queen gestures with her head to her daughter, and another stream of fire races out, separating Nate from the rest of us. When we try to fight to get to him, the circle of flames rises higher, the roaring of the fire crackling in my ears as my skin heats.

"No!" I cry.

"No?" The word drips with venom as it comes from Queen Vespera's mouth. "This shifter, Nine Lives, as they call him, tried to kidnap my daughter. My guards found them before he could take her through the gateway, and though he killed the guards before he escaped, Prince Callan remained with Mirelle. After some questioning, the prince explained the situation."

Prince Callan's eyes are dark. "There was no harm done, Queen Vespera. The shifter isn't here for her."

Her gaze cuts to him. "For once you've done well, my son. I had all but lost hope that you would be of use to me, but you've brought me the shifter as promised."

What? My blood turns to ice as realization slithers through me. I think of how many times Prince Callan had told me not to go to the palace. Had he meant any of it, or had he only said it to avoid suspicion? Undoubtedly, he had to know I would follow him here, and the betrayal stings in a way that no physical wound could.

"And you'll release Mirelle as agreed?" Prince Callan asks, his voice cold.

"Release her?" The queen cackles, turning to her daughter with mock affection. "Does your sister look imprisoned?"

Prince Callan's hard expression doesn't waver. "Sister!" he calls out, his voice hoarse.

Mirelle's only response is to turn her head, not meeting his gaze.

Queen Vespera's cackling grows louder. "You see? She does not wish to leave. But that doesn't mean I won't enjoy finally getting justice."

"No, no, no—this is all wrong! The queen can't take Nate. He's the barbed one!" Shade rambles in my head, squawking in panic.

"What? Why are we talking about his penis right now!" I hiss back.

"I don't know," she shoots back nervously. *"I'm just trying to think of what his best feature is!"*

Ignoring her, I glower at the queen. "I don't care what Prince Callan promised. Nate is my fated mate, and he is destined to become a demon royal. Once we are bonded, he will rule by my side. While the crime he committed is despicable, the princess stands unharmed. To kill a demon royal would be an act of war against the demons."

"Ah yes, *once* you are bonded is correct," Queen Vespera replies gleefully. "But if I am not mistaken, there is no bond between you and these five males. Five is an unlikely number for a demon princess, and the idea that you are all fated is merely hearsay. So my judgement stands. Nine Lives must be punished for his crimes."

The flames burn hotter around Nate, and his growl turns to a hiss of pain.

"Stop!" I yell. "You can't."

"Oh, but I can little half-blood," the queen

mocks. "And I suppose if he is your mate, then I won't have to worry about a power shift amongst the demon royals."

Rage makes my body tremble, but I don't let it get the better of me. It wouldn't do any good. Not now.

Dante tries to get to Nate, but the moment the flames touch his hand, he cries out, jumping back. His entire hand is burnt, and the flesh isn't healing.

"I wouldn't touch that if I were you," Queen Vespera sings.

My gaze goes to Alaric. I'd been hoping he could change into his giant form, but he couldn't do that without touching the fire.

I turn Prince Callan toward me, and for a moment, he looks lost. "What did you do?" I snarl.

"It doesn't matter," he mutters. "I have failed her."

"Failed who? Your sister? Sorry if I'm not sympathetic when she's about to burn us alive!"

"You don't understand."

"Of course not! But right now, all I know is that Nate is about to die because of you."

Guilt stains Prince Callan's expression.

"How do we get ourselves out of this?" I snap at him. "How do we save Nate?"

He shrugs. "There is no escape from her."

The fury I hold at his betrayal softens a little then, because I see it. That hopelessness in his eyes. That regret, and the overwhelming pain that seems to consume him. I think of the recording of him being tortured. Of how distant and cold he's been from the moment I met him. How he's always pushed me away. He's known it might come to this, and there's always been that part of him that rebelled at the idea.

"This isn't you," I tell him. "Your mother isn't who you are. I know you did this for your sister, but she's the one standing on the dais while we burn. Tell me, what can we do? Your sister must have a weakness."

When he doesn't answer, I growl in frustration.

"You would really risk starting a war with the demons over a crime that never happened?" I say to the queen. "We just put our necks on the line coming to the aid of your angels in Sailyn."

"A choice you made, yourselves," the queen says dismissively.

"If you take Nate, you'll have to kill all of us," I growl, sweat beading on my brow from the heat of the fire.

Queen Vespera's eyes flash, and she taps her chin thoughtfully. "My my, you are determined to save this street cat, aren't you?"

Nate scowls, and I lift my head higher. "Like I said, he's mine, and if you try to take him from me, I swear you'll regret it."

The queen glances at the angels across the ballroom before looking back at me. "You know I lost some good archangels in that ridiculous competition of your father's. All for what? For you to find these five? Well, I'll tell you what. Seeing as I know how you demons like to play games, how about another competition. If you can best a selection of my finest warriors, then this...*Nate*, will be free to leave with you." A sinister gleam enters her eyes. "Fail, and none of you will make it out of the arena."

"Don't," Prince Callan warns.

I frown, thinking of her proposal.

"*Oh, you can't be serious,*" Shade squawks. "*If you agree and you lose, the queen can kill you without risking war.*"

"*What choice do we have? You said it yourself. Nate is the barbed one.*"

"*I'm serious,*" Shade goes on. "*You know she'll make it impossible for you.*"

She's right, of course, but I can't see another way out. There's no way I'm letting Queen Vespera have my shifter mate. "*She doesn't know us. We'll find a way.*"

Shade continues to protest in my head, but I yell, "Fine. We'll play."

"Excellent," the queen says happily, clapping her hands together.

The dark cloud comes from nowhere, soaring over the fire and smothering us with the queen's magic. I hear my mates calling my name. Strong hands grab me, and I fight to keep my eyes open, but the darkness still takes me.

CHAPTER
TEN

~ Princess Blake ~

I'm woken by the roar of the crowd. The cries of thousands fill my ears, and I groan as I lift myself up. Grains of golden sand filter through my fingers, streaming from my hair and clothes. My nose itches, and I sneeze as I stagger to my feet, my head throbbing.

"Shade?" Panic sets in, but I spot my crow on the ground seconds later, her body half-buried in sand. Dropping down, I ignore the pain in my head and lift her into my hands.

She stirs, shaking the sand off her feathers. *"Well, it's official. Angels are just as deranged as demons, because this move seems like it was straight out of the demon king's playbook."*

"You scared me," I tell her.

"Enchantress?" Alaric's growl is faint, almost drowned out by the din of the crowd, but it's enough that I turn my head in his direction. The assassin lifts himself from the ground a few yards from me. He shakes his head, as if to clear it.

I blink, bleary-eyed back at him, and then I turn, searching for the others. My mates are on the sand, all of us separated a few yards from one another. Alaric was the first to wake after me, and Mason is next.

"My mate!" the centaur shifter calls, struggling to right himself. He staggers toward me, but Alaric remains where he is, his gray gaze going to our surroundings.

The others stir as well, and I copy Alaric, turning my gaze to the giant amphitheater we're in. There are too many rows of angels to count, the curved seating area stretching high into the sky. Some of the angels laugh, bumping one another with excitement, but just as many sit there with dark expressions.

I spin until I spot the royal box, and the golden throne where Queen Vespera smiles down at us. Beside her, Mirelle sits on a smaller but no less lavish throne, the smooth gold of the chair inlaid with sparkling stones.

The sight of the royals sickens me. The queen should be concerned with the fight against the witches. Not busy toying with us.

"I wonder why Prince Callan never mentioned her?" Shade asks, now perched on my shoulder, and I guess that she's referring to the princess.

"He never mentioned a lot of things," I reply simply, the wound from the prince's betrayal still a gaping hole inside me. I knew he was an asshole, but I hadn't expected this from him.

My gaze goes to the archangel prince who stands a few yards from me on the arena floor, but he doesn't look at me. He keeps his gaze fixed on the royals. On his sister.

"We shall get out of this, my mate," Mason says, now beside me in a fighting stance. "I've seen worse."

My lips thin, and I can't stop staring at Prince Callan. When we'd first met, I'd known he was a dud mate, but this is so much worse than I'd anticipated. *"So much for Lady Fate knowing what she's doing when she made our matches,"* I grumble to Shade.

For once, the crow doesn't have a witty comeback. She merely says, *"Blake. Where's Nate?"*

My head snaps to the side as I realize I'd miscounted my mates, and my shifter isn't anywhere around us. *Fuck.*

A horn blares, and the angels in the amphitheater quieten, all attention going to Queen Vespera.

The angel queen smiles down at me and my

mates. "How delighted we are that you have finally decided to join us," she says, her shrill voice somehow amplified and ringing throughout the enormous space.

Dante and Mason both stand with me now, and Dante's tail flicks as he stares at the queen with hatred, his burnt hand still raw, though the flesh is finally starting to heal.

"Where's Nate?" I yell.

Queen Vespera smiles wickedly. "Well now, I couldn't make it too easy, could I?" She motions to someone behind her, and the ground beneath our feet starts to tremble. My mates and I move back as the sand shifts in the middle of the arena, and from below, a giant cage rises, the thick golden bars alight with white fire.

I gasp when I spot Nate trapped inside. The shifter is suspended upside down, held by a chain that hangs from the top of the cage. Golden barbed wire covers his entire body, the metal slowly moving as if it were dozens of golden snakes, and a thick layer of clouds covers the bottom of the cage.

No!

Dante lets out a stream of curses beside me.

"Now that you've agreed to this little competition, it seems only fair that I create a game befitting the daughter of the demon king," Queen Vespera says, tapping her long nails on the armrest of her throne.

"You're playing a dangerous game," I warn her.

"I may have agreed to fight for my mate, but my death could still result in a war."

The queen sneers. "Your father already played a dangerous game by luring some of my best archangels into that pathetic competition of his. Then he had the indecency to come here, advising me to call on the allied realms for aid when Toralyn is easily the strongest realm of all five."

My stomach twists, because the queen isn't entirely wrong. King Dalton *had* made some angels lose their lives, all so I could find my mates. The angels may have come to the ball willingly, but if they'd known about the competition they might have stayed away. "He came here to help and to warn you about the witches and their plans."

"Your father is a fool, and he spouts the idea of unity after wasting innocent lives," Queen Vespera spits. "And now justice must be served."

"Then take it up with the demon king," Alaric growls. "Or are you in the habit of convicting innocents yourself?"

"Unfortunately, murdering the demon king would have dire consequences, though I had been weighing my options when you so happened to walk into my palace," the queen replies, giving me a gleeful smile.

"So, this has nothing to do with Nate," I say coldly.

"Oh, let's not get confused," she replies. "The thief must die for attempting to kidnap my daughter. But you know the saying...two birds and all that."

I scowl.

There's a muffled sound, and I turn to where Nate is still hanging. One of the wires is wrapped around his mouth, and when he tries to speak, it makes shallow cuts in his skin. The queen flicks her hand in the air, and the clouds below Nate dissipate. Hundreds of gold-tipped scorpions come into view, crawling around the base of the cage.

Alaric growls in the back of his throat.

"How bad are they?" I ask him.

"Those are creatures made of magic. One of the assassins in the order got his hands on one once," Alaric explains. "He intended to use the creature on his next target, but somehow, he got himself stung. Their venom targets the magic in our blood and will inflict a true death. They found him the next day, nothing but a husk of the male he was."

"So, it's really bad then," I say, nodding like it's no big deal.

The chain fastening Nate to the top of the cage rattles and starts to lower. It's moving incredibly slowly in small increments, but it's enough for me to realize Queen Vespera's intentions.

"One day I will be queen," I tell her. "We could be forging an alliance rather than battling as enemies."

"An alliance?" Queen Vespera laughs. "Your father didn't care much about that when he took my angels, but if you defeat my soldiers and survive this, perhaps we can discuss it. Free your shifter, and in turn save yourselves, and I might even call on the allied realms after all."

Dante and I share a look, his midnight blue eyes piercing into me. "We can do this, princess," he says casually, though his body is rigid.

I don't bother to entertain the thought that the queen might actually let us walk. I've been around enough psychos in my life to know the queen doesn't intend to let us leave here alive. After all this fanfare and her admission about wanting justice for my father and Nate's crimes, she knows there's only one real way that I'm leaving here. And it's if I take her head from her body. Something she has no intention of letting me do.

Nate lowers another inch, and the queen clucks her tongue. "Better hurry now, your highness."

I let a breath out through my nose and think of the different rules Dad taught me when I was young. *Rule number one: Never show weakness; Rule number two: Never show mercy; and Rule number three...Never surrender.*

At least fifty angels swoop down from the open space in the middle of the stadium, and they land in perfect formation, their boots slamming to the sand as they form a long line to one side of the arena. Dressed in gleaming battle armor, they face us, their helmets pulled low, and their wings flared out behind them.

Nate growls, trying to struggle against his binds,

but the golden wire only tightens, trails of blood trickling from various places on his body.

"He can't shift," Alaric growls. "The wire will only tighten as he tries to change."

Mason, Alaric, and Dante move with me, the four of us taking up battle stances, but Prince Callan stands apart, that lost expression still on his face.

"And what about your son?" I say, staring down the queen's angels. "You would condemn him so easily?"

"He never wanted to follow the path I set out for him," Queen Vespera replies. "And I've grown tired of having to manage his...outbursts. I have long since known that he worked with the shifter to try and organize my daughter's kidnapping, and she is worth one-hundred sons. Prince Callan chose his fate long ago."

"She knew?" Prince Callan mutters under his breath, his gaze finding his sister again.

My mind works as I struggle to understand. Struggle to fill in the missing pieces of Prince Callan's story. I think of the recording we'd heard of Prince Callan getting tortured. The sound of the flickering flames is still vivid in my mind along with the voice of his sister...urging him to tell the queen about Nate. To blame it all on the shifter. I'd thought the sister was trying to help him, but those flames... was she the one burning him?

Nate lowers another inch, and I know the time for words is over.

"We're with you, princess," Mason says beside me, and he shifts, turning into his winged centaur form.

The queen's eyes widen with surprise, and the crowd goes wild, none of them having seen his kind before.

Dante winks at me. "Let's show this bitch queen how demons fight." And he disappears, becoming invisible.

Queen Vespera leans back on her throne, a pleased smile on her face.

Prince Callan wrenches his gaze from his sister and turns, finally coming up beside me. "There will be a barrier around the royal box," he says, though I hadn't asked the question. "And the archangel soldiers will all have a protective shield around them, too. I'd have to be within arms-length of them to use my magic."

I move my feet, adjusting my stance. "And why should I believe a word you say?"

"You shouldn't," he replies simply, and he runs out ahead of me.

I want to shout at him. To curse him for betraying us, but the archangels descend on our position, fanning out, and we need all the help we can get.

"Always knew you'd never amount to anythin', prince," an archangel spits as he sends out a burst of water magic, aiming it for Prince Callan's head. Prince Callan jumps into the air and spins, tucking in his wings as he easily avoids the blast. In a few motions, he's grabbed the archangel's sword and has knocked the soldier out.

Half of the crowd boos while the other half cheers, as if they're all just as confused as we are.

"Kill him!" the queen shouts.

Another archangel cries out, his head taken, and though I can't see him, I know it's Dante's doing.

Electricity zaps into the air from a soldier somewhere to my left, and Alaric snarls, a blow hitting his shoulder before he manages to take the soldier down. More soldiers run at him, but Alaric gives them a dark smile, and his body starts to shift, growing until he's in his giant form, an incredible mass that looms over us. He stomps around the sands swiping at the soldiers. With one blow, he throws an archangel at the royal box, and the archangel smacks into an invisible barrier not far from the queen's position before falling to the ground.

Queen Vespera glowers at us, and more archangels descend from the sky above.

Three archangels circle me, and I have two down in a matter of seconds. The third lifts his hand and a dozen sand monsters materialize around me. Mason and I cut through them, moving quickly, before I take the archangel's head.

One by one we spill blood, carving our way through the archangels. Shade flies from my shoulder watching from above and commentating on the activity. By the time all the queen's archangels are down, I stand there covered in blood, my chest heaving. I don't let myself think about the waste of life. At the fact that these soldiers would have been better used defending against the witches. This is the queen's doing and there's nothing I can do about that.

Going by the way her face is contorted with anger, I'm guessing Queen Vespera had expected this to be a much easier fight for her angels.

I turn my gaze to the cage. Nate still hasn't reached the scorpions, and I send a thank you to Lady Fate. *All right, now we just need to get him free.* I take a step toward my shifter mate, but the instant I do, multiple doors on the side of the arena open, and more archangel's march onto the sand.

The smug smile is back on the queen's face, and I know what she's doing. The queen simply wants to keep me busy for long enough that Nate dies. Once that happens, she knows I'll be weakened. That the loss of my fated mate will likely distract me enough that she'll be able to take me down.

Never surrender. The words sound in my head.

Gritting my teeth, I fight the closest archangel, throwing him over my head, and finishing him with my blade through his throat. Two more archangels come at me from behind, but Mason gallops to meet them, grabbing a discarded spear from the ground and throwing it into one of the archangel's chests, then descending on the other soldier.

In the cage, Nate drops lower. *We're running out of time.* Taking a deep breath, I close my eyes and call to them. I can feel them around me, their tiny hearts beating in my mind. There are thousands of them, and they fly from the forest, the tops of the buildings, and the bridges along the waterways. The sky darkens as birds descend toward the stadium, thousands of wings beating at once, and the sound a steady hum in my ears. The fighting pauses as everyone looks up, craning their necks to see what's above.

Opening my eyes, I lift my gaze to the royal box, expecting to see the queen cowed, but that smug smile is still there, pulling her lips even tighter. Immediately, I know something isn't right. And then Mirelle lifts her hand. *No! No! Oh, Lady No!*

My heart slams against my ribcage as streams of white fire race up the walkways of the amphitheater, curving up, racing higher with every second.

Go back! Please, please go back! I scream in my mind, trying to warn them. Trying to save my birds. I tell them to fly away from the amphitheater, but some of them are already too close and they swoop down.

Stretching out my wings, I launch into the air, spearing straight up. I flap my wings hard, pushing my muscles to get to them.

Shade stares at me as she flaps in the air, panicked. *"No Blake, you can't!"*

But I have to try. They're here because of me. I've

lost birds during battle before, but not this many. Thousands of the birds are still descending, still trying to get to me and answer the call I'd put out.

"Stop, my mate!" Mason calls, launching into the air behind me, but I only flap my wings harder, rising higher, racing Mirelle's fire.

"Sister, no!" Prince Callan's rough voice is a guttural plea to the princess.

"I said go back! Please, go back! Why aren't you listening?" I scream in my head as Mirelle's fire keeps climbing.

Alaric reaches up, as if to grab some of my birds. To pull them to safety.

I'm almost to them, almost to the top of the amphitheater, but her magic is too fast. Flames curve around the top of the amphitheater, creating a wall of fire in front of me and Alaric, and I only just manage to stop in time, heat blasting my face as I curve to the side, inches from the flames.

I hear as they fly into it, their little bodies sizzling as they impact with the fire, and their squawks and cries fill my head. My birds turn to ash in seconds, and the flakes rain down on us, the ash so thick it's like snowfall.

"Oh god, Blake," Shade's voice trembles in my mind.

I lift my palms to the sky, cupping my hands like I'm still hoping to catch them. To save them, but the only thing around me is death.

"Selfish. I was so fucking selfish to call them here."

"It's not your fault," Shade counters. *"You can't have known that would happen."*

"They still came here because of me."

The angels in the stands are silent as the ash falls, the amphitheater a haze of gray flakes.

Cackling comes from the royal box, and the queen's laughter is like a spark that ignites the fury inside me. I turn to the angel ruler, and the scream that comes from me is a raw, guttural, wounded sound. I'm not sure what happens next. One moment, I'm focused on the anger, drowning in sorrow for the birds, and the next a cold calm settles over me.

Yes, just like that. Let me in, little demon. An ancient voice speaks in my mind, but I don't have time to realize what its presence might mean. Power builds within me, filling my every pore, and tattoos appear on my body. Only, instead of my tattoos that shine with golden light when I'm with my mates, the intricate lines are like black tar against my skin.

I don't question it. I direct the dark power inside me toward Queen Vespera, and she's helpless to stop it. Dark power erupts from me, spearing through the magical barrier around the royal box, and it takes the queen, climbing down her throat until she explodes, becoming a mess of blood and bone.

Mirelle jerks her head, the princess staring at her mother in shock, and I fall from the sky, crippling exhaustion making me drop like a stone.

Down. Down. Down, I fall, the air whistling by my ears and tearing at my wings.

Shade screams in my head, and then there are strong arms around me. *Mason.*

He flies down, landing on the arena floor, but he doesn't let me go. The queen's remaining archangels don't move around the arena. They merely watch us from a distance, confused now that their ruler has been slain.

"Blake!" I feel Dante's hands on me now as well, and Alaric is nearby in his smaller form again, his scent of dark chocolate in my nose. The dark power that had been inside me moments before is now completely gone, and slowly, my energy begins to return.

"We've got you, princess." Dante's voice is soothing, though worry shines in his dark eyes.

Prince Callan's gaze is full of regret, and he stands near me, but he doesn't approach.

There's a muffled cry, and it's only then that I remember the cage. "Nate!" I'd thought when I killed the queen he would be spared and whatever magic was tied to the cage would be broken, but my shifter is mere inches from the scorpions now. They gather beneath him, their golden tails glinting. White flames still cover the bars of the cage, and my gaze connects with Prince Callan's.

"Sister!" Prince Callan calls out. "Release him! It's over."

Dante gives me a look like he's reluctant to leave

my side, but I struggle from Mason's arms, and we all move into action, circling the cage and looking for a way to get Nate out. The golden wire is still wrapped around the shifter, but the fire on the bars is the first barrier. Nate struggles more, and blood drips from where the wire has cut into his skin.

Mirelle flies from the royal box, landing on the sand of the arena a few paces away from us.

And she smiles.

CHAPTER
ELEVEN

~ Prince Callan ~

I can hardly meet Princess Blake's gaze. I'd warned her not to come here, but even I had not expected this. I peer at the queen's bloody throne in the royal box, and no sympathy goes through me. Queen Vespera deserved this, and the ash continuing to float around us is a reminder of how ruthless the queen could be.

"Release the shifter," I tell my sister again as she lands not far from us. "The queen can't control you any longer."

I expect my sister to remove her flames from Nate's cage, but she stands there watching us.

"Now why would I do that?" she says calmly, her voice as smooth a silk, and nothing like the voice of the timid sister I loved. "After all, he has wronged me," she goes on. "In my mother's eyes, he tried to kidnap me, and in yours, he left me behind to rot, not honoring your agreement to take me to the beast realm. Either way, he should be punished."

Her words surprise me, and I study my sister. She stands tall, a smile spread across her face. She looks nothing like the cowed girl my mother abused for all these years. I should be happy to see her appear so free, but there's something about her smile that makes me pause.

"With the queen dead, as the rightful heir, Andal will take the throne," I remind her. "End this now, and our new king can place judgement on the shifter." Our eldest brother has turned a blind eye to the queen's actions in the past, but I feel without her influence, he may prove to be a fair ruler. In any case, I should be able to break the shifter out by then.

"Andal?" Mirelle laughs, and it's a strange sound. Nothing at all like the soft peals of laughter my sister has let out on rare occasions in the past. "You are out of touch, brother. Didn't you hear? Just days ago, the queen declared me to be her heir. I guess, she sought to honor all my past sacrifices."

Sacrifices? She says it as if she had a choice.

Princess Blake walks forward, her expression livid despite the lines of exhaustion that remain around her eyes. Mason stays by her while the others stay next to the cage.

"Release my mate, *now*, or you'll receive the same treatment as the queen," she says, her voice cold.

I step between her and Mirelle. "Stop," I say to Princess Blake. "Queen Vespera deserved her fate, but no one has endured more from the queen than my sister." The promise that I made to Mirelle a long time ago rises to the forefront of my mind: *I'll get you out of here and away from her. I promise.*

I've held onto that promise, staying here in the castle, close to my sister, but the queen has been ever vigilant.

Nate drops another inch, and Blake's anger continues to simmer. She grits her teeth. "I understand you believe Nate has wronged you, but you can't kill my mate."

Mirelle shrugs. "You see, I think I can. And mother wasn't completely wrong. It's better to defeat you before you can unlock your power. Better that the demon realm is ruled by one of your power-hungry clan leaders who might be more easily manipulated, don't you think?"

I stare at my sister, unable to speak. She's never spoken like this. *More easily manipulated?* "Princess Blake is my Ahalian Touizda," I blurt.

"Yes," Mirelle says, turning her sweet expression on me. "And what good did that do for her? You betrayed her by bringing them all here, no doubt still hanging on to that ridiculous promise you made to me. As far as I can see, you're not being the best mate, brother. You're supposed to love your Ahalian

Touizda more than any other. Maybe you'll all be better off alone."

The ridiculous promise? Her words repeat in my head, but I can't accept what they mean.

"What promise is she talking about?" Blake snaps at me, but all I can do is stare at the stranger who has taken the place of my sweet sister.

"Oh, he didn't tell you, did he?" She laughs. "No, of course he didn't. You see, my darling brother has always taken it upon himself to see me as a victim who needed saving. I tried to tell him in the beginning that he was wasting his time, but he was all insistent, talking about saving me from a life of inflicting death and letting mother use me as a weapon." She flicks her eyes up, thinking, then she counts on her fingers. "Yep, eight times I think it is. There's been eight times when he's come close to getting me out of Toralyn. At first it was annoying, but then it became a little game to see how many times I could foil his plans without him noticing." She grins. "I must say, your persistence has been admirable, brother."

"All those attempts..." I trail off, my voice rough. "I thought it was the queen—"

"Oh, don't insult me," Mirelle snaps. "That old goat never had control around here. Not without me pulling the strings." Her gaze swings to Nate in the cage. "But that time when you had convinced the shifter to take me, there was a moment there, where I thought he would pull me with him into the beast realm. And why would I want to go to that ghastly place? I had to use my fire to back him into the gateway, or I swear he wouldn't have left without me. Of course, the thief chooses that moment to get all noble."

A high-pitched ringing starts in my ears, and I blink at Nine Lives. At *Nate. He hadn't meant to leave her.* I'd thought the shifter had deserted her and had gone back on his word. That he was so cowardly he fled the moment the soldiers arrived, forsaking my sister. For days as the queen tortured me, trying to get information out of me, I'd thought of the jaguar shifter with a hate that grew inside me with every passing hour. With every moment the flames touched me, mutilating my wings. My blood chills, and I lift my gaze, thinking how it had been my sister's fire that had tormented me. When she'd stood beside my mother in that cell, and my mother had barked the orders, I'd thought Mirelle had no choice but to burn me. But now, if I am to believe what she's saying...

"You made me believe the shifter fled," I croak. "You tortured me for days before coaxing me into confessing a story about Nate. You *pleaded* with me."

Princess Blake stares between us, her own anger now mixed with confusion.

Mirelle lets out an exasperated sigh and rests a hand on her hip. "It's not my fault you weren't smart enough to blame the shifter from the beginning. Why you wanted to protect him, I have no idea.

What, you spoke to him for a few days, and suddenly he was your friend? Pathetic," she wrinkles her nose with disgust. "But anyhow, as fun as it was to see you suffer, it was getting rather tiresome by the end, don't you think? Besides, blaming the shifter gave mother something else to obsess about. And it provided the perfect opportunity for all this." Opening her arms, she indicates to the bloodshed around us. "Someone had to take care of mother, and it couldn't be me. That barrier protection spell she's always had around her has been a constant annoyance, but it looks like your pretty little demon had no problems getting past it."

My breathing becomes short as everything I thought I knew is turned completely upside down. I turn to Nate. To the male I've hated for so long. To the male I'd shared stories with in that prison cell all that time ago. And then I turn to Princess Blake. My mate. My Ahalian Touizda. "Release the shifter. You admitted it yourself. He's done nothing wrong."

Nate lowers another inch, and sweat drips from his nose, plopping onto a scorpion just below him.

"If I am to rule successfully, I told you, I can't let your demon princess bond with you. Five mates? It's unheard of. Better that the shifter dies now."

"You don't know what you're saying..." I mumble.

Mirelle glares at me, and I'm stunned by the hatred in her gaze. "And you, my darling brother, have always underestimated *me*."

Princess Blake snarls, launching for my sister, but Mirelle is waiting for her. Her flames circle Blake, cutting her off from all of us. Shade swoops down, her claws outstretched as she aims for Mirelle's head, but I use my power, gently diverting the crow before she's killed.

"No! Blake!" Mason shouts, and Mason, Alaric, and Dante advance on Mirelle, wielding their weapons as they sprint toward her.

With the flick of her hand, white flames race out, encircling them, and creating a dome of fire, trapping them within.

My sister laughs, her expression maniacal. "Oh, I am going to have such fun! Killing you all is going to be the perfect start to my reign." Her eyes flare wide as she bares her teeth, staring at Blake and my mates, and I don't think about what I do next. For years, I've remained submissive. I've appeased the queen and kept close to my sister. All so I could try and find the next opportunity to get her out. To get Mirelle away from the bloodshed and abuse. For years, I was so desperate to free her. But now I find out that Mirelle is the one who had been making the cage.

She doesn't expect my magic. Not even as the air lifts her off the ground, trapping her hands behind her back so she can't use her power, and wrapping around her neck, squeezing. Mirelle struggles, her face reddening, but I maintain my hold on her.

There was a time in the past when I'd told the

queen to use me as her weapon instead of Mirelle. Queen Vespera had laughed and asked for a demonstration against my sister. I'd hesitated, and before I'd even been able to use my power, Mirelle's fire had engulfed me. Mirelle had later said that she'd been afraid of what mother would do if she'd failed. That her magic was out of control, but I now realize my sister had always wanted to be by my mother's side. If only to make sure she was able to orchestrate the queen's death and take her place.

Mirelle's legs flail as I restrict her air supply, and with her hands restrained, there's nothing she can do to fight me. Around the arena, the soldiers stand watching, confused as to whether they should help.

"Stop, brother," she wheezes. "I know you love me. You've always loved me. You wouldn't do this."

I step close to her, and as I watch her struggle, a wave of cold indifference washes over me.

As Mirelle suffocates, the circle of fire around Princess Blake and her mates disappears, as does the fire on Nate's cage. The others rush to the cage, and I hear them bend the bars.

"Callan," Mirelle rasps again, her face now an unnatural shade of blue.

I think of my mother's radical changes in mood and the decisions she'd made over the years. Queen Vespera could be cruel, but now I wonder how many times it was Mirelle who was the one pulling the strings.

"The angels deserve better than you," I tell my

sister. "From what you've shown, all you would give them is cruelty. You would usher in a time of darkness."

"The angels need someone to control them," she snarls, wheezing. "And with you and your mate out of the way—" She manages to break one hand free from my hold, but before she can send out her flames, I close my fist, and the air around her neck squeezes so tight it takes her head.

I stare as Mirelle's body thuds to the sand, but Princess Blake's voice pulls me from my thoughts. "Callan!" she yells.

Princess Blake and the others stand by the cage. The bars have been twisted open, but Nate still hangs, the golden wire tight around the shifter. "No physical being can touch him without the wire contracting," I tell them. As the scorpions prepare to sting Nate, I send out a burst of air that lifts him higher before they can lash out with their tails.

Nate's nostrils flare, and I launch from the ground, landing on the top of the cage. Now that it's not shrouded in fire, I work on the metal box that holds the roll of chains and wire connected to Nate. It's complicated magic created by a powerful archangel in Toralyn, and created using the blood of the one who wishes to control it. I can't be sure if Queen Vespera or Mirelle ordered its creation, but it doesn't matter. Taking out my blade, I slice a line into my palm, and I turn my hand, letting my blood drip onto the wire. Because no matter what they did, they were my family by blood. If in no other sense of the word.

Instantly, the wire turns from gold to a dull gray, and it loosens from Nate. Using my wind power, I free the shifter and move him through the open hole in the bars. Princess Blake and Dante grab him, and they pull him to the sand.

Princess Blake grabs Nate's head in her hands, and she searches him for wounds. "Were you stung?"

He shakes his head, and she sends a thank you to Lady Fate before crashing her lips to his, the rest of her mates crowding around her. All her mates, that is, except for me.

I stare around at the angels in the stands of the amphitheater. A few of the angels applaud, but most of them look lost. As if just like me, they're surprised at what I've done.

CHAPTER
TWELVE

~ Princess Blake ~

We stay at the angel palace until word reaches Prince Andal about the deaths of the queen and princess. With Princess Mirelle's claim to the throne no longer an issue, the oldest Prince is set to become the new king of Toralyn.

It's hours before Prince Andal arrives, and Prince Callan stands facing his brother. The older prince remains silent while Prince Callan recounts recent events, the prince's expression darkening the longer Prince Callan speaks.

"Do you think this one's a psycho just like his mom and sister?" Shade whispers in my mind. She's still salty at Prince Callan for forcing her away when she

had tried to attack Princess Mirelle, though it's obvious the archangel was trying to protect her.

I stare at Prince Callan, not sure how I should feel about him. The sting of his betrayal still hasn't left me, and I think of my birds, their ashes scattered in the wind. There's a cold space inside me, and even though I now know the truth about Prince Callan trying to free his sister, I'm not sure if I can forgive the archangel for betraying us. Not yet, anyway.

"Let's hope not," I reply to Shade. I don't bother saying more than that. Only Prince Andal can choose what kind of king he wants to be.

"You should have told me what happened the last time you were here," I tell Nate, still annoyed at the shifter for almost dying.

"It was Prince Callan's secret to tell," he defends. "And it's not like I thought I was gonna get strung up."

I wince as the image of him hanging in the cage flashes in my mind. "And do you have any other secrets that might take me by surprise?"

He rubs his chin thoughtfully. "Only that I don't plan on returnin' to Toralyn for a very, very long time."

"That's not a secret," Dante drawls. "You're merely stating what we're all thinking."

"We should have stayed at the hot springs," Shade laments.

Reaching up, I scratch her neck. *"We can do better than that. How about we go home?"*

She perks up, and I watch as Prince Andal passes a silver flask to Prince Callan. Prince Callan pockets it, and then the pair are striding toward us.

"Prince Andal has just come from the battle in Danora City," Prince Callan says when they stop in front of us. "The witches are proving to be much more organized and powerful than the angels expected, and he's agreed to call on the united realms for assistance."

Shade relaxes on my shoulder. *"Finally."*

I keep scratching her neck, mostly to give myself something to do, and my crow laps up the attention. "That's good news," I say. *At least, Dad will be happy.* "And the coronation?"

"It will be held within the next two days," Prince Andal replies, his face kind. Like Prince Callan, he has large golden wings, but his hair is a stark white in comparison to Prince Callan's honey-colored locks. "I had hoped, my brother might stay for the ceremony."

I shift uncomfortably.

Before I can comment, Prince Andal smiles. "But it seems he's certain his Ahalian Touizda would wish to return home immediately."

My heart pounds, surprise filtering through me.

Prince Callan's gold-flecked gaze connects with mine. "That is, if you will still allow me to accompany you, princess?" His words are tentative, and there's a hopeful plea in his voice.

I hesitate. A part of me feels like telling him to

stay here. From the moment I met him, the archangel has been cold and determined not to let his guard down. But I think of how he'd killed his sister. Of how he'd freed Nate. Since then, he's been quiet, and that cold edge has been missing from his eyes, replaced with something else. I can't tell if it's grief or simply relief. Likely, it's a mixture of both. The archangel is hurting, and as much as he's an asshole, he's still my mate. My gaze drops to those gold-brushed lips before lifting back to his face.

"You're my mate," I tell him simply. "We can't bond without you."

He nods once.

Prince Andal gives me a polite smile. "Then I suppose, until the next time we meet." He dips his head to me and my mates, and he says a final farewell to Prince Callan before striding away.

When Prince Andal is gone, Prince Callan turns to Nate. The pair of them haven't spoken since the arena, and the shifter's slitted eyes narrow on the prince.

"There's no point bothering with excuses," Prince Callan says. "But I remember you having a particular fondness for this." He digs into his robes and holds out the flask I'd seen Prince Andal give him. "I hope you may one day forgive me, bond brother."

Nate takes the flask and unscrews the lid, lifting the opening to his nose. A lop-sided smile crawls onto his face, and he slams his hand onto Prince

Callan's shoulder. "Only you would bring me prison wine as an apology, brother." The shifter laughs.

Prince Callan clears his throat. "That's actually one of the finest wines in Toralyn. The grapes are grown in the vineyards on the floating hills in the north. A single bottle of wine costs a small fortune."

Nate's brows lift. "Well then, that explains why it doesn't taste like piss. Apology accepted."

I stare at the shifter, surprised that his forgiveness came that easily.

Nate shrugs. "This isn't the first time I've been betrayed, nor is it the first time I've almost died. But it is the first time a prince has apologized to me." Grinning, he takes a swig of his wine.

Prince Callan turns to me next, but he doesn't have any gifts this time. Instead he kneels, bowing his head. "No apology could express my regret, but know that I will always fight to be worthy of you. You are my Ahalian Touizda, my mate, and it sickens me that I've already failed you. My blade is yours, Princess Blake, as am I."

I squirm uneasily, because this isn't the Prince Callan I've come to know. I don't reply, because I have no idea how I'm supposed to answer to that. Not too long ago the prince had been cold and telling me to stay away from him, and now he's claiming to be mine? My stomach clenches, as the fated mate connection sparks between us.

"Get up, prince," Dante murmurs. "You're making us all uncomfortable."

Mason's brows draw down. "His apology is admirable. Even if he has already proven himself to be a horrible mate."

I scrub a hand over my face, because life with my mates continues to be complicated.

"Okay," I tell my archangel mate awkwardly. "I... appreciate the thought. But can we go home now?"

Nate winks at Prince Callan, holding out his hand and helping the archangel up. I turn to Mason who passes me his portal ring.

"Yesss girl," Shade squawks in my head. *"Bring on the demon realm."*

"I can't believe we're finally home," Shade squawks in my head as I breathe in deep, taking in the musky and smoky scents of Seral.

The forest is dark, stars littering the sky overhead.

"Where are we?" Nate asks. His shoulder brushes a nearby tree, and a dozen pairs of tiny eyes appear in the darkness. "What the fuck?" he stumbles back into me, and I steady him.

"Careful now," I whisper in his ear. "Someone might think you were afraid."

"Of them?" He points to the small furry creatures clinging to the tree trunk, and he squares his broad shoulders. "They're lucky if they don't become a snack."

Like they've understood him, the little creatures bare their pointed teeth and hiss. The shifter curses, taking another step back.

"Right, a snack," I tell him sarcastically. "Relax, they're not going to hurt you. They just like the tree bark."

"And this is where you live?" Mason asks, curiously observing the creatures.

"We're in the forest that grows beside Seral City," Dante explains, scrubbing the back of one of the creatures with his fingers until its warning hiss turns into a low purr.

"The forest?" Alaric asks.

"We can't head straight to the castle," I explain. "Not until we know what the situation is there. So, we're making a stop here first."

Prince Callan doesn't speak as he stays at the back of the group.

It's a short walk through the trees, and then I stop before a darkened building. "I trained out here a lot when I was younger. When I was learning to control my power," I explain. "And when I was older, I would come to this spot when I needed a moment to breathe, away from the castle. There are multiple rooms, and there should be enough supplies for us to last a while, though I don't suspect we'll be here long."

I move to the front door, and the moment I touch the handle, a retina scanner zaps my eye, and there's a click as the door unlocks. I swing it open, and the lights blink on, lighting the main living area as I walk inside. My mates follow me, and soon we're all standing in the common room surrounded by plush couches. A red fire bursts to life in the fireplace, casting shadows on the decorative blades lining the walls, and on the far end of the room is an eating area and an open kitchen.

Nate whistles. "Nice hideout, gorgeous."

"It's not a hideout," I reply.

My mates all stare at me, but I ignore them.

Lifting my hand, I point to an archway that leads to a wide hallway. "Down there you'll find the washrooms and the bedrooms."

Nate goes to flop onto one of the couches, but Dante's tail snaps out slapping him on the ass.

"Ow, what the fuck was that for?" the shifter says, rubbing his ass cheek, and looking more intrigued than irritated.

"I highly doubt the princess wants your blood and sweat all over her furniture, shifter." Dante peers pointedly at the hallway. "Washroom now, asshole."

Nate rubs the back of his neck, and he looks at me sheepishly. "Yeah, right. Sorry 'bout that."

I bite my lip as I fight to hold back my laughter. Truthfully, the blood and the sweat does it for me, but Dante has a point about the furniture.

My demon winks at me, and when he starts toward the hallway, Nate rolls his shoulders and follows.

Mason smiles walking after them. "Join us, our mate. The water will be cold without you."

The idea of my mates all being in the washroom together makes my thighs tremble, but when I turn back, Prince Callan is still standing there, watching me silently.

"Uh yeah, so I'm just gonna go check out that washroom as well," Shade mumbles in my head, hopping from one foot to the other on my shoulder.

"Shade," I warn, because she might be my friend, but that still doesn't mean I'm down with sharing.

"Relax," she says with a giggle. *"I'm going to go nap in one of the bedrooms so you guys can have some space."* As she lifts from my shoulder, she adds, *"Tell Callan that he's going to have to kiss your feet before I forgive him. I don't care how sexy he is."*

"He was worried about his sister," I say wearily. *"He made a promise to her."*

"Yeah, but he still didn't have to be such an asshat," Shade counters.

When my friend is gone, I turn my attention back to the archangel. Before I can say a word, he drops to his knees, and for a moment, I think he might just be about to kiss my feet like Shade suggested, but he remains kneeling and he stares at the floor, not giving me eye contact.

"What are you doing?" I ask, because he's making me uncomfortable again. It was bad enough the first time he did it. I'm used to the demons bowing to me, but Prince Callan is my mate.

"Tell me what you want me to do, Blake. Name it," he says, his voice a low rasp. "I don't have any excuses. Only regrets."

I release a breath through my nose. Demons hardly ever apologize, so this is strange for me. In his weird way, Prince Callan is doing it for a second time.

When I don't answer, he goes on, "You helped me and the angels, and I am grateful. I have not been a good Ahalian Touizda. If you wish to bond with me to get your power, and then reject me, that is your right. I will suffer it."

"Reject you?" I sigh. Truthfully, the thought had crossed my mind. To let him back in after his betrayal goes against the second rule of being a demon royal: *Never show mercy*. But I'm quickly learning that the rules I grew up with don't exactly apply to my mates.

Pain shines in Prince Callan's eyes when he peers up at me, and his chest rises and falls as he lets out a breath. "I pushed you away, even when I should have known better."

He's not wrong, but then I think of him taking his sister's life. A sister he'd fought for over and over again. He wasn't trying to deceive us, he had just been choosing his family and was trying to save his sister. And now everything he'd believed about his sister turned out to be a lie. The betrayal he must feel is undoubtedly much deeper than what I'm experiencing, and the idea of leaving him to go through that alone makes me feel sick.

"You have been an asshole," I say slowly, licking my lips as I think of what to say. "And there definitely are a few things you can do to make it up to me, but..." my expression becomes more serious, "I'm not going to reject you."

He looks confused. "Why?"

"Because I'm starting to realize why Lady Fate matched us all."

"And why would that be?"

I shrug. "Because who else would she match with such broken individuals?"

The hint of a smile touches his golden lips. "Only an extremely tolerant and insanely beautiful she-demon?"

I snort. "I meant all of us. For a long time, Shade has been the only one I've really felt close to," I admit. "My father only cares about making me stronger, more powerful, and prepared for life as a demon royal. I'm sure that's his way of showing his affection, but it's not until I met the rest of you that I realized..." I take a deep breath, "that there's more to family than blood."

Prince Callan watches my face, and my cheeks flush.

"So, I guess, this is my way of saying that despite your crappy attitude, somehow, I still...care," I blurt, suddenly feeling silly. "But I swear, you betray us again, and you'll learn the meaning of true regret."

The look on Prince Callan's face chases away my embarrassment and makes my heart squeeze. He stares at me like I'm the most perfect being he's ever laid eyes on, and he can't believe I'm in front of him. Tears make his eyes glassy, but he blinks them away.

He's on his feet in an instant, and I'm in his arms before I realize what's happening. He presses a kiss to the side of my head. "I swear to you, Princess Blake, I'll spend my life proving that I'm worthy of you. Of us." His lips drag lower, and he kisses just below my jaw. "And I will never stop showing you, how much I have wanted you from the first moment I laid eyes on you."

A brisk wind whips around us, making the flames dance in the fireplace, and teasing my hair.

I can hardly breathe when there's a shout from down the hallway. "Hey! Stop makin' it breezy in here," Nate calls out.

Laughter bursts from me, and Prince Callan smiles. There's still darkness shadowing his eyes, but it's a real smile, and my heart flutters at the sight of it. It's weird being in the prince's arms, but at the same time, it feels so natural, like our bodies have known each other for a long time. His scent of crisp apple and bergamot smells stronger than usual, and as he carries me down the hallway toward the others, he holds me possessively like he never intends to let me go.

I'm still not entirely used to being carried, but I can tell he needs this, so I don't protest.

When we enter the washroom, the other three are in the massive pool that stretches across the back wall. They're all naked, but they stand on opposite sides, like they're purposely keeping their distance from one another. Prince Callan places me on my feet, and my heart races as he starts undressing me, peeling off my layers slowly while my mates watch intently.

When I'm naked, Prince Callan strips off, tossing his clothes to the side, then he lifts me again and carries me into the pool. The water is warm as it licks against my skin, and when we reach the middle of the pool, I expect Prince Callan to release me, but he only kneels down and holds me there.

I turn my head toward him, and his lips go to mine. For the first time, he kisses me like he's not holding back. It's a punishing, desperate kiss that leaves me gasping for air. And when our lips finally break apart, he kisses a trail down my neck, one of his hands finding one of my wings. His fingers trail along the sensitive membrane, and I whimper, still not used to the sensation.

Nate prowls toward me, the pair of them focusing solely on me. My shifter's chest starts rumbling as he moves closer, and then I'm between them. Prince Callan lowers me, and my arms wrap around Nate's neck as I kiss him. His hands press into my back as he devours my mouth, and then he lets me go, letting me kiss Prince Callan again as he comes up from behind. His hard cock prods at my ass, and my eyes shoot wide as I think of how his barbs would feel there.

"Don't get any ideas," I warn him, because as good as his barbs feel, that isn't something I'm willing to try. Not yet, anyway.

Nate chuckles and kisses my shoulder, his teeth dragging against my skin and making me shiver. "Oh, I have so many ideas, gorgeous," he rumbles, and he bites down, his teeth sinking in. I let out a small cry, but the noise is swallowed when Prince Callan captures my mouth with his. His hand pushes my legs apart, and his fingers slide to my center. Teasing, testing, and making me squirm.

Reaching around, Nate squeezes my breasts, rubbing his thumbs over my hardened nipples, and I moan as Prince Callan massages my clit, the pair of them working me into a shivering mess. Prince Callan pushes the tips of his fingers into me, and I buck my hips, wanting more.

Instead of giving me what I want, the prince pulls back, teasing my clit again, and I squirm in their hold.

Nate chuckles. "Knew he'd be fun when he finally came around," he purrs in my ear. Before he knows what's happening, I turn my head, biting Nate's lower lip. "And yet, if one of you doesn't fuck me soon, you'll be kicked out of this pool," I tell him sweetly.

Not far from us, Mason and Dante watch me with heated stares, their hands below the water.

I'm about to suggest swapping with them, when Prince Callan lifts me up higher, his hands gripping under my thighs. He positions me so I can feel the slide of his hard cock as he teases up and down my center. Nate is behind me, and he grips Prince Callan's cock guiding it.

"Do you want this, gorgeous?" Nate purrs in my ear. "Do you want this cock inside you? Makin' you scream?"

My mouth falls open as he angles Prince Callan's cock, and the head pushes into my pussy before he stops.

I whimper, and my legs shake as need drives me crazy.

"Yes," I gasp, and I'm starting to feel tempted to take matters into my own hands, when Prince Callan's hooded gaze goes to my face.

"Then I'll make you scream always," he promises me, and he slams his cock inside me. I cry out at the sheer size of him as he fills me, stretching me, and then he's bouncing me on his cock. My wings flare out as he moves me at a steady pace, and I can't seem to catch my breath.

Gasping, I let go of his shoulders, reaching out and stroking the membrane of his folded wings. A tortured sound gurgles in his throat, and he thrusts faster, his cock burying so deep my cries grow louder.

"Mmm," Nate muses from the side, watching with keen interest. "She is perfect, isn't she?"

"Her wings," Prince Callan tells him, like he's reminding the shifter not to neglect them. Nate's answering grin is feral.

"I can't take much more," I rasp, because I'm already feeling too much, but then Nate's teeth clamp onto the membrane of my right wing, and I scream as the orgasm tears through me.

"Mine," Prince Callan pants, still thrusting into me as the pleasure consumes me, tattoos lighting up on my skin as I find my release. "You were always mine, Blake. My...everything." The emotion in his voice makes my heart crack, and he groans as he spills into me.

The orgasm has barely ended when Dante and Mason are there, crowding around as well. When I stop shuddering, Nate spins me, pulling me onto his cock instead, and Dante takes me from behind. Soon I'm screaming again, the feeling of both of them filling me driving me crazy. Nate's barbs push inside me, pressing against the inside of my walls, and I'm a quivering, shaking mess by the time I come again.

When I climb off Nate, Mason pulls me into his arms, and he kisses my temple gently. "If you've had enough, my mate..."

But I could never have enough of any of them. When Mason takes me, he moves slowly at first, giving me time before he makes me orgasm again, dragging out the pleasure for as long as possible. When I stop shuddering, I sag against his muscled chest, my breaths labored as I peer at my mates.

They're still crowding me like they can't get enough. They take turns cleaning me while still covering me with kisses.

Wait... My brows lower when I sink back into the water. "Where's Alaric?" I'd been so distracted that I hadn't noticed the assassin was missing.

"You didn't know? He never came into the buildin'," Nate answers. "Guessin' he's still in the forest."

"What?" I stand and internally chastise myself for not noticing. "I have to go get him."

"He might need to cool off, my mate," Mason says with concern. "The assassin seemed quite unhappy while we were in Toralyn."

"He's always grumpy," I counter.

"This seems like something more," Mason says.

I don't give myself time to think about it. I wade from the water, lifting from the pool and finding a clean pair of clothes in a nearby cupboard. Luckily, I always have it stocked, and I yank a large shirt over my head that reaches to my thighs.

"I'll go with you, princess," Dante says, moving to the edge of the pool.

I shake my head. "No. I need to work whatever this is out with him."

"Then we should definitely come with you, my mate," Mason tries to insist, but I arch a brow at him.

"I think I can handle it. You guys enjoy the bath. Feel free to explore the rooms when you're ready."

Dante nods, though the others still look concerned.

"It's fine," I reassure them again. "This is my home, remember?"

No one says anything more as I stride through the house toward the front door. *Time to go get my giant.*

CHAPTER

THIRTEEN

~ Alaric ~

I cannot enter the house. The moment we arrived in Seral, the anger I've been keeping trapped since meeting the demon king in Toralyn, became too much.

I didn't follow Princess Blake as she led the way inside a house located deep in the forest. And she didn't notice as I slunk away, keeping to the trees.

Now I stand at the edge of the forest, overlooking the demon city—Seral City. It's a strange place, alive with activity now that the night sky is overhead, the buildings lit up with light, and vehicles traveling the tarred streets. The city reminds me of the human realm. Much of their technology has been borrowed from the unsuspecting humans, who know little of our realms besides the occasional embellished story, usually twisted from a human's brief encounter with someone from the other realms. Humans create stories of monsters and angels, with little understanding of who any of us truly are.

My gaze lifts, and I pinpoint the black stone structure that stands like an imposing landmark in the middle of the city. Several stone towers stretch into the sky, and a large stone wall stands strong around the structure, no doubt patrolled by a small army of guards. *The royal castle.*

I've only visited it once. The night when the king put on the ball for Princess Blake to find her mates. Or, I guess I should say, for the king to gas us all and leave us in Perstalia in his twisted competition.

That night I'd gone to the ball with one mission. One target—the demon princess. To kill her in front of the king, and make him suffer for what he'd done to my brother, West.

And now I stand here, watching over the peaceful city. Anger twisting in my soul. Seeing Queen Vespera had only made it worse. As Blake's birds turned to ash, and I heard her scream, I wanted to make the queen hurt. To make that wicked bitch suffer for what she'd done. But then that power had come from Blake—something unnatural and dark. *Enchantress.* The demon princess might be my mate, but that doesn't mean Lady Fate was right to match us.

And now that I'm here in the demon realm, I

can't escape everything that's happened. And everything I've been working toward since my twin brother was taken from me. I couldn't kill the demon king's daughter, nor could I kill the demon king when we were in Toralyn, but I could kill him here. I could finally avenge West.

...And lose my mate in the process. I shake my head. *My enchantress.* Even now, I doubt myself.

Like I've summoned her, Blake's scent fills my nose, warm honey and cinnamon instantly working to disarm me, but I don't let it consume me. No, when the little demon tries to sneak up on me, I pivot, my blade in my hand. She curses, dodging my attack as I knew she would. My blade swipes at the air above her head, and I lunge at her again. She's quick, ducking out of reach, and it's only then that I realize why she's not deflecting me using her own weapon.

She's in a different outfit, an oversized t-shirt, and she doesn't have her weapons belt. Her hair is soaked to the tips, and the scents of her other mates are all over her. Instantly, my cock hardens at the thought, but this all just makes me more irritated. I can tell she's toying with me, taking it easy like she's playing some kind of game.

Growling, I don't hold back as I attack her, no longer completely myself but a mess of emotions, fury flooding my veins.

"Fuck, Alaric," she curses as she darts around a tree, and my blade sinks deep into the trunk with a loud *thwack*. I wrench the weapon out, snarling, and toss a spare blade at her feet.

"Pick it up," I rumble, and I run at her again.

She leaps to the side, making no move to grab the weapon. "I'm not going to fight you, asshole! I thought we were past this."

Past it? When we were in The Haven, I could almost let myself pretend she wasn't *his* daughter. The demon king's. But now I'm faced with reality, torn and broken.

"Pick it up, *Enchantress,*" I say again through gritted teeth, and she lets out an exasperated sigh.

"Look, I get that as a Drozac assassin you were ordered to kill me, but we're mates, you dick. I thought you'd realized that."

"I have," I admit quietly, because it's true. We've been through too much for me not to realize it. "But Lady Fate chose wrong."

She flicks a loose strand of hair away from her eyes. "Yeah, that's what I thought at first, too."

This shocks me a little. "At first?" She twists, missing my sword that was aimed to puncture her stomach.

"Yes, *at first,*" she says between breaths. "But clearly, Lady Fate knows us better than even we do."

"What are you saying?" I bite out.

"I guess, I'm saying," she pants, still dodging my attacks. "That despite the fact you're the grumpiest asshole I've ever met, I can see how Lady Fate wasn't all that crazy placing us together."

I get over my surprise quickly, moving again, spinning, slicing the air. "Even if that's true, it changes nothing. Because you can't bring him back."

"What?" Confusion fills her face. "Who?"

"One of the Drozac," I say. "He came here, and King Dalton murdered him."

Frustration shows on her face, and her mind ticks. "Is that what this is about?" She blows out a breath. "And killing me is what? Some fucked up revenge because I'm King Dalton's daughter? Let me guess, this is how you think you'll make the demon king suffer?" She stops moving, and I halt my attacks, my gaze pinned on her. On the female who keeps making me question everything. Except now.

She lifts a single finger into the air. "Firstly, given the pain dear old dad has put me through, I'm not sure torturing me in front of him would have the desired effect," she says. "And secondly," she looks me straight in the eyes, lifting another finger, "your Drozac friend must have known what would happen if he came here. If I'd been the one to find him..." she pauses before finishing, "I would have killed him myself."

My head lowers, and I breathe heavily, pain going through me. "He was my *brother*," I snarl. This time when I lunge forward, Blake doesn't dodge me. I slam her against a tree, pinning her there, my blade pressed tightly to her throat.

Understanding shows on her face as she peers at me. My hand trembles, and I struggle to hold the blade there, conflicted because it feels so wrong to have a blade to her throat. To have a blade at my *mate's* throat.

"Look, I'm sorry about your brother," she says softly. "But if it's the guy I'm thinking of, the king found him as he was about to assassinate the leader of one of the high clans in Seral. What do you expect? That the king would just let him walk?"

I hesitate, and my hand trembles more. "It doesn't matter why he was here. All that matters is that he was murdered."

"He was an assassin," she says. "You can't blame the king for protecting one of his subjects. Any Drozac must know the risks of coming here. Just like the demons know the risks if they break any laws in the other realms. I never met your brother, but I'd be willing to bet that he wouldn't have wanted this for you."

My nostrils flare, her words cutting into me. The last time I'd seen West, he'd talked about finding a way out of the order of the Drozac. He'd said he only needed to take care of one last target, and then he could be free. When I'd discovered he was killed by King Dalton while on the job, I'd been so focused on getting revenge for my brother, that I hadn't thought about anything else. And when the order offered me West's place, and a chance to get my revenge, I'd accepted.

My stomach hardens. But no, it isn't what he would have wanted for me. West had always been telling me that I should find a female to warm my cabin in the mountains. That I should have the big family I always wanted, and when he was out of the order, he'd build a cabin not far from mine where he could start his own family. But the moment he was taken, I'd forgotten all of that. And as much as I hated the demon king for taking my brother from me, Princess Blake was right. West would have known the risks of trying to assassinate a demon leader.

I stare at the demon princess before me. My mate. Because she'd always been mine, even when I struggled to accept it. Honey and cinnamon swirls around me, and her golden eyes watch me. We're a mess—Princess Blake and her mates. And I realize why I've been so afraid. Because finally, I've found my mate, and that's something West will never get to have. For so long I've seen demons as the enemy, but it wasn't their kind that I hated. I hated that West was taken from me. And I hated the Order of the Drozac for sending West to Seral. I wonder now, if the order would have even kept to their agreement and let my brother go if he had succeeded.

Blake's throat bobs against the blade as she swallows, and there's not a trace of fear in her eyes. Reaching up with my free hand, I run my fingers through her dark locks, tucking her hair behind her ear. "West would have loved you," I rasp, and the truth of the statement vibrates through me. I've always like fiery females, but none of them have been as headstrong and stubborn as Blake. West would have loved having Blake in our family. In fact, I'm pretty sure West would have liked Mason and the others as well.

For the first time, the pain that's been in my chest since my brother's death shifts. It's still there, but it's not as noticeable. And that desire for revenge I'd held on to for so long—the hate, the anger—it starts to fade. I'd thought I was dishonoring my brother by not being able to kill the demon king and his daughter and get revenge, but I finally realize, that to honor West, I have to live. I have to finally give in to my fate and let myself have the family West and I had both dreamed of. Dropping my blade, I claim Blake's mouth, my tongue stroking against hers, as I finally let go.

Blake claws at me as I push her hard against the tree, my thigh pressing between her legs. A moan hums from her, and I groan as she rubs against me. I'd been so worried I couldn't have her. That I would have to kill her, and relief washes through me as I finally let myself give in to the she-demon.

"So, I'm guessing this means you don't want to kill me again?" she murmurs, an edge of humor in her voice as my lips tingle against hers.

I growl at the thought of her being taken from me, even by my own hand. "I've known I wouldn't be able to kill you from that first time you fought me," I rasp.

Her lips curve. "Yeah, because I kicked your ass."

My hand closes around her neck, and she gasps.

Leaning closer, I brush my lips against the side of her head. "I knew because when I was close to you, instead of desiring vengeance, all I wanted...was you. And it was torture."

My thigh presses harder between her legs, and her mouth falls open even wider.

"You always were the sweetest with words," she teases.

"But it was only torture because I was afraid I could never have you," I growl under my breath.

"Alaric," she says softly, and I reach down, freeing my aching cock. Gripping her ass, I lift her higher. She's not wearing anything beneath the shirt, and when the fabric bunches at her waist, I growl at the sight of her.

"Like I've said before," she pants, "You're mine. Just as I am yours."

I tease her with the head of my cock, and the next time she says my name, it's a plea from my enchantress, and I'm helpless to resist. I thrust my cock into her, one hand still on her throat, and her mouth falls open in a silent scream.

"Fuck," she gasps, and her lips twist. "Guess you're a grower then, huh?" Before I can respond, she snorts with amusement. "Then again, I guess it makes sense considering you're a giant."

Of course, my cock when I'm in my actual giant form is way bigger than now, but I don't mention that. "Don't tell the shifter," I rumble at her. "He seems sensitive about these things."

She laughs outright at that, but her laughter dies off when I squeeze her throat tighter and start pumping into her. Her body stretches to accommodate me, and I let out a tortured sound.

Her bottom lip trembles as I hold her firmly. "See? Isn't this better than fighting it?" she pants.

I snarl, fucking her harder until she's screaming, her mind only focused on the pleasure I can give her. Fuck, I never want to stop hearing that sound.

When I pull my cock completely out and thrust it in again, she falls over the edge, screaming my name as her golden tattoos light up on her skin. I slam my lips to hers, swallowing the sound, and my balls tighten before I spill into her, my own release crashing through me.

My enchantress.

Mine.

Despite all my doubts, the she-demon fits perfectly against me, and we shudder through the aftershocks together. When she stops jerking, I gently move my hand from her throat and set her on her feet.

"Alaric, you've been holding ou—" Princess Blake pants, but her words abruptly stop when we both hear it at once. The sound of a cracking twig comes from close by, and I shield my mate, grabbing a smaller blade from my boot and sending it into the darkness.

The blade connects with flesh, and there's a grunt as someone stumbles forward and comes into view.

Princess Blake peers around me. "Dante?"

The demon grins, his tail flicking as he watches us. "What?" he says, giving Blake an innocent look. "We voted that someone should keep an eye on you in case this prick was up to no good. It's not my fault I was the lucky one chosen." He smirks. "Of course, that may have also had something to do with my abilities."

The demon has a raging hard on, and I think about snapping it off, but going from Blake's grin she's happy to see him, so I settle with glowering at the male for his intrusion.

"Which, I must say, I'm glad to see you two have sorted things out," Dante drawls, his eyes crinkling with amusement.

Blake pats me on the back. "Better late than never, huh, big guy?"

She starts toward the house, and I lift her into my arms. My release drips down her legs, and I'm not going to leave her like that.

"Why do you all insist on carrying me?" she protests, squirming in my hold. "I have legs *and* wings, if you haven't noticed."

"Of course, I've noticed," I point out bluntly.

"Then why—" She lets out an exasperated sigh, and shares a look with Dante who's busy smirking.

When it's clear she'll have to fight me to get me to release her, she relaxes in my hold.

Dante directs me to the washroom and insists on helping me bathe our mate. She grumbles about being treated like a babe, but she lets us fuss over her, cleaning her and then exiting the pool. When we're all dry, our hair still a damp mess, Dante gestures with his head to the hallway.

"The others have sorted out our sleeping arrangements," the demon says with a mischievous glint in his eyes.

Blake stares at him suspiciously. "Oh, they have, have they?"

The demon doesn't say any more as he leads us down the hall to one of the rooms.

When we enter, Blake laughs. Squeezed against the far wall, multiple beds have been pushed together, filling the space from one side of the room to the other.

"You grabbed the beds from the other rooms," she says in surprise.

Mason, Prince Callan, and Nate grin at us, the three of them stretched out on the mattresses.

"This way, there'll be no arguments," Prince Callan explains simply, and it's strange seeing the archangel there, lounging so casually. Obviously, he's accepted his fate just as I have.

I set Blake on her feet, and she walks over, crawling on to the mattress and flopping into the space they've left for her in the middle. Dante stalks over, easing onto the bed behind Mason, and I stand there with my arms crossed.

Blake shakes her head at me. "Not this time, buddy. Get your ass over here." She pats the space to her left and Nate grumbles, shuffling back to give me room.

"You heard her," the shifter says, and despite myself, I stride over taking my place beside my mate. *My enchantress.*

FOURTEEN

~ Princess Blake ~

I blink my eyes open blearily, wondering if I'm still dreaming. I'm cocooned in warmth, the scents of my mates all around me, and I swear I haven't slept that deeply in my entire life. Alaric has me tucked up right against him, one hand braced under his head, and I've never seen him look so peaceful. Mason is on my other side with Dante's arm draped across his waist, and Nate is behind Alaric.

It's only then that I realize Prince Callan is gone. The thought that he'd left us, that he might have changed his mind about everything makes my stomach drop. I sit there for a moment when I hear a faint clanging coming from down the hallway. Carefully wiggling from Alaric's hold, I slide from the mattress and silently grab one of the daggers I had hidden under the mattress on one of my previous stays here.

I'm quiet as I make my way down the hallway, and as I reach the entrance to the common room, I grip the hilt of my dagger tighter. There aren't many who know the location of this house. "Callan?" I peer around the corner and freeze.

The archangel prince turns at the sound of my voice. He's shirtless, wearing only his pants, and instead of his hair being slicked back in its usual style, the golden strands are tousled, sticking out in all directions. He smiles, holding a frypan in one hand and a spatula in another. "Good morning, angel." The greeting is like a smooth caress, and I stand there gaping. My mouth instantly waters, and I'm not sure if it's because he looks like a domesticated god right now, or if it's due to whatever he's cooking.

"Uh, you might want to close your mouth before you start drooling," Shade chuckles in my head, and I notice she's perched on the edge of the kitchen island.

"Speak for yourself, perv," I shoot back, knowing full well why she's there.

"What?" she replies innocently. *"I thought you'd appreciate me keeping an eye on your mate. And*

speaking of, I'm guessing this is his way of trying to make amends?"

Shade turns her head, and I follow her gaze to the dining table which is laden with food. Much of it is prepared using the stock I had kept in cool storage, but it's obvious Prince Callan must have gone hunting and foraging in the surrounding forest. My gaze roves over the spiced venison, fried mushrooms, herb salad, and a number of other dishes that I would have no clue how to make myself. There's a selection of freshly baked bread rolls, and my brows lift. "How long have you been preparing this?"

He walks to the table, flipping the eggs from his pan onto an empty plate and placing the frypan back on the stove. "It doesn't matter."

"I found him in here about three hours ago," Shade comments. *"Who knows how long he was up before that."*

I'm still gaping when firm arms wrap around me from behind, and Nate squeezes me before planting a kiss on my cheek. "Mmmm, what's smellin' so good?" He scans the room, and when he spots the spread, he grins widely. "Well, damn, Callan, you have been holdin' out on us."

Pulling me along, Nate gracefully slides into a chair at the table and drags me onto his lap.

Dante, Alaric, and Mason, come down the hallway, and Dante brushes his fingers against my cheek before taking a seat opposite me. "Sleep well, princess?"

Before I can answer, Alaric drops into the seat on my right. He grabs me from Nate's lap, pulling me onto him instead.

Mason shakes his head at the possessive assassin, and Shade gushes in my mind. *"Hold on, what'd I miss? Because that's not the grumpy Alaric I know."*

I smile. *"Let's just say, my assassin has finally come around."* I wiggle on Alaric's lap trying to get comfortable, and he grunts, growing hard beneath me. *Oops.*

I can practically feel Shade pouting in my mind. *"What? You guys are too cute! This is so unfair. I need my own harem of sexy men."*

"I'm sure your bird mate is out there somewhere," I assure her.

*"Yes, but I don't want **one** mate. I swear, if I was human—"*

"If you were human, I never would have rescued you from the human realm," I interject. "And I'm pretty sure humans only have one mate."

"Actually, they have husbands, not mates, and there are some who choose more than one partner," Shade corrects, and then she squeals in my head.

"What, what is it?" I snap, surprised at her outburst.

"He's trying to feed you, girl. That is next level adorable."

I frown, but when Alaric lifts a forkful of venison up to my lips I realize what she's going on about.

I make an unimpressed face. "Okay, being carried around is one thing, but this is too much."

Alaric doesn't lower the fork. "You wanted me to treat you like my mate, so eat, enchantress."

"And I will," I say forcefully. "But I can feed myself."

"I'm sure he knows you can, princess," Dante drawls, "but if you don't start eating something soon, I'm going to be tempted to feed you something else, and we wouldn't want all the archangel's hard work to go to waste."

My cheeks heat as Dante's midnight blue gaze holds mine. The only empty seat is next to him on the other side of the table, and he slides it closer to him like he's making me a promise, one that is all too tempting. But he's right about not wanting to waste all the delicious warm food.

I force myself to ignore his seductive stare and look over at Prince Callan who's now seated a few chairs from me. "This is amazing," I tell him, and before I can close my mouth, Alaric has shoved a forkful of food in there.

I glare at the assassin, but I'm soon distracted as layers of flavor explode on my tongue. *Merciful Lady.* My eyes shoot wide with surprise.

Nate's chest rumbles as he swallows his own forkful, and gives the archangel a lopsided grin. "Definitely holdin' out on us, brother."

I don't complain as Alaric continues to feed me, but then I slip from his lap and make my way over to my seat, because there's no way I'm not getting my own plate. Dante watches me with a hawkish gaze, but he doesn't pounce on me like he'd teased, though his tail does wrap possessively around my leg, pinning me to the chair.

Shade goes straight for the bowl of seeds and nuts that's on one side of the table, clearly left there for her. There's also a large selection of prepared fruit. *"Mmmm....have I mentioned that I love this archangel?"*

"Actually, I'm pretty sure you were anti-Prince Callan the last time we discussed him. You're swayed that easily then, huh?"

"I'm just saying, I could get used to this," Shade says. *"Besides, don't pretend you weren't easily won over as well. I heard all of you last night."*

I can't really argue with that, and the others don't say much as we devour the food. It's only when we've eaten our fill, that I realize all eyes are on me again.

Dante is the first one to speak. "So princess, now that we're home, where do we go from here?"

"I'd like to know that, too," Shade chimes in. *"What have the crows been telling you?"*

My stomach churns. Even now I can feel them— my crows spread throughout the city. It wouldn't take much for me to connect with each of them and find out what they know, but I shudder, remembering what happened to the birds in Toralyn. Logically, I know Princess Mirelle isn't here, and that I don't have to worry about her fire harming them, but I still can't bring myself to command them. Not yet.

I clear my throat. "We need to find out what's happening in the city," I say aloud, ignoring Shade's question. "When I left, there was already evidence that at least one of the demon clans has been working with the witches, and we need to find out who else is involved and what the plans are. Clearly the witches have their hands in a lot of pies, and we need to figure out how this all pieces together before it's too late."

"And why aren't we headin' to the castle?" Nate asks, popping another mushroom into his mouth and moaning.

"Yes, would the king not be expecting you, my mate?" Mason asks.

"I'm sure he is," I say slowly. "But the thing is..." I go on to tell them all about the secret vault. I don't explain how to access it, but I tell them all about the forbidden door and the power I can sense on the other side. I also tell them about how Dante was attacked when he was disguised as Kai. "So you see, I'm not willing to risk taking any of you to the castle just yet. At least, not until we've bonded." I pause. "That is...if everyone's interested in bonding?" I'm not sure why I feel so hesitant to ask. All of my mates have now shown that they're committed to me, but it's one thing to share our bodies, and it's another thing entirely to bond yourself to others for eternity.

Everyone's silent for a moment, and it's not until Mason reaches out, linking his fingers with mine, that I realize how tense I am. Lifting my hand, Mason kisses my fingers, and I let out a long breath.

"I want nothing more than to seal the bond between us, my mate," Mason murmurs, and my heart pounds.

Dante's tail tightens on my leg. "Of course, princess. How could I want anything else?"

Nate grins at me and winks. "Let's do this."

Prince Callan nods his head. "Anything for my Ahalian Touizda. If she'll have me."

I peer at Alaric last, and he stares back at me, his grey eyes unreadable. "What do you think, assassin? Want to bond with the enemy?"

He sets down the fork he had been gripping tightly. "You were never my enemy, Blake. I see that now." His voice is gruff and raw, and bumps prickle over my skin.

"*Well, damn,*" Shade says, hopping from one foot to the other. "*Do you guys need a minute?*"

"It's settled then," Dante says. "We're finally all agreed that we'll bond."

My heart races even faster as my mates all keep their attention on me. I'm not sure why I'm nervous about this. Finding my mates and bonding has been my goal since Dad announced his retirement. I need the power boost if I'm going to be able to keep the demons in line, let alone keep on top of this witch problem, but it suddenly all feels like too much pressure.

I swallow thickly. "Looks like it."

FIFTEEN

~ Princess Blake ~

Prince Callan, Mason, Alaric, and Nate clear the table, and Dante leads me over to one of the couches, pulling me down beside him. When they're done, the others join us, sitting around the common room.

Shade finishes preening her feathers, and she pulls her beak out from beneath her wing. *"Okay, well I think that's my cue to give you guys some space. I'm going to get some fresh air for a bit. Have fun, girl, and try not to destroy the house."*

"Why would I destroy the house?"

"Uh, no reason other than you have five mates who finally want to bond with you, one of whom is a literal

giant." She chuckles. *"Let me know when it's safe to return."*

"Will do."

She leaves through a small high up window, and the moment she's gone, I turn back to my mates. They're all staring at me intently, and I squirm at the attention.

"Soooo, bonding huh?" I say awkwardly, because honestly, I feel out of my depth right now. I can face off demon bugs and witches, but bonding with five fated mates? Yeah, I wasn't ever prepared for that.

Dante chuckles, and his tail curls possessively around my leg.

"Fated mate bonds are rare for my kind," Mason says. "What exactly does bonding involve?"

"From what I hear, a demon has to bed all of her mates at the same time," I reply.

"They all have to be touching," Dante adds.

"And mentally, they have to be open to the bond," I finish. My gaze finds Alaric then, but the assassin doesn't shy away. He simply stares at me, those soulful gray eyes never leaving my face.

Nate leans back in his chair and grins. "Sounds easy enough."

"It's not supposed to be easy," Prince Callan says. "We're supposed to worship our mate, and in return, Lady Fate will grant us with more power. We're supposed to be the ones to balance our mate. To protect and cherish her." As he speaks, he moves positions, coming to sit on my other side. His golden wings drape over the back of the couch, and instinctively I reach over, tracing my finger slowly down one wing. He shudders and cups the side of my face. "Are you ready to bond, my Ahalian Touizda?"

My heart thuds as I stare back at the archangel's ridiculously handsome face. "Yes," I reply, my throat suddenly tight. "Are you?"

"I couldn't be more ready," he answers. His golden lips quirk up, but there's so much emotion, so much...love, in his eyes, that my bottom lip trembles. He brushes his thumb across my cheek, and my heart beats so loud it's like there's a steady drumbeat in my ears. I have the startling thought that after this, I won't ever truly be alone again. That somehow, after all these years, after all I've endured, I've found my family, and I would die to protect them. *...And die without them.* The thought is both thrilling and terrifying, because life won't be the same if they're ever taken from me.

My gaze sweeps over the rest of my mates as they rise from their seats and come closer. For once, Nate has no jokes, and there's no casual banter. My mates are serious as they surround me, and for just this moment, it's as if time has stopped.

A sudden spark of panic goes through me, and I blurt out an irrational thought that pops into my head. "But what if I'm not a good mate? Five of you is a lot to keep happy."

"You could place us in your dungeons and throw

away the key, and we would still think you are the perfect mate," Prince Callan says.

I laugh at his ridiculous answer. "You would no —" I don't finish, because my archangel presses his lips to mine, and the worry that I might not be enough for them vanishes in an instant. The kiss is soft and gentle, and it fills me with a warmth that chases away all the dark thoughts buried in the depths of my mind. I lean into him, deepening the kiss, my tongue stroking over his, and the archangel responds, claiming me like he's been waiting an eternity for this moment.

Dante's tail releases my leg, and he brushes his fingers across my neck. "Come, Blake," he whispers.

I pull my lips away from Prince Callan and stand, watching as Dante and the rest of my mates undress, exposing ridges of hard muscle and sculpted abs. Prince Callan comes up behind me, pulling off my shirt, and he drags his lips against my bare shoulder. I'm still not wearing anything beneath the shirt, and my nipples pucker as they're exposed to the cool air.

We make our way to the bedroom, and Nate lays on the mattress. I crawl over to him, anticipation winding through me as I climb on, and I gasp as I feel every bump and groove of his cock as it slides inside me. *Merciful Lady.* My golden tattoos flare to life instantly this time like the power inside me is already awakening. Like it already knows what we're about to do. *Mine.* They have always been mine. I can feel it in my soul, in the very depths of my being. These males are my fated mates.

Nate grips my hips as I ride him, whimpering as I move up and down his length.

Mason comes up behind me. "Can I, my mate?" he asks me tenderly. I nod and stop moving, leaning forward so the centaur can work himself slowly into my ass. When I start moving again, it takes a short while for me to adjust to the feel of them, and then I'm moaning as Mason cups my breasts.

Still, it's not enough. I need the others. Like Dante can sense what I'm thinking, he comes onto the bed, kneeling on my left, and his tail curves around to flick my clit. Alaric climbs onto the bed and kneels on my right. I reach out, gripping their cocks and stroking them, loving the sound of their groans in my ears.

Prince Callan is the last to move onto the mattresses. He makes his way near Nate's head and kneels. His cock juts out proudly, and I bend over enough to grab it in my mouth.

He curses, his golden wings flaring out as his cock hits the back of my throat.

Five mates. *Five.* Their scents mix in the most intoxicating way, and as I breathe them in, something settles in my chest. There's this feeling that no matter what happens in the future, this moment is right. I was always meant to claim these five. From the moment I met them all, I knew they were mine, but I never really realized how badly I wanted this. How badly I *needed* this, until now. And it feels so good to finally have them. To finally let myself bond with them.

I keep my mind open to them, and my heart feels like it's about to burst as pleasure consumes me. We move in tandem, finding a rhythm, the six of us all touching. The power inside me grows, the magic spreading to my fingertips and racing to my toes as the tattoos light up on my skin, so bright I squeeze my eyes shut.

"Fuck, Blake," Nate curses, his fingers digging into my hips as I cry out.

My shifter's barbs explode inside me, and the pleasure, the power, becomes too much. The house shakes, dust and rubble falling from the ceiling, and there's a buzzing in my head as I feel the mental connection between me and my mates snap into place. My power builds in pressure until it explodes, and the orgasm hits me with a force so intense I scream. Just when I think I can't take anymore and the power is going to tear me apart, the connection with my mates grows even stronger, and my power starts flowing into each of them. My mates find their releases at the same moment, and their groans fill the air.

It takes moments for the power to stabilize and regulate, the magic like a pulsing heartbeat inside me, and when our orgasms end, the house stops shaking. I still feel the power bubbling under my skin, but it's contained, constantly flowing inside me and my mates.

"Holy Fates," Mason mutters in awe, and my chest heaves as I realize I've just heard him in my mind.

I let go of Alaric's and Dante's cocks, and I swallow Prince Callan's release before pulling my mouth from his cock. When I open my eyes, for a moment all I see is light. It takes seconds for the light to fade, and then I stare at the golden circle tattoos now on my mate's chests, the whirls and marks matching the tattoos covering my body.

"I feel you," I say to them, my eyes wide as I speak to them in my mind.

Mason kisses my sweaty shoulder. *"And we feel you, our mate."*

My heart is so damn full, tears prick at my eyes, and I smile.

Dante rocks back on his knees. *"Well, that was... intense."*

"So, this is what it feels like," Prince Callan murmurs, tucking his wings in again.

Mason gently pulls his cock from my body, and I climb off Nate. Alaric moves back, and I flop onto the bed. *"I guess so,"* I say with a soft smile.

My mates all stare at me, and there's so much love in their gazes that I feel as though my heart has grown two sizes.

"For so long I have felt empty inside," Mason says out loud. "And not just from the pain of losing my family, my friends, and the betrayal of my brother. It was as though there was something missing, but I couldn't understand what it was." He smiles at me. "Turns out it was you, my mate."

My throat is so tight that all I can do is smile back at him, and when Alaric lays beside me, gently curling his arm around me, I bury into his chest, wishing I never had to come up for air.

We take our time cleaning up and dressing, and then we're back in the sitting room.

"I feel incredible," Dante says, holding his hands in the air like he can see power traveling along his veins. A funny smile crosses his face, and he walks to a wall. Lifting his hand, he presses his palm against the dark paint, and the entire house freaking *disappears*. Not just Dante, but the entire building and everything inside it, including us.

My skin tingles as I blink at the scene around me. Though I can still feel Dante and my other mates in exactly the same positions as we were seconds ago, the forest surrounds us now, trees and grass lining the space on all sides. A short distance beneath us is the large stretch of flattened earth that the house was built on. *Whoa.*

Nate curses.

"So, I think we can confirm I've leveled up," Dante drawls. "Considering, I only used to be able to make myself and small items invisible, like the clothes I was wearing or another person I was touching."

The house comes back into view, the fully furnished room and my mates appearing around me as the tingling stops.

Dante is holding his hands in the air, staring at them in awe again. "Looks like the limitations of my power have changed."

Nate prowls around the room. "Let's take this outside. I want to try something."

We all follow him, and once we're standing beneath the stars, Nate walks a few paces away from us. He winks at me. "You all might want to stay back." And then he's shifting. Fur rushes over his body as his form changes and morphs, and he turns into a jaguar that's twice the size of his previous form. He shakes his huge head, his large claws digging into the earth, and he opens his mouth revealing a set of massive fangs.

His chest rumbles, and I hold up my hands. "Don't!" But Nate doesn't stop. Before the roar tears from him, Prince Callan whips his hand up and a tunnel of wind forms around the powerful jaguar, stopping the sound from escaping. The wind tunnel becomes larger, stretching wider, and uprooting a few surrounding trees.

"Uh, Callan—" I start, surprised by how fast his wind turned into an out-of-control vortex, but just as quickly, Prince Callan forms a fist with his hand, cutting off the flow of power. The vortex grows smaller in size until it disappears, and all we're left with is a giant cat with ruffled hair and a pissed off expression.

I smother my laugh. "We don't want to draw attention."

Nate glowers at Prince Callan, looking like he wants to snack on the prince's wings.

Mason decides to try his power next, changing into his shifted form. While he's not double his size like Nate, he is larger, his coat more glossy, and I could swear even his muscles are bigger. He takes one of his knives, aims at a nearby tree, and throws it. The blade cuts straight through the trunk of multiple trees before it stops.

"And, what about you, our mate?" the centaur says, giving me a breathtaking smile. "How have your powers changed?"

I bite my lip, my power continuing to flow outward. The others can't sense it, but I can feel them around me. The birds, that is. My reach is much further than it was before, stretching far across the realm. My power reaches out to the animals, touching them, coaxing them to me without me even uttering a command. A bush rustles nearby, and Nate's cat eyes fix on the spot, the giant feline ready to pounce. Before anything springs free, I pull back my power, severing the connection. The bird that had been about to appear flies away, and all five of my mates turn to me.

"I can sense more of them," I explain. "The birds, that is." I don't give them a demonstration and summon the innocent creatures to me. I still can't forget what happened when I failed the birds in Toralyn.

From their worried expressions, I'm guessing my mates can sense something is wrong, but I force a smile to my face and shrug. "I feel stronger, too. More in control." That last part, at least, seems to appease them.

"And what about you, assassin?" Mason asks. "What are your gifts?"

Alaric frowns, staring at his hands.

"Maybe we should find that out another time, hey big guy?" Dante points out. "Something tells me the demons will notice a hulking giant in the forest outside the city."

"That's probably wise," Alaric growls.

"Ahhhh!" Shade screeches in my mind, and I whip my head to the side in time to see Nate leap into the air, catching her in his paws and cradling her as he lands.

She struggles in his hold. *"Bad kitty. Very bad kitty! Oh god, this is like that time with Jessie's house cat all over again."*

I'm there in a second, prying Nate's paws open.

Nate hisses, and his tail flicks back and forth as he reluctantly watches Shade hop away and then fly onto my shoulder.

"Oh, thank god. For a minute there, I thought he

might eat me," Shade says. *"Blake, what is happening? Why is Nate so big? I mean, I knew he was big, but I'm talking about his cat form, not his..."*

Dante stares at Shade, a bewildered expression taking over his face. *"Is it me, or did that bird just speak?"* he says via our mental connection.

Prince Callan steps up beside him. *"She spoke."*

Shade stares at them with beady black eyes. *"Uh Blake, I must be hearing things, because I swear I just heard your sexy mates chattering in my head."*

"Hmmm is it weird that the bird thinks I'm sexy? I feel like I should find it strange, but I can't blame her," Dante muses out loud this time.

"What the— Did he just— Blaaaake!" Shade squawks.

I can't help it, I burst out laughing.

"Unbelievable," Shade says, sounding pissed though there's an undercurrent of excitement in her voice as she perches on my shoulder. *"They can hear me, can't they?"*

"Looks like it's not only me who will have the pleasure of your company," I say to her. "Let's hope they catch on to your humor real quick."

"Shall I punish Nate for scaring the bird, my mate?" Mason asks seriously.

"Uh, yes please," Shade replies, suddenly chipper. *"Seriously, this guy knows the way to a girl's heart. He's still number one."* Her gaze goes to Alaric. *"And I have to say, aside from his previous grumpiness, Alaric has come a long way."*

"Number one?" Dante says incredulously. "Well, now that won't do." He moves closer to her, and starts rubbing his finger on the side of Shade's neck, making her cock her head with pleasure.

"Mmmm, I'm completely okay with this. Sure, you can be number one, demon."

I roll my eyes as Shade laps up the attention.

Prince Callan watches Dante and Shade. "Have you always been able to hear her speak?"

"Ever since I found her," I reply with a small smile.

"And the matter with Nate?" Mason asks, still looking like he wants to punish the shifter.

I shake my head. "He's fine. He wasn't going to eat her. He just struggles with impulse control."

Nate crouches playfully, his tail flicking. *"Is that right, gorgeous?"* His voice is a low purr in my head.

"Yes, it is," I reply, even though the sound of his rough voice is driving me crazy. "Because you wouldn't dare eat my best friend. Not if you wanted to keep on living, bonded or not."

"You heard her," Shade adds. *"Keep your grubby giant paws off me."*

Nate's tail continues to flick back and forth. *"If you keep tempting me—"*

I give Nate an unimpressed look, and then I peer around at the others. "My demon gift allows me to speak with birds, but Shade has always been chattier than most. And it looks like now that we're connected, you can hear her, too."

Nate shifts back to his human form and grins. "So this entire time, this little ball of feathers has been chattin' to you about us?"

Shade lifts her beak higher, puffing up her chest. *"That's right, asshole. Welcome to the party. Looks like this is a group chat now."*

"Group chat?" Alaric rumbles.

I shake my head at him. "She doesn't always make sense." Then I plant one hand on my hip, staring at Nate as I answer his previous question. "How else did you think she understood your directions to find the rebels when we were in The Haven?"

Nate shrugs. "Honestly, I hadn't thought she'd be able to find them."

Dante strokes his chin. "It does explain a lot."

Alaric doesn't say anything, but I get the feeling he'd pieced together my connection with Shade a while ago. The demons always thought I was simply able to control the birds, so I'm not surprised the others didn't realize.

"She's mouthy and a little pervy, but you'll get used to her," I assure them.

"Hey! I am not pervy!"

I shoot her a look.

"I simply appreciate," she defends.

Dante's lips curve upward. "Well, I for one, like her more already."

I smile at Shade, but my brows lower when I notice her claws. "Shade, what is that?"

She looks behind her in an exaggerated manner. *"What is what?"*

"That," I say, pointing to the sticky orange residue she's left on my shoulder. "Please don't tell me that's worm guts or something disgusting."

"All right, it's not something disgusting," she says, shifting uneasily.

Making a face, I reach down, touching the sticky residue and bringing it close to my nose. I breathe in. "Shade," I say sternly. "Why the fuck do my fingers smell like Dante?"

She makes a grossed-out noise in my head. *"Hey, where you stick your fingers in your mates is your own—"*

"Shade!" I snap via our mental connection this time. *"You know what I mean. Why is there apricot juice on your claws? And not just any apricots, but the same incredible ones we can only find at Dante's mansion."* My jaw drops. *"Have you been eating them...without me?"*

Dante smirks, and the others look simply clueless.

Shade sighs in my head. *"I was going to bring you back some. But then I heard them, and I guess I got distracted."*

"Them?" I give Dante a worried look. "We're supposed to be laying low. What happened?"

It's only then that I think about how fast she'd been flying through the forest toward us before Nate caught her. I'd been too distracted to question it.

Shade peers around at all the inquiring faces and huffs out a breath. *"So, I know you said not to go to the city just yet, but I figured I could sneak to Dante's house and grab some apricots to go."* She pauses. *"It was going to be my happy bonding present for you."*

"I don't think demons usually give bonding presents," I point out, but my heart still warms.

"Well, they should," she counters. *"Gifting is some people's love language, you know."*

"And Blake likes...apricots?" Mason muses thoughtfully, and I get the feeling he's stashing that information for later.

"But you didn't bring any," Dante says. "So what happened at my clan house?"

"Well," Shade continues, *"I was busy finding the best apricots."*

I grin. "You mean, you were busy eating them."

"Yeah, that," she agrees without missing a beat. *"And that's when I heard them arrive—Luna and Noah."*

Dante's eyebrows rise. "Are they all right?"

"They're fine," Shade assures him. *"And I would have continued right on with my business, except it's what they were talking about that concerned me."* Her beady black eyes go to the side of my face. *"They were talking about someone who'd propositioned them. Sounds like it's not the first time either. They were saying that they weren't sure what to do, and that they wished Dante was there. Something about if they don't turn up*

at the meeting they're dead, but if they do go and the king finds out, then they're also dead."

"Could this be about the witches?" Prince Callan asks.

"Maybe," I answer. "Or this could simply be about who is going to succeed the throne when the king retires, and the power shift between the clans."

Dante curses. "I need to speak with them. We have to find out what the situation is. I'm the Coilan Clan leader, and the responsibility should be on my shoulders. Not theirs."

I rub the back of my neck, wishing I had the eyes of my crows. But again, the moment I think about sending them out there, just the thought of commanding them makes me feel sick. "I let us have too much time here, when I should have been in the city."

"Now that we're bonded, can't we go to the castle and speak with the king?" Nate suggests. "Whatever power is being hidden in the castle, I'm sure we can face it."

I rub my temples. I had wanted us to stay away from the castle and the dark power there until we were bonded and at our strongest, but... "Despite our power, even now my absence from the castle can work to our advantage," I say. "If this meeting is about the Seral throne, it could be worth finding out what's happening between the clans now while they still don't realize I've returned."

"I'll go to my clan house without mentioning

anything about you, princess," Dante says. "I'll find out the information from Luna and Noah, and I'll attend the meeting. It's our best way of gaining inside information."

I purse my lips. It would be the easiest way for us to find out the information, but my stomach roils at the idea of my mate walking into danger without me. "If it's simply a meeting between the clan leaders it should be relatively safe, but demons have a habit of getting stabby when tempers flare, and I imagine things will be tense when discussing a new ruler for Seral. Unless of course, the meeting is to discuss the witches...which brings a whole new set of challenges."

"I can go with him," Mason volunteers. "To protect our bond brother."

Dante rests his hand on Mason's shoulder. "Thank you, but you're not a demon. There will be too many questions."

"There would have been demons who saw us together in the Perstalian ruins," Prince Callan points out. "They'll remember Dante was with the princess, and may have even pieced together that you're mates,"

I pace, thinking about this. "Okay, then what if we're all disguised?"

My demon mate frowns. "What?"

"What if we're all disguised as demons with different faces," I explain, and my gaze collides with Dante's. "Can you get word to Luna?"

CHAPTER
SIXTEEN

~ Dante ~

The little crow chats constantly in my head as she flies back to Blake's house in the forest, with Luna and Noah following her in Noah's car. It's strange listening to the bird who has zero filter, but I feel honored I'm able to share this with Blake. I'd always suspected the princess could speak to the birds rather than simply command them, but I hadn't expected the crow to be such a mouthy little thing.

It's not long before Noah's car pulls up out the front of the house. The rumbling of the engine shuts off, and there's a knock at the door. Mason answers it, and Shade flies into the sitting room, perching on Blake's shoulder.

Noah and Luna stride into the room, the pair of them wary. Luna's auburn hair is a mess, and she looks as though she hasn't slept in days. Noah doesn't look much better with ruffled hair and a weary expression. They both keep their gazes trained on Blake, not having spotted me yet as Alaric is somewhat blocking my view.

"Thanks for coming," Blake says with a smile. *"And thanks for fetching them,"* she says to Shade.

"Don't mention it," the bird replies.

"Of course, your highness," Luna says, placing her fist to her chest and bowing low before she straightens. I think of the message Shade had delivered to them. The small piece of rolled up parchment had simply said they were to be escorted to the princess immediately. It hadn't said anything about me.

I step out from behind the giant, and my friends immediately spot me.

Luna lets out a noise of surprise. "You asshole!" she blurts, momentarily forgetting about Blake. Launching at me, she crushes me in a hug.

"We thought you were fucking dead," Noah says, whacking me hard on the back.

Then, remembering where they are, they both stare uncertainly at Blake.

Noah clears his throat like he's about to apologize, but my mate grins. "It's all right." Her tone is casual, but her gaze lingers on Luna for a little too long, and my pants tighten at the possessiveness in my mate's eyes.

Getting the hint, Luna takes a step back. "Hold on," my friend says slowly, clearly picking up on the power coming from us. Her eyes snap wider. "You're bonded?"

I smirk, and despite the fact I'm happy to see my friends, a part of me wishes I was alone with my mate and my bond brothers. If only so we could make Blake scream again.

"Sure are," Nate says, baring his teeth in a smile that isn't exactly friendly.

Luna is still gaping, and it takes her a moment to digest the news. She stares at Blake, and then the five of us. "Wait...you're *all* bonded? Damn, the power coming from you is making me shiver." She makes a show of looking at the goosebumps on her arm.

"Guess it's a good thing Dante likes to share," Noah jokes, and my tail flicks out, lashing his leg.

He curses, and his face pales when he stares at Blake again. He dips his head. "Sorry, your highness."

My mate raises a brow, her eyes dancing with amusement. *"Please tell me these are two of the few demons you haven't slept with."* She says it casually in my mind, though from the tightness of her body, I'm guessing this is affecting her more than she's letting on.

"Would it matter?" I muse back.

"Uh yes, asshole," Shade answers for her. *"Because if you have slept with either of them, this might not end well."*

I chuckle through the bond. *"Asshole? I'm starting to think that's a term of endearment."*

"Insult? Endearment? Who cares. Answer the question, demon," Shade replies dryly.

"Hmmm are you always this demanding?"

Blake grins. *"Oh, this is nothing. You wait until she's hangry."*

"Hangry?" Mason asks.

"Angry because she's hungry," Alaric growls, then he scowls like he's annoyed that he knows that.

"Yep, she gets attitude," Blake adds, beaming at the assassin like she's a teacher praising her pupil who just got the answer right.

"This is her without attitude?" Nate asks with amusement.

"Actually, I could use a snack," Shade replies thoughtfully. *"I forgot to bring the apricots."*

"Again?" Blake sighs.

"You're avoiding the question," Prince Callan cuts in.

"What question?" Shade asks. *"Is this still about the apricots?"*

The prince rubs the bridge of his nose. *"No. The question of whether Dante has slept with either of these demons."*

Shade perks up again on Blake's shoulder. *"Oh righhhht."*

My mate and the others all look at me, and I give them a devilish grin. "No, I haven't slept with them," I say aloud, and the others all glare at me like I've just revealed a big secret.

"What?" Luna snorts.

I curl my arm around Blake and smirk. "The princess here, was just wondering whether she needed to teach you a lesson for daring to touch her mate."

Luna raises a brow, not looking the least bit intimidated by the thought. "Oh, yeah no, Dante is like a brother to me. We grew up together, and the thought of that," she uses her finger, making a circular motion toward my crutch, then points to herself, "near this?" She makes a disgusted face. "Yeah, it was never going to happen."

She winks at Blake, and my mate grins, already won over by my friend. *Typical.*

Shade cackles in my head. *"Ohhh I love this she-demon already. Can we keep her?"*

"Is anyone else concerned that when we bonded we ended up not just sharin' a mental connection with one female, but two?" Nate points out, indicating at Shade with his head.

Alaric, who's next to him, punches him in the stomach and the shifter lets out an "Oof."

"What? Don't pretend you weren't thinkin' it," Nate defends.

"That's our mate's friend," Alaric growls.

Blake lifts a hand to her face to stifle her laugh.

"Someone blow Alaric a kiss. He needs a reward for that," Shade chatters. *"Mason?"*

The centaur doesn't even hesitate. He takes it one further and leans over like he's about to peck Alaric on the cheek. Before he can, Alaric's hand shoots out, gripping the male's neck and stopping his lips from touching him. "No," he growls and pushes him back.

"Holy crap," Shade cackles. *"He was really going to do that. Mason is **definitely** my favorite."*

Alaric let's out a resigned sigh.

"She has a short attention span," Blake explains. *"You'll get used to it."*

"Okay, I'm not going to pretend I know what's happening here," Luna says, staring at Alaric and Mason, and the rest of us like we've lost our minds. Her gaze goes to the tattoos on Alaric's arms, and her brows rise. "Also, is that a Drozac assassin?"

Noah squints, taking a step closer. "Fuck, it is."

"Relax," I tell them. "He's with us."

"Well, I get that," Luna replies, "but how did this happen?"

Blake shrugs. "Who the hell knows?" She indicates with her head. "That's Alaric, and yes, he's a Drozac assassin. Next to him is Mason, he's a foreign prince and winged centaur." Luna opens her mouth, but Blake adds, "Don't even ask."

My friend closes her mouth again.

"Then we have Nate, he's a jaguar shifter," my mate continues, "Prince Callan from Toralyn, no explanation needed there." Prince Callan bows, making a show of it. "And of course, Dante," Blake finishes.

Luna blinks and takes a moment before speaking. "Okay, I think I followed all that." She fixes her gaze on my mate. "And what can we do for you, your highness? For you to request that we come here, there must be a reason, and I'm guessing it's not just so we can see Dante is alive."

I don't miss the fact that Luna says 'requested' rather than 'ordered,' even though we all know when the princess makes a 'request' of one of her demons, it isn't to be disobeyed.

My mate crosses her arms. "Some time ago, you used your power to disguise Dante so he could enter the palace without me realizing his true identity," she says.

Luna sends a worried glance my way and bows, bringing her fist to her chest again as she stares at the ground submissively. "Princess, it was not my intention to deceive—"

"Dante..." Noah starts to protest, but Blake continues on.

"I didn't bring you here to punish you," my mate says quickly. "I brought you here because we need your help."

Frowning, Luna slowly rises, pulling her fist away from her chest.

"We need you to use your powers to disguise us," I say.

Luna's gaze cuts to me before she turns her attention back to Blake. "Disguise you?"

My mate strokes Shade's feathers. "It's come to our attention that during Dante's absence, you've been approached, and individuals have requested that you attend a meeting."

"They've been by every day for the past three days," Noah admits.

"Who has?" I ask.

Noah shifts uncomfortably. "Ivar's minions. There has already been one gathering since the princess's ball and King Dalton announced his retirement. I'm sure there are more that we don't know about."

"Ivar from the Fallon Blade clan?" Blake asks, her back snapping straight.

"According to the rumors, the Fallon Blade clan has a new house in the city, but we don't know where it is," Luna answers.

"*What is it?*" Alaric growls in our minds, his question clearly directed at Blake.

"*About a week before Dad drugged us all for the competition, we found a demon with witch contraband. Weapons,*" Blake explains. "*He was from the Fallon Blade clan. Our top general was sent to investigate, but apparently the clan house had been cleared out before he got there. The general torched the building to send a message to them.*"

Nate curses.

"So this meeting," I ask Noah. "Is it a gathering of the clan leaders or are there others set to attend?"

Noah looks at me strangely. "Only a few of the clan leaders as far as I'm aware."

"Let me guess," Blake says, "the ones who would choose a different ruler for Seral?"

Noah dips his head. "I can't be sure, your highness."

My mate blows out a breath. "They're so predictable."

I rub my hand soothingly against Blake's arm. "Is there any other news?" I ask my friends.

When they both hesitate, Blake prompts. "What is it?"

"I can't be sure," Luna says reluctantly, "but there have been whispers in the city."

"What whispers?" Alaric growls.

"About a new power," Luna answers. "We can't tell you much more than that."

"You think she's talking about the witches?" Shade asks.

"All we know is that things aren't right," Noah adds. "The moment the king announced his retirement, fights have been breaking out all over the place. Some say it's because King Dalton destroyed the Fallon Blade clan house without provocation."

"No provocation?" Blake scoffs.

"Whatever message was intended, it sounds like the narrative has changed, my mate," Mason says.

Blake's jaw ticks, and she stares at Noah. "When and where is the meeting?"

"Daybreak," Luna replies. "At the Bleeding Hearts club."

"Bleeding Hearts? That belongs to the Silver Sun Clan," I say. "They've always been closely allied with the Fallon Blade Clan."

"Well," Blake says, cracking her neck. "Looks like there's no time to waste."

CHAPTER
SEVENTEEN

~ Mason ~

"**W**hat? *No, tell her she can't mess with this perfection,*" Shade complains, flying over and settling onto my lap. I'm sitting on one of the chairs beside the table, and the she-demon, Luna, is sitting opposite me. Luna pulls back, staring at the crow uncertainly.

"Shade, this is the whole reason we brought Luna here," Blake comments aloud, but the bird stays where she is. "We need to know what's going on at this meeting, and to do that, we all need disguises."

To Luna's credit, she keeps a straight face, not commenting on the fact that my mate is speaking to her bird.

"Yeah, well I've changed my mind," Shade squawks. *"C'mon Blake, these are **your** mates. Aren't you worried about what will happen if they can't change back?"* She stares up at me with her beady black eyes. *"Seriously, look at this face! Wouldn't you miss staring at this?"*

Blake rolls her eyes, but her lips quirk into a grin. "We *will* all change back," she assures her friend. "Luna has done this many times before. Isn't that right, Dante?"

Dante smirks. "More than she would ever admit to you, princess."

"Okay, well I'm going to try not to read into that," Blake replies, shaking her head. "But see? It's completely reversible. And besides," she peers down at me, and just having my mate's gaze on me has my heart pounding, my pants tightening, "let's be honest, he could have the face of a goat, and I'd still bed him. He's my mate." The warmth and honesty with which she says this is everything to me. Even if I have no desire to ever be a goat.

"Whoa, I know you guys just bonded, but can you do something about this," Luna cuts in then, blatantly looking at the massive bulge in my pants. There's no point trying to hide it because my efforts would be futile. Besides, it's nothing to be embarrassed about. Not when my mate looks at me like that.

"I apologize," I tell Luna sincerely. "I seem to have little control around my mate."

Luna shakes her head, side-eyeing Blake. "Don't worry. Can't say I blame you, buddy."

"*What are you guys talking about?*" Shade lowers her gaze, and she squawks in surprise. Reeling back, she stretches out her wings and flaps up to Blake's shoulder. "*God, you should warn a girl before doing that,*" she gripes to me, sounding more flustered than annoyed. Then she adds, "*Wait, when Luna works her magic, will it change that as well?*"

Nate pales, his hands lowering to the front of his pants. "Hey, no one said anythin' about changin' things down there."

"Relax," Dante says, exasperated. "Her magic only changes your outer appearance, and she only changes as much as you ask. I very much doubt Luna will want to go anywhere near that area."

"*Oh, I don't know,*" Shade says. "*I go back to my previous argument. Have you seen that face?*"

"*Okay, fine,*" Blake replies via the mental link this time. "*No one in Seral has seen Mason before anyway. Will you be happy if we keep that?*"

Shade doesn't reply, and Blake says to Luna. "Sorry, can we keep Mason's face the same, but give him the features of a demon?"

"Easy done," Luna replies.

I find it interesting that the bird is focused on my appearance. I've always known that I'm attractive, but for the entire time I was in Celzar's mine, I never had access to a mirror. At most, I saw my warped reflection in the crystals I mined, and the strange image felt like a reflection of who I was inside. Someone broken made from the shattered pieces of the male I once was.

But with Blake and the bond now humming in my chest, I feel complete. Despite everything, I know my appearance pleases my mate, I do not wish for that to change. Still, I was the first to volunteer as this is what my mate wants, and I would do anything to bring her happiness.

"Your magic will also mask our power too, right?" Blake asks Luna.

She nods. "Your power will still be there, but others won't be able to sense it."

"Good."

"But the moment you use your power," Luna goes on to explain, "it will shatter the illusion magic. So, use old-fashioned steel or other weapons if needed unless you're ready to give away your identity."

"Hold on, so we're goin' to this meetin' without our powers?" Nate asks.

"We shouldn't need to use them," Blake says. "We're only going to be there for information, remember? We can't have anyone knowing who we are."

The shifter scratches the back of his neck. "Great. We just get a boost, and we can't even use it."

"Unless you'd rather wait here while the rest of us go?" Dante teases.

Nate's slitted gaze settles on our mate. "Not happenin'" he murmurs.

"So that's it then," Blake replies. "All right, ready Mason?"

"Of course, my mate," I answer, my gaze snagging on Blake's perfect lips.

My mate turns to the red-headed female. "Okay, Luna, we'd better do this."

~

~ Princess Blake ~

It feels wrong asking Luna to disguise us and mask our powers, but I need to know what's happening between the clans. I keep assuring myself that at least if we need to use our power, all we need to do is reach for it.

When Luna is finished with Mason, I can't help but gape. My centaur mate still has the same face and dark hair, but protruding from his head are now twin brown horns like that of a mountain goat. His long-forked tail curls around, and Mason stares down at it without concern. I guess it isn't too different from having a tail when he's in his winged centaur form.

Luna leans back in her chair, dusting off her hands as she stares at him with satisfaction. "How do you feel?"

Mason tilts his head to the side. "Strange," he

admits. "I can sense my magic is still there, but it's like it's just out of reach."

"That's good," Luna says. "Keep it that way unless you want the illusion to fall apart."

With a curt nod, Mason lifts from his chair and moves to the side.

"I'll go next," Alaric offers, and Luna goes about working her magic on the assassin. The process seems to take longer, but when she's finished, Alaric peers down, running his fingers over the smooth skin of his arms. Where there used to be the distinct black tattoos, marking him as a Drozac assassin, now the skin is completely bare, and there's something about the way Alaric is staring at it that makes my chest tighten.

"Are you all right?" I ask him. "Don't worry, they'll come back."

When I say the last part, I swear he flinches a little, though he continues to touch the skin. "The last time my arms looked like this my brother was alive," he murmurs.

"Before you joined the order of the Drozac?" I ask softly.

"Yes. It feels...odd."

I reach down, placing my hand over his.

For a moment, he simply stares at my hand, but then he clears his throat and stands, moving away from the chair.

"Your turn, Nine Lives," Dante says with a grin.

Nate still doesn't look too impressed with the

idea, but he moves and slumps onto the chair. "Go easy, will ya," he tells Luna.

"It's his first time," I say to the she-demon with a mischievous grin.

She stifles her smile. "Nothing to worry about, tough guy."

Nate squeezes his eyes shut, and Luna is finished in a matter of minutes. "All done," she says, still grinning.

Nate peers up at me. "Still want me, gorgeous?"

Instead of his shaggy reddish-brown hair and reddish-gold eyes, his eyes are now turquoise like the sea, with matching-colored twin horns. Nate reaches up, feeling his horns, and his gaze shoots to Luna. "They're smaller than the length of my thumb," he grumbles. "Is that even normal for a demon?"

Dante's lips twist into a smirk as he watches Nate with wry amusement. "Be honest, Luna, you did that on purpose."

She shrugs. "What? He was only worried about me messing with the size of his cock."

"Hey now, it's not about the size, it's how you use it," Noah says, winking at Nate.

I lean down, kissing my perplexed shifter on the cheek. "We're bonded, Nate. I'll always want you." Then I turn to Luna. "But the less we stand out, the better."

"Yeah, I know," she replies, still grinning. "But I couldn't help but tease." Lifting her hands again, her magic fills the air, and Nate's horns grow larger.

This time my shifter grins when he reaches up. "Now, that's more like it."

I can't help but roll my eyes.

"We're never going to stop hearing about this, are we?" Shade says, staring at Nate's horns which are now the biggest.

Ignoring her, Nate lifts to his feet, grabs me and crushes our lips together in a punishing kiss. It's weird, seeing as he has a different face, but our bond is still strong between us, and I melt against him, losing myself. It's only when Noah clears his throat that Nate finally releases me. "All right," Nate muses. "It'll do." He slaps my ass as he moves to make way for the others, and he goes to stand with Alaric and Mason.

Prince Callan finds himself on the chair next. I expect the archangel to hate the idea of losing his wings, even if it is only temporary, but he simply stares at me, his gaze fixed on my face as Luna changes his features. And then he's no longer my golden-haired archangel, but a demon with tan skin, violet eyes, and ash-colored hair.

When she's finished, he rolls his shoulders, lifts, and presses a kiss to my cheek before stepping to the side.

"And what about you?" Luna asks Dante. "Demons have been talking about how you were last seen leaving with the princess in the Perstalian ruins. Not everyone believes the rumors, but the demons will have questions."

"Then disguise me as Noah," Dante replies, sitting opposite her. "You said they keep inviting him in my absence. So I'll go as him."

Noah grins. "Always knew you wished you could be me, brother."

Dante arches a brow at his friend. "If only to get a reprieve from the ladies," he teases.

Noah shakes his head, pretending to be unimpressed despite the grin threatening to break out on his face.

Luna turns to me, and I nod. "Do it."

Once again, magic prickles the air, and then there aren't one, but two Noah's in the room.

The real Noah admires Dante, grinning as he appreciates his copy. "I'm such a sexy beast. Promise me you won't get me into too much trouble?"

Dante slaps him on the shoulder and goes to stand with the others.

And then all eyes are on me.

My heart pounds as I settle onto the chair.

Luna stares at me. "Are you sure about this, your highness?"

I chew my bottom lip. Truthfully, I'd been all in, but now that I'm sitting here, my stomach is a mess of knots. I hated being powerless and under King Celzar's control, but I remind myself this is different. "Yes," I say, steeling myself.

Shade flies from my shoulder, settling onto the table and watching me intently.

Luna swallows, reaching up. No doubt, she's worried that if I don't like the result she'll be punished. It's what Dad would do. My instincts are telling me this is wrong. That I shouldn't be letting the demon tamper with me and my power, but it's the only way for us to attend the meeting in disguise. Or at least, it's the most reliable way.

Magic flows from Luna's fingers, making my skin tingle, and it feels like ice passes over my skin, washing over my wings. Seconds blur to minutes, and then Luna leans back, her expression serious but pleased.

For a moment, I don't move, but then my tail flicks around and my heart nearly stops.

My. Freaking. Tail.

It's long and black, and the forked tip comes up, resting on my knee. It feels so strange, like another limb, and my mouth goes dry.

"Whoa Blake, you look..." Shade trails off, and I lift my head, peering at Dante. Because out of all my mates, I know he'll understand.

His midnight blue eyes are soft as he steps forward and takes my hand, lifting me to my feet.

I swallow hard. *"I'm...I'm a real demon,"* I say to him via our bond, because I can't seem to say it out loud. I *know* the words are wrong, but I say it anyway.

He frowns, lifting his hands to cup my face.

"Having horns and a tail isn't what makes someone a demon," he tells me. *"Your heart is here, princess. Your soul is in this land, and no one deserves the throne more than you."*

My heart pounds, and that's all I allow myself. One moment of vulnerability while Dante holds me. One moment, to let all the crushing slurs from the past weigh me down. That I'm not worthy. That only a true-blood demon should be the one on the throne. And then the moment has passed.

"Thanks," I whisper.

Taking a deep breath, I close off my emotions, letting indifference flow through me. *Never show weakness.* This can't be the thing that defines me. I need to attend this meeting, and this is simply a way to do it.

Besides, I may have gained horns and a tail, but it's shadowed by the loss I feel for my wings. My back feels incomplete without them.

I pull from Dante's hold. "We'd better find something suitable to wear and get moving."

CHAPTER

EIGHTEEN

~ Princess Blake ~

It's not long until daybreak when we step outside the house and the forest air greets me. We're all wearing clothes suitable for the club, and Mason passes me his portal ring.

"Why not take Noah's car?" Luna asks.

"Hey!" Noah protests. "No one's taking Jesebel anywhere."

Mason frowns. "Jesebel?"

"While it would make sense for our pretend Noah to be driving his car," I say. "I doubt the six of us are going to fit. Besides, we're running out of time."

Noah breathes a sigh of relief. "Well thank fuck for that."

Squeezing my eyes shut, I concentrate hard, feeling the build up of energy in front of me. Thankfully, creating a portal uses the magic of the ring, and all I have to do is focus that power. When I open my eyes, a ring of fire flickers before me.

"You know, I'm never goin' to be able to look at a portal the same. Every time we go through one, we end up in trouble," Nate comments, staring warily at the gateway. "I still vote for the car."

"Relax. This portal leads to a club that's been abandoned for years," I explain. "It's walking distance from the Bleeding Hearts club."

"And when was the last time you visited this building?" Prince Callan asks, just as wary.

I shrug. "I don't know, a year, maybe? But no one goes there. They say it's haunted."

"Haunted?" Nate groans. "This just keeps gettin' better."

Prince Callan tilts his head. "By haunted, do you mean there's a gateway there to the shadow realm?"

"No, I checked for that a while back," I reply. "I think it's more that the demons believe the place brings bad luck."

"So why not take us somewhere else, my mate?" Mason asks.

"Because this is the only known abandoned building in the area. Now, let's go," Dante explains. He winks at me before walking into the circle of fire.

"You know, maybe Nate has a point," Shade says in my head. *"You know how I feel about spooky things."*

"There's nothing spooky about this empty building," I assure her and follow my demon mate. Shade squawks as we enter the portal, but within seconds we're on the other side, stepping into a dark room that has a stack of broken chairs on one side. Dust plumes in the air, and neon paint glows on the walls.

"It's weird to think this used to be one of the most exclusive clubs in Seral City," Dante muses. "And now it's simply a dustbowl. You know, I considered buying this place once. If it weren't for the fact that the demons are too afraid to come here, I could have made this great again."

I smile. "I would have come."

"Likely to check you weren't breaking any more of the king's laws," Shade mumbles.

Dante presses a kiss to my hair and chuckles. "And I would have lured you in for a dance."

"And Blake would have ended up stabbing you as part of your weird foreplay," Shade adds.

"It wasn't foreplay," I defend.

"Oh phuleez, anyone could see the sexual tension between you two," Shade snickers.

"Why are we talkin' about foreplay?" Nate asks a little too eagerly as he steps up behind me.

Heat rushes through my body, but I force myself not to get carried away with my mates. Pulling back from Dante, I turn to the others as they all step through the portal. "There's no foreplay happening right now. The meeting starts in thirty minutes. Let's go through our stories again before we leave here.

Dante is covering as Noah so he should be set, but the rest of us will pretend to be demons from the Warsky Clan. It's one of the clans that's the least involved with higher clans, and so the members are lesser known. We'll find a back entrance to the meeting while Dante goes through the front door. Shade, you stay outside and scout the area. Let us know if anyone suspicious turns up."

"But what if this ends in an orgy like the last meeting we busted? You can't let me miss that," Shade protests.

"An orgy?" Alaric growls.

I wave my hand in the air dismissively. "We had to break up a gathering between two clan leaders a while back. They were discussing illegal weapons. One of the members is an incubus, and when I arrived, he sent out his power hoping to influence me so I'd go easy on them."

Dante's brows rise.

"But his power didn't do anything to Blake, and it just worked on all the clan members. They all stopped fighting and ended up fucking instead," Shade finishes. *"It was hilarious. And sweaty. Hmm... actually maybe a little too sweaty."*

"That's not going to happen this time," I say. "And Shade, you can't come or that will give me away. Just try not to be seen."

She grumbles at that but doesn't complain again.

"Time's not on our side," Dante urges. "Any longer and we'll miss the meeting."

"Okay, remember we're all demons," I say as a final reminder. "No reaching for your power unless it's absolutely necessary." On that note, we make our way up a flight of creaky wooden stairs and pass through another door before we enter the upstairs space that looks just as dusty. The windows have been boarded up, and we make our way to the back door.

"Stay safe," Shade tells us.

We stop opposite the Bleeding Hearts club, keeping out of view as the first rays of sunlight peek over the buildings. There's no line at the front entrance to the club, and two burly demons dressed in black suits stand sentry before the doors.

"Wish me luck," Dante says with a mischievous smile, and he presses a kiss to my cheek before crossing the street.

"We'll find a back entrance into the club," I tell him through our mind link. *"Make sure you keep us informed."*

"Of course, princess," Dante replies.

He reaches the front of the club, and after a small conversation with the bouncers, they let him inside.

The moment he's gone, the rest of us backtrack, crossing the street further down before maneuvering around buildings until we reach the back of the club. Two more bouncers guard the exit.

I turn my head to Nate. "Any ideas on getting in?"

Before he can answer, a large group of intoxicated demons stream out of the club, ushered by two more guards.

"Don' see why we 'ave to leave," a scruffy looking demon slurs as he sways on his feet. "We was just havin' some fun."

"Go sleep it off," one of the bouncer's growls, as all four bouncers lead them away from the door. A bouncer places his hand on the demon's shoulder, and the drunk demon snarls, shrugging him off. "Why you puttin' your hands on me?"

"That's our chance," I say to my mates, pointing to the door that's no longer guarded.

We move quickly, crossing the distance in a few strides, and then we're slipping into the back of the club.

Dance music pounds in my ears the moment we enter a darkened hallway, and we move quickly, making our way down a series of passageways until we reach the main room of the club. Spread before us, a horde of demons are still on the dance floor, grinding and dancing with one another like they intend to have fun long into the day.

"Now this is a party," Nate says with a wide grin.

Lifting my gaze, I look up to where three cages are suspended high above the crowd. The two smaller cages on the sides hold she-demons who are almost completely naked. They dance in time to the music, moving fluidly with one another in a mesmerizing display. In the larger cage in the center, a she-demon is busy enjoying the company of a male. They're both completely naked, and he grips the back of her neck as he fucks her from behind. She arches her back, her cries of pleasure drowned out by the thudding tempo.

Smoke drifts through the air that's thick with the scent of sweat and brimstone, and I'm pretty sure there's at least one incubus in here. The demon's magic isn't affecting me heavily, but I can still feel the drag of magic against me as someone in the crowd feeds on the sexual energy.

"Better than the bunny burrows?" I ask Nate, remembering what he'd said about the pleasure house back in the beast realm.

My shifter wraps his arms around me, pulling me close and nuzzling his nose into my neck. "Anywhere with you is better than that place, my queen."

I grin. "Good to see you're learning, shifter."

His lips find my neck, but the sound of animated voices comes from the passageway behind us, and I pull him into the crowd. Prince Callan, Mason, and Alaric follow, the five of us moving further into the throng of demons.

"Dante, where are you?" Prince Callan asks my demon mate.

There's silence and then Dante replies, *"Upstairs. Near the balcony. The meeting hasn't started yet."*

I look up again and this time I see the long balcony to the left side of the room, not far from the cages.

I'm about to ask Dante a question when I'm distracted by the sound of grumbling behind me. Twisting my head, I see that back near the passageway, two of the bouncers from outside look irritably at the crowd of demons. Blood is splattered on one of the male's faces, and I get the feeling he's just looking for a reason to kick someone else out.

"We need to blend in," I say to the others. *"And then we find a way to watch the meeting."*

"Blend in?" Nate says, looking way too eager. *"Thought you'd never ask."* He grabs my hand, pulling me further into the crowd, and he spins me until my back is pressed to him. Swaying his hips, he grinds against me in time to the music. The others follow, and Mason and Prince Callan start dancing around us, though Alaric simply stands there scowling.

"Shade, how is it outside? All quiet?" I frown when I realize I can't connect with the crow. *"Something must be blocking us from talking to her."*

"The bird will be fine," Nate tells me reassuringly.

I hope he's right. *I'm sure she's perched on a roof somewhere out of sight.*

Nate moves behind me, and slowly my body loosens. My tail flicks in the air, and I laugh at it. It's such a strange sensation having it there, and while I always wondered what it would be like to have one, now it just feels...odd. I miss my wings and their constant weight on my back. It was like they helped ground me, and yet, also gave me the means to escape when I needed it. To soar high above all my problems.

Reaching up, I grab onto Prince Callan's shirt, pulling him closer to me. "Do you miss them?" I ask him.

His eyes sparkle in the light as he stares at me. "Them?"

"Your wings," I say. "It's weird, right? Being like this." As if to punctuate my point, my tail flicks around, tightening on one of his legs possessively.

Prince Callan's lips quirk up. "From the moment I met you, life has been...unexpected, my Ahalian Touizda." His eyes soften, his expression becoming serious. "But you accepted me even after I proved myself to be unworthy, and life is much sweeter now that I can have you. I trust you, even when it comes to my wings." His tail wraps around my leg mimicking the way my tail acted.

"Oh, don't start soundin' like Mason," Nate groans. "It's hard enough keepin' up with that guy."

Prince Callan grins. "Don't worry, there's plenty of our mate to go around. I doubt she has favorites."

Nate chuckles, and he leans down, gently biting my earlobe. "Is he right, gorgeous? No favorites?" His hand snakes around my hip, sliding to the front of my short dress, and between my thighs. My breathing quickens as he pushes my panties to the side and runs his fingers up and down my center. My mates crowd around me, and my body tightens as the music pounds in my ears like it's keeping time with my rapid heartbeat.

"Nate," I rasp as he teases me with his fingers, the hard press of his body behind me.

"Yes, my queen?" he purrs in my ear.

"We don't have time for this. We're supposed to be finding a way to watch the meeting." I attempt to wiggle free, but I don't try too hard. Nate's hold on me feels too good, and I can't stop thinking about his fingers between my legs.

"Relax. I've already got it sorted," the shifter tells me. "We just need to stay here for a little while longer."

"Why? What have you figured out?"

My shifter ignores my questions, his fingers relentlessly torturing my clit. I lean back against him and Prince Callan presses in closer to my front, his hands sliding up my arms as he kisses my neck.

"Not helping," I chastise the archangel.

Prince Callan shares a look with Nate, and then he turns his head like he's checking something in the crowd.

"The meeting's about to start," Dante's voice sounds in our heads. *"Are you in position?"*

"Time to go," Nate says with a shit-eating grin. He pushes two fingers deep inside me, making me gasp before pulling them out, and taking a step back from me.

I glare at him, entirely sexually frustrated. "So what's your great plan?"

Nate's grin becomes feral, and he licks his fingers clean while staring at me intently.

I bite my lip, desire making my core clench, but then he looks up, and I follow his gaze. Slowly, the three cages descend toward the ground, and I realize what Nate had been getting at.

"Wait. You want us to get in one of those?" I ask.

"It would give us a nice view," Alaric admits.

I think of when we'd been in Toralyn. "But...are you sure you want to get in there?"

Whether the idea of being in a cage again bothers Nate, he doesn't let it show. "Gorgeous, I'd go anywhere with you. Now, are we claimin' one or not?"

The cages reach the ground and the gates open. The demons inside them start piling out, and other demons start to gather around them.

"Come on then," I say, darting between the mass of demons and heading toward the cages. I dodge past a couple who were headed for the middle cage and step inside, watching as my mates follow. *Fuck, I hope I'm not going to regret this.*

CHAPTER
NINETEEN

~ Princess Blake ~

Prince Callan, Mason, Nate, and Alaric step into the cage with me, and the moment the cage door is shut, a demon at the side of the room pulls a lever. All three cages lift into the air simultaneously, and I widen my stance as the cage rocks a little. In the cages at our sides, a handful of half-naked demons dance to the music, and I look at my mates and then at myself.

"We need to strip," I tell them.

"What?" Alaric growls, looking unimpressed.

Nate and Prince Callan are already lifting off their shirts, exposing panes of hardened muscle, and Mason follows their lead. I slide down my dress, and my mates' gazes heat as they stare at me in my lacy black bra and matching bikini bottoms. I hadn't expected to end up in a cage, but it's always best to be prepared when visiting a club on the Devil's Lane —the stretch of street in Seral City where the most exclusive clubs are.

"We need to look like we belong here," I explain to Alaric, and he begrudgingly pulls off his shirt before removing his pants like the others. By the time the cage stops in line with the balcony, all five of us are half-naked.

Copying the dancers in the cages around us, I start moving to the music. The thudding tempo isn't as loud up here, so we should be able to hear the demons speaking at the meeting, but first, we need to blend in. If we fuck this up, we might be revealing our identities sooner rather than later, and we have one chance to get the information we need.

Trying to be subtle, I peer over at the balcony which leads onto a private floor of the club. There's a small bar, a selection of leather couches, and a long table, surrounded by seating. Eight clan leaders are seated there, including Dante, who's positioned facing us, a drink on the table before him.

"We see you," I tell him, *"But don't make it obvious when you spot us."*

"You say that as if you're somewhere close," he drawls, intrigued, and the moment he spies us, a slow smile pulls across his face. *"Now I knew tonight*

would be entertaining, but I didn't quite think it would be this exciting. You do realize what that middle cage is for, I presume? And the entertainment you'll have to provide to avoid suspicion?"

Heat blooms low in my belly. *"As long as we get the information we need."*

Dante's dark chuckle vibrates in my head.

Trying not to think about it for the moment, I glance at the demons at the meeting using my peripheral vision before looking away again. *"Seated on Dante's left is a clan leader named, Gloria,"* I explain to the others. *"She runs the Blackthorne clan, which is one of the demon clans with the most members. Gloria has been the leader for over two centuries."*

"And the demon to his right?" Alaric asks.

I eye the skeletal male with a wicked scar that traces over his lips and down his chin. *"That's Scyro from the Zetar Clan. He's known as one of the most ruthless clan leaders in Seral. He killed eight members of his family to get his position."*

"Tortured some of them, too," Dante adds grimly.

Slowly, I list the names of all the demons around the table, with some input from Dante every so often. They're all easily identifiable and all from influential demon clans, including Hanz from the Silver Sun clan. The clan that owns the club.

I've just finished explaining their backstories when a tall demon in a navy suit walks from the staircase. An impressive number of knives hang from the belt around his waist, and a distinct tattoo of a blade is visible on his collarbone. He strides toward the table, flanked by six muscular demons who break off and take up positions around the space.

"And that would be Ivar," I tell the others. *"Leader of the Fallon Blade clan."* Despite already hearing that he's the one behind the meeting, I'm still surprised when I see the clan leader. After General Josek tore down the Fallon Blade clan house, I left orders for the demon guards to scour the city for the Fallon Blade clan members. I thought Ivar would stay in hiding, and it feels like a bad sign that the clan leader is willing to risk such a meeting.

"Ivar has a history of opposing the laws put into place by King Dalton," I say. *"He's unpredictable but cunning, and shouldn't be underestimated."*

"Sounds like a charmer," Nate comments dryly.

We watch as the demon leader claims the only unoccupied chair left at the table. His gaze sharpens as he peers at the demons already seated, and a smile tugs at his thin lips when he sees Noah. Or at least, when he sees Dante disguised as Noah.

Dante smiles at Ivar and lifts his drink into the air before bringing the glass to his lips. *"I've never liked this bastard,"* my demon mate murmurs. *"Whenever he's at a party, you know there's going to be trouble."*

My gaze is still fixed to Ivar when Nate's hands roam over my body. *"You need to keep movin' gorgeous. If you keep starin', someone's bound to notice."*

I hadn't even realized I'd stopped dancing, and I

curse, diverting my gaze and rolling my hips against my shifter mate when Ivar's glance slides to us in the cage.

"You'll need to do more than dance, princess," Dante points out, his lips curving up at the sides. *"Unless you wish to draw attention."*

"You mean something like this?" I say, pulling from Nate and reaching for Alaric, pressing my lips to his. If anything, the grumpy assassin was going to be the one to get us caught out, but thankfully, his muscles loosen at my touch. He cups the back of my head, kissing me back hard.

"That's a good start," Dante muses.

Mason presses in behind me, gripping my hips, and despite the fact I'm still trying to pay attention to the meeting, my body flushes with heat.

When I lift my leg, Alaric grabs my thigh, holding it at his side. Mason's hands rove over me, exploring from behind, his lips brushing against my skin, and despite where we are and *why* we're there, I need my mates. Like they can sense it, Nate and Prince Callan stalk closer, crowding around me. I take my lips from Alaric's, and turn my head, kissing Prince Callan and then Nate.

With every touch, every caress, the bond between us hums to life.

"Whatever happens, you can't let me come," I tell them, my breathing heavy. *"The last thing we need is my tattoos letting off a light show."*

Nate gives me a feral grin. *"I think we can handle that."*

The look in his eyes has my heart beating wildly, anticipation thrumming through me.

"I mean it," I tell him, because I get the feeling he hasn't gotten the point. *"You guys can't come either. Our tattoos, remember?"* Luna has disguised our marks, but considering what happened with our tattoos when we bonded, I'd rather not risk it.

"Like I said," Nate replies. *"I think we can handle it."*

I glance back at the meeting, only to find a few of the demons are watching us expectantly. Ivar is busy talking about the current state of Seral, and how he disagrees with the way the city has been run, but the demons around the table keep glancing my way. *Fuck.*

"Can't they just focus on the meeting?" I grumble.

"You are rather distracting, princess," Dante drawls. *"You might not be wearing your usual face, but even with Luna's magic suppressing your power, these demons can likely feel it. They're drawn to power, and without knowing why, they'll simply be looking to you as a cage entertainer."*

I let out a long breath. *"Then I guess we'd better give them a show."* I run my hand down, grabbing at the front of Alaric's pants, and the male's nostrils flare.

~ Dante ~

It's hard to concentrate while my delectable princess is being pleasured in a cage for the entire club to see. Nate and the others bring her to the edge over and over again never letting her find her release, and my balls ache. I grip my leg under the table and wish I was gripping my cock instead. I want to be with them, making our mate writhe, her cheeks flush with heat as her pleasure builds. I want to be the one sinking into...

I let out a rush of air through my nose and force myself to focus on Ivar. The meeting. That's why we're here, and I'm well aware that later Blake will be questioning me, searching for any information she missed while in the cage.

At the thought, my gaze connects with my mate, and my lips curve as she whimpers while Alaric drives his cock into her. Even with another face she's still perfect. My mate. My princess.

The Fallon Blade leader is now talking animatedly, and I lean back in my chair, drumming my fingers on the table as I turn my attention back to him.

Ivar rests his elbows on the table. "We all know this has been a long time coming. We need to act. The balance between the clans has always been fragile, and it's time we do something about it."

Ah, a meeting to discuss the overthrow of the king. How predictable. So far there's been no mention of the witches, and it's mostly just been Ivar dribbling about how he thinks he could be a better leader than King Dalton. Which is laughable. The clan leader has always been too quick to reach for his blades. King Dalton might be ruthless, but he's always been strategic.

"But it is a balance," Gloria counters, her lips pursed. "What do you propose? That we put you on the throne?"

Ivar's expression darkens as he stares down the she-demon, opening his arms wide. "If there's another here who you think would be a more suitable candidate, then please, I'm all ears."

Gloria hesitates before saying, "We could let the demon princess—"

"That halfblood?" Ivar sneers. "You'd rather have her rule rather than a true-blooded demon? The angels never wanted her, and neither should the demons. She doesn't have what it takes to rule."

My tail flicks down by my legs, and I struggle to contain my anger. My gaze finds Blake's, and while her eyes are hard, she subtly shakes her head. Mason, Alaric, and the others are still giving her attention, but going by their hard-set expressions they're just as pissed as I am.

"As much as I'd also like to cut that sneer from Ivar's face, stopping him now won't help us," Blake says.

"No, but it'd make me feel better," Alaric growls.

Blake grins.

Around the table, a few of the clan leaders look

around nervously. Likely, they're searching for Blake's crow spies. Even now, the demons fear my princess, and my lips twitch with amusement.

"I would rather have peace," Gloria replies shrewdly, sitting straighter in her chair. "The princess has shown strength, and I believe she could keep this realm together. What do you have to offer?"

"Demons respect power and experience, and the only power the princess has is because of her father. Without him, the throne is there for the taking," Ivar snaps back. "As for experience, she's never seen a war. I was there when the witches came all those years ago. I haven't forgotten the battlefield."

"So you're a soldier," Gloria says. "That doesn't mean you'd make a good leader."

Ivar has one of his blades out in an instant, and he stabs it into the table before him. "I can unite this realm like no other!" he snarls. "The clans are divided, but with me leading, we could be one clan. And if we take the throne before the princess returns to Seral, everything will already be in place before she has time to act."

"You talk of unification, but all I hear is a demon wanting to rule us all," I drawl, unable to help myself. "You seem to forget, the clans weren't created by the monarchy. The decision was made by demonkind. So the different clans had the power to deal punishments and rule their clans as they saw fit. As long as we followed a set of overarching laws, demons were given more power."

Ivar's right eye twitches, and he smiles cruelly as he turns his gaze to me. "And look how those overarching laws have grown over time. This freedom you speak of is false. Creating clans wasn't the answer. All we needed was the right leader."

"And you believe that's you?" Gloria scoffs.

Ivar's nostrils flare, but he schools his expression before speaking. "If I rule, the clan leaders would become my advisors, and they would have their say in the laws that are created. For example, I could make it that there is no punishment for visiting the human realm. Why shouldn't we feast on such easy prey? They are the ones who call us. All we're doing is giving them what they seek. Wouldn't you agree, Noah? We all know your leader, Dante, has a habit of bringing humans here."

I've said the same thing to Blake many times when she'd caught me with humans, but now hearing it from Ivar's mouth makes me sick. I never harmed the humans, and my demons only bedded those who consented. Within hours, they were also returned to their homes with little memory of what occurred. There was good reason for the laws against demons taking advantage of the humans, and I hadn't realized how damaging my actions were until now.

I avoid Blake's pointed stare though I can feel her attention on me.

Ivar stares at me expectantly, and I'm forced to give him the answer he desires. "It would be a...relief to have some of the laws lightened."

The demon leader's eyes shine with approval. "You see! I can make Seral a much more...pleasurable city to reside in. *Together* we can reshape the city."

In theory, I do see some sense in Ivar's argument. It's a pity that the demon is as untrustworthy as they come, and I highly doubt he would listen to the voices of the demons for long, if at all.

"For such an impactful change, the demons should have the chance to vote again. To voice whether they wish to disband the clans," another demon says.

Ivar's eyes twitches again, and he forces a smile. "Something we can discuss when I'm on the throne."

There's a beat of silence as all the leaders digest this.

"I may not always agree with King Dalton," Gloria says slowly, "but he's maintained peace for this long. We've not seen another war since the witches, and I believe the princess would uphold his legacy."

"His legacy?" Ivar sneers again. "Since the war with the witches, the king has hardly offered much to our realm. He's been so concerned with keeping us battle ready that he closed himself off to any other possibilities that might present themselves."

"Other possibilities?" asks Scyro.

Ivar noticeably shifts, not necessarily

uncomfortable, but uncertain. "Possibilities that could mean big changes for the demons. Since the war with the witches, we've been seen as the realm that needed to call for aid. The ones who couldn't handle our own when the time came."

"Any realm would have needed assistance," Gloria counters. "It was simply unfortunate the witches targeted our realm rather than one of the others."

"None-the-less the demons don't hold the respect that we once did. But I can bring that back. When I'm king, I can make Seral great again." Ivar's eyes sparkle, and I don't miss the fact that he said 'when' not 'if.'

Ivar has always been a vocal leader, but he's never been this brazen before.

"You speak of taking out the king before the princess arrives. King Dalton is one of the strongest demons to have lived. How exactly are you proposing that we defeat him?" Scyro asks.

Fuck. That's all it takes for the conversation to change.

Ivar beams at Scyro. "Going by my intel, the king is weak. It's why he's retiring. So now is the time to send in an assassin."

"An assassin? Presumably, one who won't fail this time?" Gloria mocks.

"This time?" I drawl, curiosity getting the better of me.

"*Careful, Dante,*" Blake warns, though from her

intense gaze, she's as interested in the answer as I am.

Grabbing the dagger he'd stabbed into the table, Ivar pulls it out, examining the sharp edges of the blade. "We had a Drozac assassin on board to help us some time ago," he says, surprising me with an answer. "Assigned by the order. Unfortunately, the king turned up during my initial meeting with the assassin, and I had to make it seem as though the assassin had come after me. It was unfortunate timing."

A Drozac assassin? My brows lift, and my gaze goes to my bond brother in the cage before flicking back to Ivar. "And what happened to this assassin?"

Ivar shrugs, spinning his blade, handle upward on the table. "The king had been quick to take care of him, with my assistance of course. It was a disappointing time for all involved."

I nod like it's the answer I expected, but considering the sudden pale shade of Blake's skin, I know she heard every word. Alaric squares up his shoulders and he pulls away from Blake, his eyes blazing with fury, but then Blake and the others are there, surrounding him. Blake runs her hands up his chest, trying to soothe him.

"He's talking about West," Alaric growls, his fury rumbling like thunder in our minds. *"I was told West was killed in Seral when he tried to assassinate a clan leader. But if what this Ivar says is true, then it was only a cover up, and the leaders of the order of the Drozac*

were involved. West was never here to kill a clan leader. He was here to kill the king."

"And Ivar turned on him," Blake says softly. *"I'm sorry, Alaric. All I knew was that a Drozac assassin had tried to kill a clan leader and was executed. I never knew who the clan leader was. I promise we'll make Ivar suffer before this is over. But not now. Not yet."*

"So, who is the assassin this time?" Gloria asks. "And how do we know they'll be able to get the job done?"

"We need to know this won't be traced back to us," another says. "If the king hears of this, it'll be us in the royal dungeons."

Ivar leans back. "This assassin will not be traceable. Not that it will matter when the king's head is rolling on the floor."

"What does that mean?" Scyro growls.

Ivar hesitates before saying, "On this you'll simply have to trust me. The less you know the better in the off chance I'm captured. Above all, your safety is my top priority."

"Yeah, right," Blake mutters.

"And what do you need from us?" Hawke, a burly demon with a scruffy beard, and the leader of the Bloodsky clan asks gruffly.

"Everyone here leads either one of the largest, or most respected, clans in Seral City," Ivar says, smiling. "I need to know that when the time comes, and the king has been taken care of, you'll back me for the position of king. With your support the other demons will find it easier to accept the... transition."

For a moment, no one speaks. The clan leaders all peer at one another, trying to gauge their responses.

Ivar pockets his blade and drums his fingers loudly on the table. "So, what do you say? Who's ready to unite the demons and bring about a new era for our realm?"

I'm not surprised when one-by-one hands slowly go up around the table. My hand is one of the last. I don't need a target on my back, and voting against Ivar won't stop this.

"Well, I hope the princess doesn't find out that you're supporting a traitor," Blake jokes in my head. Her words are light-hearted, but it's obvious she's seething about all of this.

Alaric is still tense, but the rest of them are back to kissing and touching one another, pretending not to watch the meeting.

"Mmmm I'm hoping I'll be able to ask for her forgiveness," I murmur back.

There's a dark gleam in Ivar's eyes as he stares around at the show of hands. Everyone has given their support, including Gloria, despite her earlier doubts.

"Well then," Ivar says gleefully. "I'll set the assassin in motion in the coming days, and I'll be in touch when it's done. Thank you all for coming." He grabs the drink on the table before him, and he toasts the air before sculling the contents. Slamming the glass back on the table, he stands and straightens the collar of his shirt. Gesturing with his head, his guards around the room form up behind him as he heads for the stairs.

The clan leaders hardly speak as we file from the room after him.

~ Princess Blake ~

"Soooo *is someone going to explain what happened?*" Shade asks as we walk from the Bleeding Hearts club. She lands on my shoulder, and my mates and I dart down the alleyway, hiding behind a dumpster. "*The moment you entered the club, I couldn't connect with any of you! I was practically pulling my feathers out with worry.*"

Reaching up, I stroke Shade's wings trying to calm her. "*The demons are plotting to take the throne,*" I reply bluntly. "*No surprise there.*"

"*Ivar plans to become king,*" Dante explains as he exits the club after us. I wave him over, and he moves quickly to our position. "*Despite the incredible fact the demon has never cared for anyone but himself,"* my demon mate adds.

"He's organizing an assassin to take Dad out," I say, scowling at the thought. Dad might be merciless but he's fair, and he's still the king. Gloria was right, King Dalton has maintained relative peace in our realm, aside from the occasional clan war. If Ivar were to sit on the throne, something tells me Seral would see much more bloodshed.

"Okay, so we kill Ivar before he contracts the assassin," Shade suggests. *"Problem solved, right?"*

I frown. *"I thought of that too, but I get the feeling there was something Ivar wasn't willing to tell the others. Something tells me this goes deeper than simply hiring an assassin."*

Dante's expression grows thoughtful. *"There aren't many who would be brave enough to try and assassinate King Dalton. And if they tried a Drozac assassin last time, who do you think he'd use now?"*

At the mention of a Drozac assassin, Alaric's body tightens, and I rest my hand on his arm. *"He'll pay for what he did to your brother,"* I assure him.

"Hold on. Hold on. Ivar killed Alaric's brother?" Shade squawks.

"It's a long story," I sigh. *"Right now, we need to figure out what Ivar is up to. That demon is hiding something."*

The door to the back of the club opens as a few of the last clan members exit the club, climbing into their cars and leaving the alleyway.

"*I picked up on that, too,*" Prince Callan agrees.

"*You want us to follow him, my mate?*" Mason asks.

"*It all just doesn't sit right,*" I say. "*I've never seen Ivar look so confident.*"

Nate's brows lower. "*You think Ivar is plannin' on contractin' a witch assassin?*"

I shake my head. "*I don't know, but I can't help but feel like we're still missing a big piece of this puzzle.*"

"*It could be days before Ivar makes contact with the assassin,*" Dante points out.

"No," Alaric growls. "*The decision has been made. He'll make contact and soon, before any of the clan leaders have a chance to second-guess their support of him.*"

A long black car stops at the end of the alleyway, and the driver keeps the engine on. "*That's Ivar's ride,*" Dante points out. "*I recognize his driver.*"

"*Okay, well we need to—*" My words die off as I turn and see Nate further down the alleyway. His elbow is wrapped in strips of his clothing, and he smashes the driver window of a beaten-up black van before jumping into the vehicle. In a matter of seconds, he has jump-started the van and is driving slowly toward us. He stops opposite us and winks at me. "*Want a ride, gorgeous?*"

I grin.

"*I thought these are metal death traps?*" Mason asks with a confused expression, reciting my words from earlier when we'd first been discussing if we should take Noah's car.

All four of us turn to look at him. *"It is,"* I say.

Mason looks taken aback. *"And you wish to enter it, my mate?"*

"Okay, I might be exaggerating slightly. It's a contraption on wheels that can get us places faster. One of the many inventions we've copied from the human realm," I explain.

Mason still looks confused. *"So...it does not kill anyone?"*

"Not demons, anyway," Dante answers, smiling.

Before Mason can ask more questions, Nate beckons us. *"Let's keep this movin', shall we?"*

We start piling into the van with Dante taking the front seat next to Nate, and the rest of us climbing in the back. Thankfully, the vehicle is empty, but it rocks when Alaric hops up, the back wheels lowering at his weight. Mason is the last of us to enter, and he peers at me warily.

I hold out my hand. *"It'll be fine,"* I tell him. *"Trust me."*

His eyes spark at my last words, and he doesn't hesitate to place his hand in mine. "Always, my mate," he replies, and my heart warms as I help him into the van.

"Let's see if he still feels that way when the car starts moving," Shade comments as Mason settles down on one of the long leather seats lining the sides of the van. *"Maybe you should get him to sit near a window."*

"He'll be fine," I send back to her, though Mason is staring at me.

"Why the window?" he asks.

"It's nothing," I assure him, shutting the back doors of the van.

Nate twists his neck, checking the back. "All right, if you guys are ready." He rubs his hands up and down the steering wheel. Just as he's about to pull away from the gutter he curses.

I jerk my head up. "What is it?"

"Ivar just exited the club," Dante explains, waving at someone through the front window. "He's spotted us."

"Fuck." I duck down, carefully peeking through the front windshield. Ivar enters his car, and seconds later, the black car starts down the street and disappears from view.

"Not to worry," Dante says. "This simply means we'll need to be more discreet."

"Discreet? What are you—" I don't finish. Tingles race over me followed by an icy sensation, and then we all...vanish.

A rush of air leaves me, and Prince Callan reaches out, pulling me onto his lap. I can't see the archangel, but his scent swirls around me, his hands tightening on my body. The van purrs beneath our feet, but all I can see is the alleyway and the street below us.

"Now, this is fuckin' strange," Nate comments from the driver's seat, but he doesn't waste time. He speeds away from the alleyway, moving in the direction we saw Ivar leave. In no time at all, we've spotted Ivar's car up ahead, and Nate stays a short distance behind him.

"Just remember, we might no longer be visible, but we can still be heard, so we'll need to maintain our distance," Dante warns.

"You know this means you've shattered your disguise," I remind Dante. The moment he used his magic, the illusion Luna placed on him would have broken.

"And thank goodness for that," Dante replies lightly. "It was rather unsettling having Noah's face."

No one says anything for a while after that as Nate maneuvers the streets, following Ivar's ride. I squirm on Prince Callan's lap, struggling to sit still. My fingers twitch, and I can't stop theorizing about Ivar's plans.

Prince Callan's hands tighten on me, stopping me from squirming.

"What are you doing?" I hiss.

His lips brush by my face. "You can't do anything about Ivar now, but I can do something to make you more comfortable my Ahalian Touizda."

"I don't want to be comfortable. I want to make him bleed until he spills the rest of his plans," I grumble, but then I feel one of the archangel's hands sliding up my dress. My heartbeat quickens. My mates drove me to the edge so many times in the club that I'm still wound tight.

"We need to focus," I tell him. "Ivar could stop at any moment."

"And you need release, my mate," Prince Callan replies matter-of-factly. Using his fingers, he pushes my panties to the side, and then his fingers are sliding up and down my center. I bite my lip, holding in my gasp as his touch makes me shudder. I'm still so sensitive. So ready that it hurts.

Sliding his fingers down, Prince Callan pushes them into me, and I pant, spreading my legs wider. I feel him hard beneath me, but he makes no move to pull out his cock. He pushes two fingers in and out of me moving torturously slow until I'm shaking in his hold.

"Please," I beg, my chest tight. "Callan."

He moves his fingers faster, fucking them into me, and when he reaches around with his other hand, rubbing my clit, I shatter in his hold, the orgasm crashing through me. I bite my lip hard, tasting blood, and Prince Callan keeps moving his fingers, making the pleasure last.

When I stop shuddering, I sag against the archangel, and he kisses my cheek. "Better?"

"It's a good start," I say with a grin.

"Maybe for you guys, but what about the fuckin' rest of us?" Nate grumbles. "This is torture. Someone else drive."

Dante chuckles. "This is the last time I go for the front seat."

"At least you guys are all getting some," Shade says so quietly in my head I almost miss it.

"Hold on, does Shade here not have a mate?" Nate questions, clearly having heard her as well.

"What? Pshh," Shade replies. *"What I said was, whoa, this is trippy."*

"Trippy?" Alaric asks, confused.

"Yeah," she says as the street goes by beneath us. *"It's like we're flying in this thing. Makes me feel like I'm on an invisible rollercoaster."*

"Rollercoaster?" Alaric asks.

Shade sighs.

"It's an amusement ride they have in the human realm," I explain. "Something you ride for fun." Alaric doesn't respond, and I doubt he gets it. Personally, I've never been on a rollercoaster, and considering I can fly, I've never seen the appeal.

Nate follows Ivar's car around another corner, and when the van straightens again there's a slight hacking sound coming from Mason's direction.

"Told you, he needed the window," Shade points out. *"He needs the fresh air."*

Crap. "Mason, are you all right?"

"Vomit on me, and you'll regret it," Alaric growls. It's funny, I always thought the assassin was just grumpy because of me, but it turns out it's simply in his nature. I'm not even sad about it, either.

"I'm just... I think I've been poisoned, my mate," Mason replies, still making gagging sounds from the other side of the van.

I move away from Prince Callan and slowly step toward where I remember Mason being. I think I'm almost there when Nate turns another corner. Instinctively, I go to flare out my wings and correct my balance, but then I remember I don't have them. Before I topple, two large, strong hands are holding me in place. *Alaric.*

The van straightens again, and I pat the assassin's hand. "Thanks," I tell him. He grunts and releases me, and I take the final steps toward Mason with my hands out.

Nate slows the van abruptly and I fall forward, my fingers jabbing into something mushy. Mason curses, and I jerk back. "Fuck, I just touched something sticky. Please tell me that wasn't your nose." There's moist residue on my finger, and I make a face as I wipe it on my dress. "I swear if it's a booger I might just start gagging, too."

"Only my eye, my mate," Mason replies, no doubt cradling his injured eye.

"Oh, good," I reply, and I reach out again, my hands sliding down Mason's arms. Carefully, I sit down beside him, and I almost regret my decision when my mate starts dry heaving again.

"Focus on the buildings outside," I tell him. "You're not poisoned. Your body is simply confused. Because we're moving and yet you're not walking, your body is acting like you're poisoned."

"It's called motion sickness," Shade adds sympathetically. *"It's pretty common unfortunately."*

"Then why aren't any of you having the same reaction?" Mason asks.

Using one hand, I rub his broad back soothingly. "Many grow out of it as they get older. Some are luckier than others."

Mason takes a few more gasping breaths, and he lifts his head, staring out the front window. Following his gaze, I peer at the buildings soaring past us—tall structures of black stone, with narrow arched windows and gray tiles covering the rooftops like dragon scales. The streets are mostly bare, the city flooded with light, and it's quiet, with most of the demons likely in their beds.

A cawing noise draws my attention, and I lift my gaze as a crow flies overhead, soaring past our vehicle.

"Your crows miss you," Shade says softly in my mind.

I stay silent as the memory of the birds in Toralyn resurfaces, and I can feel it again. Their ashes. The thought makes my chest ache.

Mason takes my hand in his. "What happened to the birds in the angel realm wasn't your fault, my mate. The burden of guilt is heavy to carry, and not one you deserve."

When I still don't answer, we sit in silence.

It's not like Toralyn was the first time for me to lose a bird. That's the thing with battle. There are always losses, and I don't command the birds. I make a request. I ask them to come, and they trust me enough to follow. But to lose so many... It still bothers me.

Mason's breathing is even now as he stares out the window, and he speaks up again. "It is beautiful, you know. Your city."

"It's not mine," I say softly, though the statement feels false.

"Oh, screw that," Shade counters. *"Whether you become queen or not, this is your city, Blake. No one knows this place better than you."*

She's right, of course. Because of my crows, I've seen parts of this city that I never would have seen otherwise. I've been training to rule my whole life, but now that Dad's wanting to step down, now that the clans are unsettled and the witches are mobilizing, everything feels wrong. Once I had my mates, everything was supposed to slot into place, but I still can't help but wonder if we'll be enough.

"Let's just focus on discovering Ivar's assassin," I reply, my voice devoid of emotion.

No one says anything else for a long while as we follow Ivar through the city, to one of the outer districts. The road changes, the dark stones changing to compact earth, and the scent of the sea drifts through Nate's smashed window as we near the harbor. I'm lost in thought when the van curves, and Nate speaks up. "Ivar is stopping up ahead. Looks like some kind of warehouse."

I jerk my head up as Ivar's car is parked out the front of an abandoned warehouse, and the clan leader exits the vehicle along with three of his guards.

I scan the building. At least half of the frosted glass windows are broken, and it looks almost the same as the last time I saw it years ago. Almost, because unlike last time, there are now numerous guards patrolling the perimeter.

Nate stops the van behind a wall of old machinery and scrap metal that's been stacked a few yards from one side of the building, and we all pop back into view. I roll my shoulders as tingles race through me, and the walls of the van appear around us again.

"Can we not do that again anytime soon?" Shade says, fluttering her wings. *"It makes me feel all kinds of weird."*

Dante opens the back doors of the van, and we all file out.

Nate cracks his neck and stretches his arms. *"So, are we allowed to use our powers now?"* Moving quietly, he peers around a broken-down truck, scouring the warehouse. *"That's still some distance to cover."*

"We stay in our disguises for now," I tell him. *"Only change if you need to."*

"I count at least seven guards," Prince Callan says, standing beside Nate.

"Ten," Alaric replies, towering over the other two and pointing to three more guards stalking the roof.

"We don't want to spook Ivar until we get the information we need," I remind them.

"*So how do we get in without being noticed?*" Mason comments.

"*That door,*" Alaric says, pointing to the right side of the building. "*There's only a single guard positioned there.*"

"*I saw that too,*" I reply. "*That door leads to an old underground storage room. That's our way in. Shade, I need you to stay out here and let us know if any other unexpected visitors arrive.*"

"*Eye-eye cap'n,*" she replies, flapping from my shoulder and perching on the roof of a rusted forklift that's resting on its side.

"*It also might be better if you don't get spotted just yet,*" I tell Dante.

He grins, and then he winks out of sight. "*Not a problem, princess.*"

It wouldn't be the first time I envied his power, but I grin when an invisible Dante squeezes my ass. "*Show off,*" I mutter.

"*You know, if we all hold hands, we could simply stroll over there,*" Dante chuckles.

"*Oh my god, please tell me you're all about to hold hands and do a hero walk to the warehouse,*" Shade squawks in our heads.

"*He-ro walk?*" Mason mutters, confused.

Alaric frowns, crossing his arms. "*Does the bird always speak nonsense?*"

Shade squawks, flapping her wings to show her agitation. "*It's not nonsense. If you're all touching Dante, he can make you invisible.*"

Nate groans and rubs the back of his neck. *"Let us have some dignity will ya. It's not that far."*

I grin. *"I don't think we need to resort to hand holding just yet."* Truthfully, the idea doesn't bother me, but something tells me Alaric isn't keen.

Leaving Shade where she is, we move closer to the warehouse, darting out quickly in intervals and ducking behind the discarded machinery until we've stopped behind a pile of scrap metal that's the closest cover to the door of the warehouse.

"I call dibs," Nate says, eyeing the guard at the door. He cracks his knuckles, preparing to shoot out, but before the shifter has even left the cover, the guard's head jerks like he's been hit, and the demon guard is lowered to the ground.

"Well, what are you waiting for?" Dante drawls in our minds, and the door opens.

Nate's eyes bulge. *"I fuckin' called dibs."*

I pat the shifter on the shoulder sympathetically. *"Next time, buddy."* Then I dart out, moving to the open door. The others follow and we creep inside, entering the darkness of the storage room.

TWENTY-ONE

~ Princess Blake ~

It takes a moment for my eyes to adjust, and then my jaw slackens. Tall rows of wooden crates fill the room reaching higher than Alaric's head. It's silent, and we walk between the crates, following the only clear pathway further into the room.

"This was empty the last time I was here," I mumble. *"There must be hundreds of them."*

Nate moves to a crate sitting on the floor on its own, and he squats, gripping the edge of the wooden box and cracking open the lid. A sharp, acrid scent fills the air, and when the dust settles, we all peer inside.

Dante curses as Nate holds up a glowing green

orb. The liquid sloshes in the glass ball, bubbling at the movement before settling again.

"*Witch weaponry,*" Alaric growls.

"*What? What's going on?*" Shade chirps.

"*We've found crates of weapons,*" I explain.

"*And a fuck ton of 'em,*" Nate adds.

"*Looks like Ivar is working with the witches after all,*" I say grimly.

Mason moves closer to the open crate, peering at the numerous orbs packaged in tightly.

"*If the witches are supplying Ivar with weapons, what are they getting in return?*" Dante asks, and I feel him beside me. "*Ivar has made it clear he wishes to be king. Why would they support that?*"

Nate starts to slide the orb into his pocket.

"*What are you doing, Nate?*" I hiss. "*Put it back.*"

The shifter's hand pauses. "*Figure it might come in handy.*"

I plant my hands on my hips. "*Or it could explode against your chest.*"

He shrugs, not looking the least bit concerned. "*Nine Lives, remember?*"

"*Put it back,*" Alaric growls, coming up on my other side.

Nate grumbles a protest under his breath and carefully places the orb back in the crate.

"*Oh, so you listen to him,*" I say incredulously.

"*That's because I know he doesn't have a soft spot for me like you do,*" Nate says to me with a grin.

I shake my head at him, smirking, but my

attention is pulled away when the faint murmuring of voices sounds from somewhere in the warehouse. Nate quickly replaces the lid on the crate, and we quietly make our way to the other end of the storage room. There's an open door that looks out onto the main floor of the warehouse, and I crouch to the side, peering out.

A few yards away, Ivar stands talking with a she-demon I recognize from the Fallon Blade clan. The pretty female beams at the clan leader, tossing her silky charcoal hair over one shoulder. "So, how did it go? Did they all agree to support you?"

Ivar smirks and closes the distance between them. Sliding his hands down her back, he cups her ass and yanks her against him.

"That's Shandi," I tell the others. *"She's been sleeping with Ivar for the last few years and slowly improving her place in the clan."* I think of the images my crows used to send me of the pair of them. Ivar wasn't a gentle lover, and I asked her in secret once, whether she'd prefer to move to a different clan. Shandi had simply laughed in my face and said she'd worked too hard to get where she was. I'd tried to point out that the she-demon would be uprooted the very moment if or when Ivar found his actual fated mate, but she wouldn't hear it.

"Have I ever mentioned that it's unsettling how much you know about clan business?" Dante drawls.

"It's my job to know things," I reply bluntly.

"Let me guess, she's hopin' to be queen by his side?" Nate comments dryly.

The idea of Shandi ruling by Ivar's side makes me scowl.

"Some of the clan leaders were resistant," Ivar replies to Shandi. "Gloria questioned everything, but I believe they all saw sense in the end."

"Good," Shandi beams, a smudge of red lipstick showing on her teeth. "And when the king is taken care of and you reveal you have the witches on your side, they'll be glad they supported you." She smiles a creepy smile. "Or they'll find their true death."

Ivar's lips twist into a wicked smile, and the pair start kissing. Shandi makes a show of moaning and rubbing her breasts against his chest, and he squeezes her ass. Just when I think they're going to fuck right there on the warehouse floor, Ivar pulls back. His dark brows lower. "You'd better go. She'll be here any minute, and I don't want you anywhere near her."

She? I frown, listening intently.

Shandi pouts. "It would be good for her to see you with me. Maybe then she'll learn her place."

Ivar gives her a wolfish grin, and he squeezes her ass again. "You're bold, I'll give you that. But you don't have to worry. The witch has no interest in the throne."

Shandi still looks reluctant to leave, but the moment a spark of green fire appears in mid-air, not far from Ivar, she shrieks and scurries off to hide in a nearby office.

Turning toward the spark, Ivar smooths his suit and runs his fingers through his hair. The spark grows, green flames bursting to life, and the circle grows bigger. The moment the portal is fully formed, a single cloaked figure steps from the gateway, emerging from between the flames. Distinct tattoos curl around the figure's fingers and travel up their hands.

My mates and I all tense.

"On time as always," Ivar says smoothly, bowing his head respectfully. "It is good to see—"

The witch moves her head, scanning the warehouse before narrowing her gaze on Ivar. "What progress have you made?" she says sharply, not letting him finish.

To his credit, Ivar doesn't look cowed. He clears his throat and puffs his chest out. "My best spy has infiltrated the royal castle. The demon king is even weaker since his return."

I clench my jaw.

"And?" The witch prompts. "Did you find it?"

Ivar smiles smugly. "It took some effort, but my spy has discovered a vault far beneath the castle, accessible by a hidden staircase. Unfortunately, he can't bypass the multiple layers of security and enter the vault, but I think it's safe to assume that's it."

"Good." The witch nods, looking pleased.

Ivar licks his lips.

"Is there more?"

"My spy mentioned he can feel something coming from the vault. A power of sorts," Ivar says slowly, like he's thinking about his next choice of words. "He says there's a force down there that's unlike anything he's felt."

"A power you say?" The witch asks, though going from her tone she's not the least bit surprised.

"He says it feels unnatural," Ivar adds, watching the witch carefully.

The witch snorts. "The only thing that's unnatural is the fact that it's locked away in that place. You've done well demon."

Ivar's smile falters before he stretches out his lips again. "And now that I've found it as you asked...."

"Yes, yes, you will have our full support to get you on the throne," the witch hisses. "We have little desire to rule this land. All we wish for is the return of what belongs to us."

Ivar's eyes are bright. "Then it is settled. I have the most influential demon clan leaders on my side, and once you have assassinated the king, we can combine forces and take over the castle. From there, we can—"

"No." The word is a cold, crisp command.

Ivar stiffens. "No?"

"If you wish to rule, you will need a clean slate. The clan leaders must be eliminated."

"Eliminated?" Ivar splutters. "These are some of the most well-respected leaders in Seral."

"Exactly. You wish to be king, do you not?" the witch questions, a cruel edge to her voice. "Those in power are often unreliable and untrustworthy. We can't risk any who might oppose us. When you've taken care of them, then I'll send in my assassins."

"But—" Ivar gapes, looking genuinely surprised. It's almost comical to watch as I'm not sure what he expected when he decided to ally with a witch. I might have learned the truth about the fall of Perstalia, and King Celzar stealing power from the witches, but any encounter I've had with the witches has shown them to be cunning and cruel.

Green fire erupts from the floor, circling around Ivar, and a squeak comes from the office where Shandi is hiding. Ivar's eyes shoot wide.

"Kill the clan leaders," the witch demands, flames billowing behind her. "Loyalty is fickle, and we don't need any more variables when it comes to this war. My sisters have lost too much." For the first time, there's a hint of sadness in the witch's voice, but it's gone when she speaks again. "I will be back in a day. Make sure it's done by then."

"You don't understand," Ivar blurts. "I need their support if I am to be seen as a legitimate king."

"My support is all you need," the witch replies, and she tosses something at Ivar.

He fumbles, catching the leather pouch as it hits his chest. "You have been useful, demon, but don't try my patience. Now that I know the location of the vault, my sisters will want to move quickly. We don't need your clan leaders getting in our way."

Ivar unties the string at the top of the pouch and stares at the contents within. "Poison?" His expression hardens.

"It's undetectable," the witch says, her lips twisting into a smile.

"And how do you propose I get this to all the clan leaders in such a short time? We finished our meeting not long ago."

"That's not my problem," the witch snarls. "Get creative. Organize a dinner party or an orgy. Whatever you demons like. I don't care."

Ivar doesn't look happy, but I can almost see his mind working as he devises a plan to gather the clan leaders again.

"We should act," Dante comments. *"This might be our only chance to capture a witch alone like this. We could question her and stop Ivar at the same time."*

The witch turns toward the portal. "One day, demon. If it's not done by then, our agreement is over." She takes a step toward the circle of fire, and Alaric draws two blades from his belt.

"Leave Ivar to me," my assassin growls.

"No, wait!" I blurt, but it's too late. A cry tears from Alaric as he sprints toward Ivar and the witch. In seconds, he's within four feet of them, but before he can attack, he slams into a magical barrier. A wave of power blows him back, and my assassin is thrown into the air. Snarling, he lands in a crouch.

The witch whips around, pulling an orb with neon pink liquid from her robes, and her lips form an ugly slash across her face. "Who is this?" she rasps.

I start to move, but before I can leave our cover, Dante grabs me with an invisible hand. *"Stay here, princess. Don't reveal your identity. Let us deal with this."*

My heart thuds as I stare at Alaric, but I stay where I am, trusting my demon.

My mates launch forward, but Ivar snatches the orb from the witch and throws it at them.

Leaping into the air, Nate catches the weapon, and the liquid sloshes and bubbles in the glass ball. "Fuck, it's ticking," my shifter shouts, eyeing a circular metal disk on one side of the orb. "It's a bomb!"

Shandi squeals, rushing from the office, and Ivar grabs hold of her. Alaric growls, rushing at the demon again with his blades, but in the span of seconds, the witch has disappeared into the portal. Ivar and Shandi flee after her, and the moment they're out of sight the portal closes, leaving Alaric to slice at empty air. He curses, spinning back to study the weapon in Nate's hands.

A steady ticking noise comes from the orb, the sound growing steadily faster.

"Get rid of it!" I shout, running over to him.

Nate pulls back his arm, and he launches the weapon toward the high up windows of the warehouse. The moment the orb is out of his hand, we turn and race toward the front door.

"Shade, get away from the warehouse!" I yell.

"Why, what's happening?"

"Just move!"

We exit the door as the orb explodes, fire erupting and creating an inferno inside the building. Glass shatters, and a rush of heat crashes into me as my mates and I are thrown high into the air.

I flare out my singed wings, my boots slamming to the ground yards from the warehouse, and Alaric, Mason, Dante, and Nate land around me. Turning, I find Prince Callan behind me with his hands outstretched. Wind whips out over the warehouse, a swirling vortex of air surrounding the flames as more explosions are set off, the fire contained by Prince Callan's power.

"It's the weapons in the storage room," Prince Callan tells me with a look of concentration on his face.

"Keep it contained," I tell him. "We don't need this reaching the rest of the city."

My archangel nods, sweat beading on his brow as he continues directing his power.

Shade flies down from high above, settling onto my shoulder. *"Sooo, I'm guessing it didn't go well in there?"*

There's another burst of light as something else explodes in the warehouse, but the light fades quickly.

Alaric steps up beside me, and I turn my head to my assassin. Anger is etched into every hard line of my mate's face, and he stares at the warehouse like he wishes Ivar was still in there, burning with the weapons he negotiated for.

I clench my jaw. "I think it's safe to say, the witches are coming."

TWENTY-TWO

~ Princess Blake ~

"We can regroup at my clan house," Dante suggests as the warehouse continues to burn, flames clawing at the sky.

It's been a while since the last explosion, and Prince Callan has removed his wind vortex. Undoubtedly, others in the city will have noticed the blaze by now, and will be on their way to investigate.

"Most of our clan members stay at other houses we have around the city, so it should be relatively quiet," my demon mate adds.

I frown, thinking of the witch's demands.

"Do you believe this Ivar will murder the other clan leaders, my mate?" Mason asks me.

Dante rubs his chin thoughtfully. "An exclusive dinner party would be the quickest way for Ivar to poison the leaders."

"In which case, Noah should get an invite," I say. "If we know where the party is being held, we might have another chance at capturing Ivar and questioning him. Maybe even the witch."

"And this vault in the castle," Prince Callan asks, his face solemn. "Is this the power you were warning us of? What could the power be coming from?"

I shake my head. "I wish I knew. I've never had access to that part of the vault, but whatever it is, I'm guessing it's nothing good."

There's a beat of silence, before I say, "I need to get a message to the king. Someone needs to warn him that Ivar's spy has infiltrated the castle, and that the witches intend to attack soon. He needs to protect the vault and himself. Especially if assassins are headed his way. And if whatever is in the vault is as powerful as I'm thinking it is, it might be our turn to call for aid from the allied realms."

"*I can go,*" Shade volunteers.

My brow creases. "What?"

"Dante and the rest of you should go to the Coilan clan house. I can pass a message on to King Dalton about the attack," Shade elaborates. "You just need to write out the message for me."

"No, I should go to the castle in person," I protest. "There's a barrier, so we can't portal inside the castle walls, but we can portal just outside the gates. Going there could be dangerous for you now that Ivar has a spy behind the castle walls."

"You'll be there soon enough," Shade tells me. "Ivar still doesn't know you're back in the city, so let's keep it that way. For now, you should stay with your mates and figure out how to stop him. Let me help. It won't take me long."

I don't want to agree. I want to go to the castle and strategize with the king, but if Ivar takes out the clan leaders, demonkind will be crippled before the battle with the witches has even begun.

I let out a frustrated sigh. "Fine. But promise me you'll try not to be seen. If Ivar's spy spots you, they're just as likely to kill you. Something tells me they won't treat any crow kindly at the moment."

"Sure thing," Shade replies, and despite her unexpected bravery, her voice wavers. "I'll be back before you know it. Now, about that message?"

"Actually, we should get Luna and Noah from the house in the forest first," Dante says. "You can ink a message there."

Nodding, I turn to Mason and hold out my hand. "Can I have the portal ring?"

He passes it to me, and I glimpse the burning warehouse one last time before turning and creating a gateway.

~

~ Shade ~

. . .

Why Shade? Just why? I chastise myself as I fly toward the castle, the wind gliding past my wings. The moment we'd arrived at Blake's secret house in the forest, Blake had ignored Noah and Luna's questions, immediately finding a piece of parchment and ink. In no time, the message was tied to my foot, and now I soar above the trees toward the imposing black towers of the demon castle.

For all you know, you could run into Ivar's spy straight away and end up in a pie or something horrible. The thought makes my heart pound wildly, but I don't slow my pace.

I know why I'm here. For Blake, who's been the one constant in my life. Or at least, the one constant I can remember. She needs me, and I can do this. *With any luck, I'll be in and out of the castle without so much as a squawk.*

The sky is quiet, and soon I'm banking to the right, curving around one of the stone towers, bee-lining to the south wing where Blake's room is. She'd had a small window installed, specifically for myself and her other birds, and I'm relieved when I find it's still open. The moment I enter the tower, power washes over me. I get the sensation that some dark and unnatural force is assessing me, but the feeling is gone in an instant. I tell myself I imagined it, but my feathers puff up. The power reminds me of the last time Blake and I had been in the vault, and I can't help but feel like it's a bad sign. *Don't worry, Shade, it's just some dark unknown power that the witches are desperate to get their hands on. Nothing to worry about.*

Shaking myself, I move across the room and hop through the little flap at the bottom of Blake's room door. Guards are stationed along the decorated corridor, but aside from some curious glances, none of them try to stop me as I flap my wings, launching into the air and making my way toward the king's chambers.

At this point, having Blake's crows in the castle is a common occurrence, and I could swear that some of the guards are relieved when they spot me. The thought fills me with pride, and I flap my wings faster.

As I enter the last corridor that leads to the king's bedchamber, I spot a familiar physician. I keep close behind him, and when the guards open the doors, letting the physician into the king's room, I hop in after him and duck to the side of the dresser.

It's still daylight outside and I half expect the king to be sleeping, but he's sitting at his desk with a pile of paperwork. Thankfully, he's fully clothed unlike the last time I was here, and he looks up, his brows furrowing when he sees the physician.

"Is it that time already, Farrex?" King Dalton asks gruffly. Dark circles line his eyes, and he leans back in his chair, his movements stiff. Tilting his head, he peers out the window to where the sun is just starting to lower in the sky.

"You should have been resting, your highness," the physician says, moving to the table on one side of the room and placing his case on it.

"Resting?" King Dalton laughs. "Let's just get this over with."

The physician's case clicks as he unlocks it, and it swings open. "As you wish, sire." He pulls out a large vial filled with white liquid, and King Dalton stands, taking off his shirt.

I have to contain my squawk when I see the demon king's chest. Long black lines cross the span of his torso, winding as they climb over his skin like the twisted branches of an ancient tree. Beneath the lines, is that same red rash Blake and I had witnessed before when we'd accidentally walked in on the king.

Holy hell what is that? I'm tempted to tell Blake, but I decide to wait until I know more.

Instead, I keep silent, watching as the physician smears the white substance all over the king's marks. When the king's entire chest is practically covered in white, the physician packs the vial back in his case. King Dalton shrugs his shirt on again, but now that I know to look for it, I notice the end of a black tendril still exposed on his neck above his collar. *Crap on a cracker, this is bad.*

The king dismisses the physician, and the doctor leaves as quickly as he came. The moment he's gone and the doors close again, the demon king lets out a heavy sigh.

"You can come out now," he rumbles.

I stiffen. *Wait. Me? What? But I—?*

"It's about time you turned up. I was starting to worry," King Dalton says, and his gaze goes to where I'm still hiding beside the dresser. *Crap.*

Sheepishly, I move out from the cover of the furniture, and the demon king watches me intently as I hop across the floor. Then I flap my wings, flying into the air and landing on his desk. His papers scatter, and I curse again internally, but the king doesn't look bothered.

His gaze drops to the tiny parchment tied to my leg, and he carefully removes it, stretching it open. His eyes skim over the message, and I study the older demon. He's always looked handsome and formidable, but now his eyes are sunken, and his skin is a paler shade than usual. My stomach tightens.

"Ah, so my daughter has finally bonded," King Dalton says with approval. "That's good. Very good."

Wait, out of Blake's whole message, that's the first thing he focuses on? I would have thought the news of the witches and an impending war in his kingdom would be what drew his attention first. In that moment, I wish I could talk to him, but of course, all I can do is stare.

"It looks like I'll see another war before I'm done," King Dalton says wearily. "Ivar has always wished for more power. I'm happy for my daughter to do as she sees fit to cleanse us of his influence. In the meantime, I will start gathering our forces and reach out to the other realms."

Before I'm done. His words echo in my head. I've never been close to the demon king, but my heart still feels heavy hearing those words. Even though King Dalton had already told Blake he was dying, it hadn't felt real. Not until now. And I know even though Blake tries to hide it, his death will hit her hard.

The demon king stares at me fondly, as though I'm an old friend rather than his daughter's pet, as he has so affectionately called me in the past.

"Don't worry, I'll sort this mess before I go, little one," he tells me. "We made a promise, and I won't leave our daughter while there are enemies circling."

I cock my head to the side, wishing I could ask more, but the king turns, striding toward the window. He releases the latch and pushes it open. "Go now, crow," he says, staring at me expectantly. "Take care of my daughter." It's a clear command, and I launch into the air. As I exit the window, the king starts coughing, but I don't look back as I head for Dante's clan house.

TWENTY-THREE

~ Princess Blake ~

I breathe in the scent of apricots as I stride past rows of fruit trees. It feels like an age since I was last here, reminding Dante about clan law.

Soon after arriving at the house in the forest, Shade left for the castle, and we spent the next short while filling in Noah and Luna on what had happened with Ivar. When we had them up to speed, I created a portal that opened up in the Coilan clan garden.

Dante walks beside me, and the others follow as we enter through the back door of the Coilan clan house. Thankfully, like he said, the mansion is mostly quiet, and Dante leads us to one of the more private sitting rooms on the second floor.

I drop onto a settee near the window, and Prince Callan takes the position on my right. Mason sits on my left, and he lifts my legs onto his lap. Stretching out, I lean against my archangel, and Mason massages the pads of my feet. Tipping my head back, I close my eyes and let out a contented hum. I'd always heard that having fated mates was bliss, but honestly, I'd thought everyone must be exaggerating. Turns out, I was wrong. Normally, in this type of situation I'd be wound tight, busy strategizing my next move, but Mason's fingers are pure magic. For just a moment, I let myself enjoy it. I focus on his touch, forgetting about all our problems.

"Feel good?" he murmurs.

"Never stop."

Mason chuckles. "I wouldn't if I had it my way, my mate."

My lips quirk up, and I crack my eyes open just as Dante stops before us, holding drinks out to me and Prince Callan.

"Here. This'll help too," Dante says, and I reach up, taking the glass.

I don't even bother asking what's in it. I drink greedily, glad that he's given me something that burns as it goes down. I've already finished it by the time Dante hands drinks to the others, and he grins, refilling my glass before pouring one for himself.

"So, it sounds like you've all had a productive day," Luna says, sitting on the settee opposite me.

I take my feet from Mason, murmuring a thank you, and planting them on the floor.

"I'm not sure productive is the word I'd use," Dante drawls, "but it was certainly enlightening."

Noah drops down beside Luna and curls his arm across her shoulders. "So what do we do now? Just wait until my invitation comes?"

"How 'bout we get somethin' to eat?" Nate suggests. "I'm fuckin' starvin'."

At that, Dante organizes us a ridiculous amount of food, and we discuss the witches and the realms while we eat. When everyone has had their fill, Dante sits at the grand piano in the far corner of the room. The conversation dies off as Dante's fingers fly over the keys, music filling the room and filtering through the house. He plays a soulful melody that tugs at something inside me, bringing my emotions simmering to the surface. The tempo increases, and I approach the demon, standing to one side.

Dante's fingers go from one end of the piano to the other, and when he plays the last note, I give him a soft smile. "I didn't know you played."

"It's one of the things that's helped to distract me," he replies, his midnight blue gaze sliding to my face.

"Distract you?"

"Distract me while I was away from my mate," he replies, his gaze so intense it makes me shiver. "I wrote that one for you, princess. As I did many others."

My heart stutters. "You...wrote it for me?"

His lips curve up. "Was it not to your liking, my mate?"

Mate. Because they're all mine now. The tattoos burn against my skin, and I smile, my chest feeling as though it might burst. Leaning down, I plant my lips on Dante's, and he pulls me onto his lap, deepening the kiss.

Luna clears her throat. "As much as I'm glad that Dante can finally stop pining, the invitation could arrive at any moment."

"We should be preparing," Alaric agrees, and it's the first time he's spoken in a long while.

I pull my lips from Dante's because they're right.

"So what's the plan for the dinner party?" Noah asks Dante. "I'm guessin' you're not going as me this time?"

I shake my head. "No, it's too dangerous. If Ivar is poisoning the food, the last thing we need is Dante eating it as well. I say once we know where the dinner party is being held, we break in and pretend to be waitstaff."

"Ivar won't be happy that Noah hasn't attended," Dante says. "Luna and Noah, you might want to lay low for a while."

"Without knowin' the layout of Ivar's house, it'll be hard for us to slip in undetected," Nate points out.

"The kitchens are usually on the ground floor,"

Dante says. "If we can take the places of a few of the servers, all we have to do is follow the crowd and we'll be led to where we need to go."

Luna frowns. "But if you know where Ivar is going to be, why not take him out before the party?"

"We need the clan leaders if we're going to survive a battle against the witches," I reply. "Despite what Ivar believes, the clans won't fight unless their leaders command it. But Ivar has swayed them to his cause. Even Gloria agreed to assassinate the king, and she was the one who seemed the most reluctant."

Prince Callan's expression is grim. "You think if we reveal Ivar's plan to poison them, it will restore their support for the king?"

"And then they'll be willin' to fight for the king again in the war?" Nate says.

I blow out a breath. "Yes."

Prince Callan crosses his arms. "If we prove to the clan leaders that Ivar was following the witches' order to assassinate them, it would also renew their hatred for the witches," he adds. "And alliances won't be so murky."

"But what if the witches don't make an appearance?" Mason asks. "How do we prove that Ivar is behind everything we say?"

I pace the room, deep in thought. "Scarlett," I say after a long moment.

Nate tilts his head. "Who's Scarlett?"

"Scarlett is a she-demon I helped out recently. She has the power to extract the truth," I explain.

Alaric's eyes darken, his fists tightening. "So do I."

"Confessions brought about by torture aren't always true," I point out. "Scarlett can use magic to force someone to speak the truth. They have no choice but to answer her questions. If we have her, and Ivar confesses, the other clan leaders will have no choice but to believe us."

"And do you think this...Scarlett, is up to the task?" Dante asks.

I think about the broken female who had been locked away by her family. Scarlett had been hidden away for years, and only recently escaped that toxic environment and found her mates.

"I hope so," I say. "But first, Ivar saw us at the club, and he also saw some of you at the warehouse. We need new disguises. Luna, do you think you can manage that?"

"Not me," Dante says. "I'll stay invisible."

The she-demon lifts to her feet. "Not a problem. Who wants to go first?"

Prince Callan steps forward. "I can."

"We want to be able to blend into the background," I tell Luna, and she nods, walking over to my archangel. It doesn't take long for her to work her magic on Prince Callan, Mason, Alaric, and Nate, and they have different faces yet again.

While she was busy at work, Noah slipped from

the room, and just as Luna finishes with Nate, the demon bursts in, red-faced. "I have it," Noah says, holding up a piece of black card with cursive gold lettering. "The Fallon Blade clan must have a secret house in the north. Ivar has invited me to attend a party. It starts in a few hours."

"Okay, then," Nate says, flexing his muscles. "So, we have a location."

"Your highness, shall I work on your disguise?" Luna asks me tentatively.

"Not yet," I reply, walking over and studying the invitation in Noah's hand. "The witches might be helping to guard the house. We need more information if we're going to simply walk in there. Just..." I lick my lips, "give me a moment."

Taking a deep breath, I think of my crows. The memory of the doves turning to ash still makes my chest tighten, but war is on the horizon, and I assure myself that it's not like I'm sending my crows into battle.

Closing my eyes, I break through the illusion magic still on me, and I reach out with my mind. For a second, I'm overwhelmed when I feel them all— the birds around Seral. Their minds all join to mine, ready to hear me. Focusing, I think of the northern end of the city, and it doesn't take me long to find the crow I'm after. *Emorie.* The connection strengthens at my command, and a thread of warmth goes through me as Emorie welcomes me. The other birds don't speak to me like Shade does, but she lets me in, and soon I'm seeing the world through her eyes.

She's perched on a slated black roof, and she peers over the city, watching as demons mill about in the streets, walking under the night sky. *"I need you to scout out a building,"* I tell her. *"War is coming to this land, and there's someone important in this house."* I send her the location of the party, and Emorie's only response is to stretch her wings and launch into the sky.

She soars over the tops of the houses, until she finds the one we're after.

"That's it," I tell her. *"Don't fly too low. We don't want them to see you."* Following my request, she circles high above, not dropping lower.

"It's a mansion," I say aloud to the others. "I have a crow flying overhead."

Everyone keeps silent, hanging on to my every word.

"It's three stories high, and there's some distance between the perimeter walls and the house. There's no garden we could use for cover, but there's a shed at the back that doesn't appear to be patrolled. I can create a portal to take us there. After that, Dante can you make us invisible until we enter the house? I count at least twenty Fallon Blade members acting as security."

"Easy done," Dante replies.

Emorie continues to circle the house, but without getting lower there's not much more she can show me. *"Thank you. That's all I needed,"* I whisper to her, and I pull back, weakening the connection.

My eyes fly open, and I find the others staring at me intently. "Once we enter the house, we'll want to find the kitchen quickly and replace a few of the servers before we're detected.

"Doesn't sound too hard," Nate says. "What are we waitin' for?"

I pause, peering at Luna. "I need to do one more thing first before you can give me another disguise." Reaching out with my mind, I find the other connection I'm after. *"Shade, how'd it go at the castle?"*

"The package has been delivered, cap'n," Shade chirps back, and I'm relieved to hear my friend's voice. *"Should I meet you all at the Coilan clan house?"*

"Actually, I was hoping you could do something else for me. Do you remember Scarlett?"

"How could I forget?" Shade replies. *"That she-demon left quite the impression."*

"Do you think you can go to her? It's time for me to call in that favor she owes me."

CHAPTER

TWENTY-FOUR

~ Princess Blake ~

I step out from the portal, careful to keep behind the cover of the shed. The structure is smaller than it looked from the sky, but it's enough to keep us hidden. Mason is the last to come through the gateway, and the moment he steps from the circle of flames, the portal closes.

Peering around the edge of the shed, I glimpse five guards who would spot us instantly if we simply stepped out. *"All right, you're up Dante."*

My demon mate grins and holds out his hands. *"Come on then, lovelies. Let's go for a walk. As long as we're touching, you'll remain invisible."*

Nate raises a brow. *"When he says it like that, it makes me want to refuse."*

Alaric scowls like he feels the same way.

I roll my eyes. *"So you have no problems sharing me, but holding hands is where you draw the line?"*

"What? You guys are doing the hero walk holding hands, and I'm not even there to see it?!" Shade squawks in my head.

"Don't make this worse," I send to her, though I can't stop my grin. *"It's not a hero walk. It's an, 'I don't want to get spotted before I've even made it to the house' walk."*

Dante wiggles his eyebrows, waiting expectantly, and I take one of his hands.

"For all we know, the clan leaders could all be in there already. Can we please hurry this up?" I tell my mates.

"Only because you wish it, Enchantress," Alaric grumbles, taking Dante's other hand.

Prince Callan, Mason, and Nate all take a hand as well until we're forming a line, and Dante's magic washes over us. Tingles race over me as we vanish, and I smile.

"We'll need to walk carefully if we're to remain undetected. We might be invisible, but they'll hear it if anyone stumbles," Dante reminds us.

"Stumbles?" Nate muses. *"Cat, remember?"*

"Not right now, you aren't," I point out. *"Come on."* I tug on Dante's hand, and we all walk out, moving from the cover of the shed.

There's a second when one of the guards looks our way and I think Dante's magic might not have worked properly, but the guard looks away just as quickly.

"*All right. Easy does it,*" Dante instructs.

I brace myself, waiting for us to be terrible at this, but somehow, we form an easy rhythm and we're at the back of the house in no time. We wait until a guard exits the mansion, and we dart inside before the door closes.

"*Fuck,*" Nate curses when we enter the hallway to find three more guards in conversation.

They finish what they're speaking about and head our way.

"*Against the walls,*" Alaric snaps. "*Now.*" He pulls me with him, pressing against the wall, and the rest of us follow.

The guard's glide past us, exiting the back door.

"*You sure I can't go into my beast form, and simply crash the party?*" Nate asks.

"*I told you, I want to catch Ivar in the act of trying to poison the leaders,*" I reply.

"*Right. Well, if you change your mind, you let me know,*" Nate says.

With the guards gone, the hallway is empty, and we move toward a kitchen bursting with activity. I peer through the open door, where a group of servers are gathering on the left side of the room. "*We can't just walk in there.*"

"*Wait,*" Nate says. "*I hear voices. In here.*" We move further up the hallway, and Nate tugs us into what looks like a break room. A group of demons finish dressing, and going by their neatly pressed black and white button up outfits, they're clearly servers here for the party.

"Make sure you don't spill a drop," one of the servers says to the others. "Ivar's made it clear sloppy service will not be tolerated tonight."

"W-what will happen if we do?" One of the younger-looking servers asks.

The demon who had originally spoken, pins the demon with a stare. "You'd rather not find out," he warns.

The other demon gulps.

"There are six of them," Prince Callan points out. *"We only need five seeing as Dante's invisible."*

"Then we'll just have to hope no one notices there's a missing server," I say.

One of the demons stands, impatiently tapping his foot. "We'd better hurry. It'll be time to serve the starters shortly, and Ivar doesn't take kindly to tardiness, either."

"Luckily you won't have to worry about that now, will ya buddy?" Nate says, though of course, the server can't hear him.

My shifter mate breaks from our group, winking into sight, and the rest of us follow his lead. Within seconds, the demon servers are all unconscious, and Alaric and Mason are dragging them behind the cover of a table.

We undress the demons quickly, pulling on the uniforms. I'm busy buttoning up my shirt when

Alaric steps up behind me, his hand going to my waist. "When the time comes, I need to know you won't stop me from killing Ivar," he growls in my ear. His hot breath makes my skin prickle, and I lean back, closing the last bit of distance between us and pressing against him. My body flushes with heat, and he groans as I rub against him, his hand tightening on my waist. "Say it, *Enchantress*," he rumbles.

"As long as we get the information we need out of him, he's all yours," I agree, my breaths coming in short rasps. "I hope you make him hurt for what he did to your brother."

Like it's all he needed to hear, he growls, gripping my chin and turning my head to the side. His lips slam to mine, and the kiss is hot, heavy, and desperate. Before either of us can get carried away, he breaks the kiss. His nostrils flare, and he keeps his lips a hairsbreadth from mine. "Oh, my mate. How had I ever denied that you were mine?"

My lips quirk up. I'm pretty sure it's a rhetorical question, but I answer anyway. "That's easy. You were delusional."

He chuckles and breathes me in before pressing another kiss to my lips.

"As much as we'd all like a taste of our mate right now, you should all move," Dante's voice sounds in my head. *"A few more servers just headed to the kitchen, and you don't want to be late."*

Alaric's tongue swipes across mine one last time, and he finally pulls back again, releasing me.

I blink rapidly, a little dazed, but when everyone goes for the door, I move with them.

"It's all clear," Dante tells us, and we file into the hallway, forming orderly lines and heading for the kitchen.

The moment we're through the swinging doors, I spot the large group of servers gathered to one side of the room. We try to act natural as we move to stand at the back. A few of the other servers glance our way, but thankfully, no one says anything.

It's a short while later when a demon in a white chef's uniform walks over and stands before our group.

"Look at his hip," Alaric says in my head, and my gaze lowers to where a familiar-looking leather pouch is tied there.

"Shit. He already has the poison," Nate comments.

The chef purses his lips, staring at us with disdain like we've all just stolen from his cookie jar. His eyes travel over me and the others, but he doesn't even blink.

"Right," he says sternly, pacing in front of us with his hands clasped behind his back. "Everyone here should know how this goes. We serve all meals within the short periods of time allotted. Anyone who hasn't delivered their plates on time and completely intact will be severely punished. Not a single drop should be spilled, and not a garnish displaced." He stops pacing and stares us down. "There are six courses, and each one is as delicate as the one before. Don't fuck it up." He turns his head to where numerous plates are all lined up on a long stone bench. "First course!" he bellows.

"Yes, chef!" the servers all shout back, and we hastily join them, mumbling the words as well.

The chef grunts, and the moment he turns, moving to the other side of the kitchen, the servers all start toward the steaming plates. My mates and I copy them, keeping our backs ramrod straight, and each lifting a single plate, and gliding out of the room. The servers form a single line as we move down the hallway, and we maintain a similar distance from each other.

We round the first corner, and Nate's curse sounds in my head. *"The fuckin' flower fell to the side of the plate."*

"What?" I hiss.

"Aren't cats supposed to be graceful?" Prince Callan comments.

"You ever seen a cat servin' hors d'oeurvres?" Nate sends back.

"We need to focus," Mason says from where he's walking behind me. *"Getting in trouble with the chef should be the least of your worries."*

We turn down another hallway.

"No one's looking," Alaric growls. *"So pick it up from the plate and fix the dish."*

"Okay, fine. I'll just..." Nate curses again, and I look in front of me in time to see the flower garnish fall to the floor. Before Nate can reach down, Alaric's boot lands on it.

"You dropped it," Alaric says dryly.

"And you fuckin' stepped on it!" Nate snaps.

I wonder why Dante didn't simply fix Nate's dish for him seeing as he's following beside us somewhere, but then I hear a faint chuckle in my head.

"I love these guys," my demon mutters.

"I'd love it more if we could get to the party already," I say, though I can't suppress my smile.

"Wow, can't say I've ever seen Ivar naked! His cock must be ten inches," Nate suddenly blurts, leaning closer to the server in front of him. Startled, the server turns his head to the portrait of Ivar on the wall. It's chest up and there's not an inch of bare skin except for the demon's face and neck.

Before the server looks back, Nate's hand darts around, grabbing the guy's flower garnish and adding it to the top of his smoked fish.

"Hey wait, have you dropped somethin'?" Nate asks the server, and the demon jolts, staring back at his plate. As he sees the missing garnish, his face pales, and he peers around. Twisting his head back, he spies the trampled flower on the ground. "No, I didn't..." he mutters, panicked.

Hearing him, the server before him, turns, her

eyes widening when she spies the dish he's carrying. "You've spoiled it!" she shrieks. "You must return to the kitchen immediately and have them fix this. Janson won't be pleased."

"But I didn't—" the server mumbles again, and then he lets out a panicked squeak and steps from our line, heading back the way we came.

Dante's dark chuckle sounds in my head.

"Was that necessary?" Mason asks.

"Well, I wasn't goin' to face Janson, now was I? That guy is far too serious," Nate jokes.

I can't help but feel a little bad for the server. I'm guessing Janson must be the chef's name, and considering the pep talk we were just given, I imagine the server is about to cop an earful. *Could be worse. He could be eating poison or battling a witch. And speaking of poison...*

"Do you think the poison is in this first course?" I ask the others.

There's a long pause, and I notice Alaric subtly crane his neck, trying to sniff his dish.

"It's undetectable, remember?" I tell him. *"Odorless and tasteless."*

"It'll be in this dish," Prince Callan theorizes. *"I don't see why Ivar would waste time holding off for a later course."*

"We won't know until someone tastes it," Alaric adds.

In no time at all, another server joins our ranks

with a new, perfectly arranged plate of food. I don't have time to contemplate what Janson has done with the other server, because soon we reach a hidden door and descend down a series of steps. When we reach the landing, we walk out into a main area and head into an adjoining room.

My senses heighten as I take in the dimly lit dining room, and the clan leaders all seated around a large rectangular table with Ivar sitting at the head. Moving in unison with the other servers, we all circle around the table, stopping a short distance from one of the clan leaders.

Ivar beams as he watches us. "And now, my friends, let us eat our first dish," he says, projecting his voice. "Smoked Dasdende fish."

On cue, the servers all step forward, and my mates and I copy them. I lean down, carefully placing the plate in front of Scyro from the Zetar clan.

The burly male sniffs me as I move toward him, and he lifts his hand as if he's about to touch me. "Mmm and are the she-demons on the menu, too, Ivar? I've never cared much for fish, but give me a different kind of meal..."

My mates all tense.

"If he dares put one finger on you—" Alaric growls, but before Scyro gets the chance, I move back to my position a couple paces from his chair.

Scyro frowns, clearly not used to being denied,

and he lowers his hand. I expect him to protest, but he only lets out a bellowing laugh. Everyone is staring, and I peer at Ivar, wondering if I've already ruined our cover. Before I can worry too much, Ivar smiles.

"I regret that the servers aren't trained to perform those kinds of duties," Ivar says. "But if you'd like, we can see that you're well-tended to after our dinner has completed."

Scyro continues laughing. "Sounds like a deal, demon."

"I dare say, I don't think Scyro realizes how close he came to losing a hand," Dante muses.

"If he tries it again, he'll lose more than that," Alaric snarls possessively.

Satisfied that he's diffused the situation, Ivar addresses the clan leaders. "Please enjoy."

I'm surprised when Ivar is one of the first to pick up his fork and start eating.

"It's not in this course," I point out, annoyed.

I was hoping we could get this over sooner rather than later, but we stand there dutifully with our hands clasped behind us, waiting as the clan leaders eat their meals. As they enjoy the food, Gloria speaks up. "I still don't understand why you've gathered us all here so soon after our last discussion." She hardly touches her food, and I have to suppress my smile. The she-demon is smart and lives up to her reputation.

Ivar gives her a broad smile. "Well, my dear Gloria, that would be because this is a celebration."

"A celebration of what?" she asks shrewdly.

The other leaders continue eating, but they peer at Ivar, equally interested in his response.

Ivar's thin lips stretch wider. "As we speak, a group of assassins are infiltrating the castle and taking care of our little...problem. So it seemed a good time for us to discuss the next steps before we move forward."

I tense, not sure whether Ivar is speaking the truth or not.

"You've alerted the king already," Dante says to me. *"He will be fine. Besides, the witch said she'd send the assassin after Ivar had taken care of the clan leaders."*

"That was before she knew we were listening," I remind him. I want to believe Dad is safe. There was a time when I'd thought the demon king was near invincible, but that was before he became sick.

A few of the clan leaders look unsettled by Ivar's news, especially Gloria. I can't help but wonder if she was hoping Ivar wouldn't be able to find an assassin to get the job done.

The moment everyone has finished the first course, we move with the servers, collecting the empty plates and returning to the kitchen. By the time we get there, the second course has just finished being prepared, and we're soon on our way back to the dining room.

"Why would Ivar drag this out?" Mason asks as we

move through the hallways, delicately made salads balancing on our plates.

"*Ivar loves a good party,*" Dante replies. "*Perhaps, he's enjoying entertaining the clan leaders this last time.*"

"*Or he's gettin' cold feet,*" Nate says. "*Let's face it. It's the witches who want all the clan leaders dead. Maybe he's second-guessing their relationship?*"

"*It doesn't matter,*" I say. "*He's in too deep now. He knows he must kill them or the witches will likely kill the leaders and him as well. Maybe the first course was to build their trust and ensure everyone eats the next dish?*"

"*Blake, I have Scarlett and her mates following me through the city,*" Shade's voice breaks into the conversation.

I think of Scarlett's three possessive mates. I'm not sure if it's a good idea to have them around for the interrogation, but I can't blame them for wanting to be with their female. "*Great job,*" I tell Shade. "*So you didn't have any trouble getting them to follow you?*"

"*Not at all. I mean sure, I don't think they were happy I interrupted them, but all I had to do was make a bit of noise, and they figured out what I wanted.*"

"*Okay. Well, when you're here, have them wait outside. I'll call for you when we're ready,*" I tell her.

"*Roger that,*" Shade chirps, and she's silent again.

I follow the others down the stairs to the dining room and carefully place the salad in front of Gloria this time. After the first incident, Alaric swapped places with me, and I struggle not to grin as Alaric leans uncomfortably close to Scyro, purposely getting into his personal space. The clan leader glares at my assassin, clearly not happy about the swap, but Alaric glowers at him so fiercely that I think he's too scared to complain.

It's an hour later when we're walking back to the room holding plates of a fine dessert with layers of chocolate and white mascarpone cheesecake topped with gold leaf and berries.

"Hold on, so you're telling me Ivar poisoned the dessert?" Shade shrieks when I lament how good it looks. *"What kind of monster is he?"*

"One who's about to regret getting into bed with the witches," I tell her.

During the past courses, Ivar spun tales of the laws he would change in the realm and how this would benefit all demons, but none more than the influential clan leaders now at his table.

"Ah, the final course," Ivar says eagerly, rubbing his hands together. "My chef's specialty cheesecake. My favorite."

As the clan leaders reach for their spoons, Gloria asks, "You've spoken about changing demon law, Ivar, but what about the witches? Rumor has it that Toralyn is currently under attack. Please tell us how you plan to ensure our survival and victory against them."

Everyone turns their gazes to Ivar, and Scyro is

the only one to shove a spoonful of cheesecake into his mouth.

"This is it," I say to my mates. *"Once Scyro is dead, the others will see how Ivar tried to poison them."*

"You should eat," Ivar insists. "The cheesecake truly is—"

"You speak about making Seral stronger, but how will your leadership protect us against the witches?" Gloria says, interrupting him. "King Dalton has fought them before, and he's the reason we're all still here. What makes you think you can handle the witches any better?"

Ivar gives her a forced smile, his gaze flicking to her dessert before fixing on her face. "Like you said, rumor has it the witches are busy in Toralyn. They're not our problem right now. The angels will wipe them out."

He indicates with his hand to the dessert. "Now, if you please."

"And if they don't?" Gloria says, making no move to eat her dessert.

"As I discussed, you would all become my trusted advisors, including when it comes time to discuss matters of war," Ivar snaps, his gaze darting to Scyro and then to Gloria. "But for now, let us enjoy this—"

Before he can finish, Scyro coughs, spittle flying onto his plate as his face starts to redden.

Gloria's head jerks to the demon leader from the Zetar clan. "What's wrong with him?"

Ivar gestures to one of the servers behind him. "Help him!" he snaps. "He's choking."

The server hurries over to the clan leader, but when they draw close to Scyro, the demon starts coughing more violently, froth starting to bubble from his mouth. He lifts his hand to his throat as his eyes bulge.

"It's the dessert!" Gloria shouts, pushing her plate away, and the other clan leaders around the table all follow her lead, placing down their spoons.

"What is this?" Another clan leader yells, jumping to his feet.

"He's choking and needs assistance," Ivar says gruffly, shooting to his feet as well. "What do you take me for?"

"You tell us," Gloria snarls as more green ooze bubbles from Scyro's mouth.

Scyro coughs, and green spittle sprays onto the table. More of the demons lift to their feet, pushing out their chairs.

Bracing his hands on the table, Scyro lets out a few more ragged coughs. His coughing changes to strange, frantic laughter, and then his laughter abruptly stops when his body turns to ash. The clan leaders stare in shock as his empty clothes crumple to the floor, and his horns land heavily on the table.

The servers start backing away, scurrying from the room.

"You killed him!" Gloria shrieks, pointing at Ivar's horns. "That's witch poison!"

In the span of a heartbeat, Ivar's expression of concern melts away and his lips upturn into a cruel smile.

Gloria's face pales at his change in attitude, and she turns with the other clan leaders, starting toward the door. Before she can reach it, Ivar's guards are there, blocking the exit.

TWENTY-FIVE

~ Princess Blake ~

"**L**ooks like we didn't need Scarlett to convince *them after all...*" I muse to the others. *"But she'll still be good for the interrogation."*

"We agreed to your terms," Gloria says, keeping her chin high as she turns back to Ivar. "Why do this?"

"It's nothing personal," Ivar replies. "But the witches simply aren't willing to risk keeping you alive."

"The witches?" Another leader spits. "What has this got to do with their kind? Tell me you're not that stupid."

Ivar's smile is unsettling. "I had tried to convince

them to let you all live," he admits. "But a change in leadership always comes with a price. And since you refuse to eat your dessert I guess it's time for plan B." He pulls a mask from his robe, strapping it over his face, and the Fallon Blade soldiers do the same. The moment they have them on, smoke starts filtering in from the vents on the ceiling.

The clan leaders shout, coughing and wheezing, and the Fallon Blade demons attack.

"*Blake!*" Prince Callan shouts, and a cool wind whips around my face, preventing the smoke from reaching my mouth and nose. I peer over to see my archangel has done the same for my mates.

"*We need to help the clan leaders as well,*" I tell him.

One of the Fallon Blade soldiers goes for Gloria who's the closest to me, but my hand shoots out, grabbing his arm and stopping his blade.

"Out of my way, server," he snarls.

I pretend to think about it before giving him a wicked smile. "Let's see, hmmm, no."

The soldier frowns, his top lip curling, but just as he tries to break free, blood sprays and his head slides from his body. He thuds to the floor, and Alaric stands behind him, a bloodied sword in his hand. "He touched you," he growls.

"Technically, I'm the one who touched him," I point out.

"It still counts, princess," Dante drawls from somewhere close to me.

"Princess?" Gloria says, still wheezing as she stares at me strangely.

I wink at her. "The one and only."

Prince Callan clears the air, and though the clan leaders are still coughing, they start fighting back.

"All right, let's get this done," I tell my mates, and I let my magic rip through my disguise. Power races through my body, flooding my system, and my wings tear through the fabric on my back. My golden tattoos burn bright against my skin, and I breathe in deep, feeling like myself again. Prince Callan is already back in his true form, but Mason follows my lead, accessing his power though he doesn't shift. Alaric and Nate stay in their disguises, no doubt realizing the dining room is much too small to accommodate them.

"Y-your highness," Gloria stammers, her eyes filled with horror as she steps away from me, staring at the tattoos on my arms. Her gaze flicks to my mates before going back to me, and she slams to one knee, placing her fist to her chest. "I meant none of what I said, princess. You have my allegiance. Always."

Around the room, the clan leaders gasp when they see me, and even Ivar's demons are stunned. The clan leaders kneel, showing their respect. It's sickening when they were just plotting my downfall, but I've long since learned that I don't need them to love me. For now, fear would have to do, and it's one thing to agree with Ivar's plans when they thought I was in another realm, but a different thing entirely when I'm standing before them.

The Fallon Blade soldiers hesitate, confusion written on their faces, but I have no sympathy for them. They might have been following Ivar's lead, but they've still been working with the witches, plotting my father's assassination and the downfall of the realm.

Never show mercy. Rule number two of being a demon royal. "Kill the soldiers," I command my mates. Taking out my own blades, the five of us work as one, and it's not long before Ivar's soldiers are all down.

"No!" Ivar snarls, his shock soon replaced with simmering hatred as he stares at me. Still holding his knives, he backs away, but Prince Callan sends out a burst of air, slamming the clan leader against the wall. His knives are knocked from his hands, and Alaric advances, pressing his forearm against Ivar's throat. Prince Callan keeps his power there, but Alaric stays where he is, his top lip curled as he glares at the demon.

Ivar doesn't struggle. He just starts frantically whispering to himself.

The clan leaders stay where they are, but they watch me fearfully. I walk over to where Scyro's horns are still on the table, and I pick one up, throwing it to one of the clan leaders. He fumbles for it, and his face pales as he struggles to catch it, and it falls with a clatter to the floor.

"This is what Ivar intended for you. *This* is your reward for your loyalty," I say, my voice hard and unforgiving. "Death by witch poison, and a future where your clans will be enslaved by the witches or dead."

"He's a bastard!" Another clan leader yells, but the moment my gaze goes to him, he silences.

"I know what Ivar offered you," I continue. "A say in the matters regarding the ruling of the kingdom, and a chance to be part of the royal council. The clans were created *for* the demons, but when I'm queen, I invite you all to say your peace on how you believe our realm should change. But first, we need to defeat the witches. We need to protect what's ours and band together or the demons will fall. As clan leaders, you need to rally your soldiers so we can face this war as one. I heard your scheming. This is your one chance to redeem yourselves, or deny me, and face the consequences."

"We barely survived a war with the witches the last time, and rumor has it that King Dalton isn't the demon he used to be," Gloria says. "You weren't alive during the great war, but I was. What makes you so sure we can win this time?"

"I'm not," I admit. "But if we do nothing then we know what the outcome will be. And if it weren't for me and my mates, you'd be dead right now. I'm not prepared to go down without a fight, and I'm hoping you aren't either." I look at them hard. "Or was I wrong to spare you? Are you ready to end it now?"

The clan leaders are silent for a moment, but Gloria is the first to rise to her feet. She straightens her spine, and the other clan leaders follow her.

"My clan will answer your call, your highness," Gloria tells me.

A few of the other clan leaders send furtive glances in Ivar's direction, but soon, all of the clan leaders are pledging their allegiance to me as well. Everyone, that is, except Ivar.

"You're fools," Ivar growls, no longer muttering to himself. "We won't be able to defeat the witches this time. By allying with them, the witches had agreed to spare the demons."

"What demons?" I say, jerking my head toward Ivar. "The clan leaders you tried to poison in this room, or the ones who are yet to die on the battlefield?"

"Sometimes you have to sacrifice a few to save the many," Ivar says coldly. "Of all demons, I thought you would understand that."

"Except you weren't plannin' to save anythin' except your own ass," Nate comments.

"Return to your clans," I command the clan leaders. "And prepare your soldiers. The witches may attack any day now. You'll hear the war siren when the time has come."

"Yes, your highness," the clan leaders chant in unison, sparing Ivar a last glance and filing out of the room, heading into the upper part of the house.

When the last clan leader is gone, my mates and I move closer to Ivar.

"You think this means something, half-blood?" Ivar snarls, still pinned to the wall. Blood trails from his head, dripping past his right eye. "Those demons turned on you the moment you were out of the realm. I was the demons only chance to avoid annihilation."

I snort. "Even I know you're not stupid enough to believe that, Ivar. It starts with the witches ordering you to kill the clan leaders, and it ends with all of us turned to ash."

"You're wrong," Ivar rasps.

"The witches only wanted you to help them locate the power in the castle," I tell him. "And for you to cripple the demon clans so we're weakened and easier to defeat. Did you really think they'd let you take the throne and rule?"

"They don't want this land," Ivar replies. "All they want is what's theirs. What the king took from them."

"And did it even occur to you, that once they have it, they may simply lay waste to the rest of us? That whatever King Dalton took, he probably did so for a reason. That it might be a weapon, or a power that may make them unstoppable?"

"We would be allies," Ivar says.

I scoff. "You're not that naive. And what do you think will happen when the witches discover you've failed to kill the clan leaders?"

There's a flicker of fear in Ivar's eyes, but he blinks, and it's gone again.

"Tell us everything you know about the witches, and the demons might actually survive what's to come," I say.

"I have nothing for a bastard princess," Ivar snarls, and he spits at me. I dodge to the side, avoiding his spit, and Alaric slams his fist into the demon's gut with his free hand. Ivar coughs, blood trailing from the corner of his mouth.

"Have it your way, then," I tell Ivar.

"Shade, are you guys outside?" I send to my crow. *"We're in a private dining hall down a series of steps. Nate will meet you at the top of the stairs."*

There's a pause before she answers. *"Got it. We'll be there soon."*

I share a look with Nate, and he nods, bounding from the room.

In no time at all, Nate is returning with Scarlett and her three protective demon mates—Tanner, Zachary, and Ezra, the leaders of the Nightfire clan. I'm not surprised Ivar didn't involve the Nightfire clan in his schemes. Scarlett is a truth teller, and she wouldn't have been an asset to keep around.

I eye where Shade is perched on Zachary's head, standing in his red hair.

"What are you doing?" I ask her.

"Hitching a ride?" she replies innocently.

"I think what my mate means, is why are you on the demon's head?" Mason says.

Shade flutters her wings. *"Oh, that. I'm, you know, asserting my dominance."*

"What dominance?" Nate says with wry amusement.

Shade lets out an exasperated sigh. *"The point is, I brought them here. Ta-da!"* She flies from Zachary's head, and I can see the relief in his eyes as she comes to land on my shoulder.

Her gaze sweeps the room, and she makes a noise in my head. *"Looks like you guys have been busy redecorating."*

Before I can respond, Scarlett steps forward meekly and bows her head, lifting a fist to her chest. "Princess. I am at your service."

From the grave expressions of her mates, it's obvious they're unhappy that I've summoned her, and I can respect that. They crowd close to their mate, looking like they're ready to fight anyone to protect her. It makes me like them just a little bit more than I already did.

"Thank you for coming. I wouldn't have asked if the situation wasn't critical." I gesture with my head toward Ivar. "We need you to get information out of him."

Scarlett's gaze goes to Ivar, and he finally starts to struggle. Prince Callan's air power keeps the clan leader pressed against the wall, and Alaric lifts a dagger to Ivar's throat.

"She's only just learned of her power," Tanner interjects, his voice gruff. "You can't expect her to—"

"If there was another option, I would have used it," I interrupt. "I get it. You're worried about your mate. But if we don't find out the information we need, you can say goodbye to Seral and everyone in it. The witches are coming, and this...*traitor* knows more than he's willing to share."

At the mention of the witches, Scarlett trembles, and Tanner's brows form a hard line.

"We don't have time to waste, and Scarlett's the only one who can help us extract the truth from him," I add.

"You think the witches are going to wage war on us?" Scarlett asks.

"It's only a question of 'when'," Dante says, coming back into view beside me.

Fear touches Scarlett's eyes. "Do you think this is part of what my brother, Jace, was involved in?"

I think of her sadistic brother who betrayed her and who's currently rotting in the dungeons under the palace. He's still alive, not that Scarlett asked. She takes a deep breath like she's gathering her strength. "All right. Let's see what Ivar has to say."

She positions herself in front of the Fallon Blade clan leader, with only a couple paces between them.

"How does this work?" Prince Callan asks.

"Tell me it hurts," Alaric growls.

Scarlett ignores them and holds out her right hand. Closing her eyes, she concentrates and a kernel of light forms on her palm.

"We're right here, Scarlett," Zachary says to her, staying by her side.

Opening her eyes, Scarlett directs her magic forward, and a thread reaches out from her palm, the tendril curling around Ivar's waist and tying them together.

"This won't help you," Ivar snarls, struggling against my mates.

"Ask your questions," Scarlett says, her voice slightly warped as gold shines in her eyes.

I pin Ivar with my gaze. "Tell us the witches' plans? How large are their forces?"

Ivar sneers. "Fuck you."

Scarlett sends out another burst of power, and the golden thread around the demon's waist shines brighter. His words die off as he makes a choking, gasping sound. His face goes red, his eyes bulging, and his next words come out in a rush. "I don't know their full numbers. Maybe hundreds? Maybe thousands? They wanted the demons to bolster their ranks and aid in the attack."

"What weapons do they have?" Prince Callan asks. "Your warehouse. Are there more like it in Seral?"

Ivar lets out a strangled laugh and shakes his head like he's trying to release Scarlett's hold on him, but the thread around his waist remains tight, the bands of light holding steadfast.

He lets out a choked sound, like his next words are being ripped from his throat. "Those weapons were gifts given to me in good faith. To arm the demons when the time came. None of those were meant for the witches. They're not what you need to worry about."

"So what *do* we need to worry about?"

Ivar shakes his head again. "The questions you aren't asking."

What?

"He's useless," Alaric growls. "The witches wouldn't have divulged all their plans to him. They would have known he might get compromised. Let me end him."

"Not yet," I say.

I give Scarlett a look and she nods her head, sending another burst of magic through to Ivar.

Ivar grits his teeth, seething at the strength of her influence.

"You must know something," I say. "What is the power in the castle? You must have been curious why they want it so badly."

He clenches his teeth, but he can't stop the words from spilling free. "All I know is that the power isn't a *what,* it's a *who.* And now that the witches know where the vault is, there's no stopping them."

My brows slam down. "What?"

"Exactly what I said," Ivar grits out. "The power isn't an object. It's some kind of sentient—" Ivar doesn't finish. His eyes flash green, and Scarlett whimpers, her face contorting with pain.

"Let him go!" Tanner shouts at Scarlett, and she releases her power, sagging into his arms as Ivar's lips curve into an unnatural smile.

Prince Callan and Alaric keep their hold on Ivar, but Prince Callan curses, as Ivar's head moves, his gaze taking in the destruction around us.

Except, even before Ivar speaks next, I know it's not really the Fallon Blade demon before us anymore.

I think of Ivar's last words and the vault. Of the door that never opens. Except...except when the king went to visit.

"I had a feeling you would stop him," a deep feminine voice comes from between Ivar's lips. Instantly, I recognize the voice of the witch we'd encountered in the warehouse.

Mason, Dante, and Nate grip their weapons tighter, scanning the room for any signs of a portal.

"And yet, you still ordered him to take out the clan leaders," I point out.

"It's better if the demons are fighting each other. Then we don't have to worry about them fighting us," the witch muses.

My brow creases. "Except your plan has failed. The demons will rally against you, and we'll defeat you like the last time you were here."

"Is that so?" Ivar's smile is a creepy slash across his face. "You truly have no idea, do you half-breed?"

I purse my lips. "Then how about you enlighten me?"

"They'll reveal themselves soon enough. For now, I had to make sure this spineless weasel didn't divulge too much. I must say, I don't remember there being a truth-teller in these lands."

Scarlett shies away, and her mates stand in front of her.

"They? Who are you talking about?" I insist.

"See you soon, *your highness,*" that strange voice hisses from between Ivar's lips, and then the green disappears from Ivar's eyes. The demon starts convulsing, his body shuddering violently.

"Help me!" Ivar lets out a broken cry, his voice no longer that of the witch, but of the demon leader.

"No! He was supposed to die by my blade," Alaric growls, but Ivar's convulsing increases, his eyes rolling to the back of his head. And then, the demon leader falls silent. Prince Callan and Alaric release him, letting his lifeless body fall to the floor.

"I had hoped to make him suffer," Alaric grumbles. "Here, let me have that." He grabs Dante's sword, and with a single blow, he severs Ivar's head from his body.

"I think he was already dead," Dante drawls.

Alaric shrugs. "Now we can be sure."

We all stare down at the clan leader.

"What do you think Ivar was talking about?" Prince Callan asks. "A sentient being?"

Nate's face is hard. "You think it's some kind of beast that's been captured and is being kept in the castle?"

I rack my brain trying to think of everything I know of the war with the witches. Of everything Dad has told me, but he's never mentioned that there might be something *alive* behind the black door.

"We need to get to the castle," I say simply. "Whatever it is, the witches are coming for it. And it's time Dad answered some questions."

CHAPTER

TWENTY-SIX

~ Princess Blake ~

"So, witches, huh?" Scarlett asks when we walk outside Ivar's mansion.

Zachary swipes his hair away from his eyes. "Should we be worried?"

I don't answer that. Scarlett and her mates all heard what the witch said. "Be ready," I tell them. "When the witches attack, we'll need everyone."

"So, it is as bad as it sounded," Zachary comments. There's humor in his voice, but his eyes darken.

Scarlett dips her head. "Is that all I can do for now, your highness?"

I smile at her. The first time I saw the she-demon she was scared and broken, but now, despite her

310

exhaustion from using her power on Ivar, there's strength in her gaze.

"Thank you," I tell her. "We'll take it from here."

She smiles, her eyes soft, and she turns with her mates, heading toward their car on the side of the street.

When they're gone, I face my mates and spread my wings. "We could portal outside the castle, but after what I've just heard, I need to stretch my wings. Who wants a ride? You have three amazing options."

Mason and Prince Callan step up on either side of me, and Alaric, Nate, and Dante share a look.

"Not this time, gorgeous," Nate says, giving me a lop-sided grin. "The beast side isn't too happy he missed the action just now. I'm gonna go for a run."

Alaric flexes his muscles, and points to a sports car up ahead on the side of the road. "Dante and I can take that."

"What, not a fan of flying?" I tease.

Alaric scowls. "The only thing that makes it bearable is you, mate. But it might look strange arriving at the castle in your arms."

I roll my eyes. "So, you're worried what the demons will think?"

"I prefer my hand around your throat, mate, not you cradling me like a baby," Alaric counters. "And seeing as shifting into my giant form would cause unwanted attention, the car will do."

Desire fills Alaric's eyes as he stares at me, and my body flushes with heat.

"I could send us all there with my wind power," Prince Callan suggests, but Nate shakes his head.

"Like I said, I need to run," my shifter says.

I blow out a breath. "Fine."

"How 'bout we see who gets there first?" Nate suggests, a playful gleam in his eyes.

Dante raises a brow, like he's interested in the challenge, and Mason shifts, changing into his winged centaur form, and pawing the ground with his front hooves.

"Where's the finish line?" Prince Callan asks.

"You can't be serious," I say. "We just learned of the witches attacking, and you're talking about a race."

"It'll help us let off some steam," Nate defends.

"The winner is the first one inside the castle walls," Dante says, smirking. "And they get to be the first one to make Blake come when we get the chance."

My brows lift, my core tightening at the thought. "What? I'm not a prize. We're already bonded."

"Loser has to watch and gets to be the last," Alaric growls, and I can't believe even he's getting in on this.

I plant my hands on my hips. "And when *I* win?"

My mates all turn to me. "Then you get to use us in any way for as long as you see fit, and we'll only come when you let us."

I laugh but need coils within me as I think of my mates on their hands and knees, worshipping me.

"Oh please, that hardly seems fair. You'd all do that anyway," Shade says.

"This is true," Mason admits.

I grin. I know instead of joking around, we should be headed to the palace by now. The witches could be already circling, but I can tell my mates need this. Usually, when fated mates bond, they hide away for weeks, simply enjoying each other's company, but we don't have time for that right now. Instead, we have this.

Before any of them move, I shoot into the air, flaring my wings out wide as I lift higher than the houses.

"She's fuckin' cheatin'," Nate comments in disbelief, and I laugh as they scramble to catch up.

Seconds later, Nate's roar splits the air, and I hear car doors slam. I flap my wings faster, trying to take advantage of my head start, but Prince Callan and Mason soon catch up to me, flying at my sides.

The wind filters through my feathers, and for a moment, I feel at peace.

"Do you wish for me to let you win, my mate?" Mason asks me seriously, and I laugh, the wind tearing tears from my eyes.

"Just get to the castle," I tell him. Honestly, I don't care about winning. Because in a way, I feel as though I've already won. Even though we'll be facing the witches soon, and none of us might survive, for

once, I feel free. And I know it's all because of them. *My mates.*

"I'm going to hedge my bets on Nate," Shade comments. *"Damn that cat can move."*

I follow her gaze down to where Nate runs in his jaguar form below us, weaving between the streets at frightening speed. Demons dodge out of the way when they see him coming, and some of them scream in surprise when he snaps at them, his massive jaws narrowly missing one of their limbs.

"That's if he doesn't get too distracted showing off," Shade adds, and I chuckle, not doubting that my shifter mate is enjoying this.

We've already covered half the distance to the castle when a familiar-looking sports car comes out of nowhere, Dante and Alaric overtaking Nate and literally driving right past the shifter's nose.

Nate snaps at them, and his powerful limbs eat up the distance between them until they're side by side.

I keep pace with Mason and Prince Callan, though honestly, I don't know how hard any of us is really trying.

It's nice being up here, and I know all that will change the moment we make it to the castle. Once we're there, I'll need to go straight to the king. To alert him of everything that's going on and hope he's managed to get more soldiers from the allied realms. If anything, I slow my pace a little.

Prince Callan turns his head, peering at me with concern. *"What's wrong my Ahalian Touizda?"*

I sigh, enjoying the cool night air on my skin and the scent of smoke in my nose. *"Nothing, and yet, everything,"* I reply. *"What happens if we can't defeat the witches?"* Before now, I hadn't let myself contemplate it. Not really. But before I met my mates, I never had much to lose. Now, my chest tightens at the thought of five males being taken from me all too soon after only just finding them."

"We will," Mason says firmly. *"There was a time when I was in the mines of The Haven, when I wondered why I was still alive. But now I know. The witches have tormented the different realms for too long. No matter what Celzar did, they need to be stopped. I was always meant to be yours, my mate, and something tells me, not even the witches are a strong enough force to break us."*

I give him a tight smile, and I peer ahead at the looming dark towers of the castle growing larger with each passing second. I thought I'd be happier to be returning home. But it's only then that I realize the demon castle never had really felt like home. Not even when I was little and mostly confined to life within the stone walls. And now that I'm bonded to my mates, I know why. Because my home never was a stone structure where I slept. It was anywhere I went with my mates, and that hole inside me that was missing? It was them. It had been all along.

"Ha! First place!" Nate laughs in my head, as he

grapples along the castle stone walls and lands on the other side.

"*Be honest,*" I say to the others. "*You all let him have that.*"

Their chuckles sound in my head.

"*No one wanted to have to listen to his complaining if he lost,*" Alaric grumbles as their sports car skids to a halt just outside the castle gates.

The demon soldiers on the castle walls shout and a volley of arrows fly at Nate. He dodges to the side, narrowly missing them, but they keep coming. One is aimed at his eye, and he snatches it out of the air with his teeth. "*Uh, gorgeous, any chance you can tell them to stand down before I have to kill someone?*"

Grinning, I tuck in my wings, soaring the last distance, and Prince Callan gives me, Mason and himself an extra boost of speed using his wind power.

I'm glad to see Dad has doubled the guards on duty, but before Nate starts tearing through them, I shout, "Stand down! He's my mate, and unless you want to lose your life, put your weapons down."

A guard on the ground who was clearly about to use his power, lowers his hands.

"It's the princess!" another guard yells, peering at me as I land beside Nate.

"*Okay, is it just me, or do they look glad to see you?*" Shade comments, sounding uncertain as she lands on my shoulder.

"*It's not just you,*" Prince Callan says.

I frown, peering at the relieved faces of the demon guards. Over the years, I've grown used to demons respecting me. Fearing me, even. But I never thought they'd be relieved to see me. *"Why does that feel like a bad sign?"*

I order the guards to open the gates, and Alaric and Dante join us before the gates close again behind them.

"Just enjoy it," Shade says, as the demons all drop to one knee, slamming a fist to their chests.

Nate shakes his shaggy head, and his body shifts, growing smaller again as he changes back from his beast form. He winks at me, a triumphant gleam in his eyes. *"I'm lookin' forward to collectin' my reward, gorgeous."*

I want to say that I am as well, but I can't stop thinking about how relieved the guards look. *Has something happened here?* I purse my lips. *"We'd better get inside."*

"So, about the castle," Shade starts, *"Blake, there's something I need to tell you."*

I push open the heavy front doors, striding into the dimly lit entrance hall. The moment I'm inside the castle, invisible icy claws reach for me, scraping against my skin. The dark power I sensed the last time I was in the vault, pushes at my mind, those claws scraping against my skull and trying to find a way in. Cursing, I fight against it, fortifying my mental walls, and I turn to my mates, panic thrumming through me.

"Did you feel that?" I rush out.

They all stare at me, blinking.

"You mean how damn cold it is in here?" Nate asks, rubbing his arms. "Yeah, hasn't the king ever heard of a fire?"

"It's summer," Dante says dryly. He moves closer to me, concern written on his face. "You can feel it can't you? The power?"

"You can't?"

He shakes his head. "All I noticed was the temperature dropping a few degrees."

I search his eyes, remembering when he was disguised as Kai and the power had tried to kill him.

"I'm fine," he says, his midnight blue gaze locked on me. "We all are. You don't have to worry."

Without knowing what the power is, there's no way to be certain that any of us are safe, but his words send a spark of relief through me. "Okay, well I guess it's probably a good thing only I can feel it. And in any case, it's gone for now." The sensation of icy claws has left me, but I can't shake the unsettling feeling in my chest.

"*I felt it,*" Shade says, puffing up her feathers. "*Or at least, I did when I came here to deliver your message to the king.*"

"What?" I stare at her. "Why didn't you say anything?"

"*You were busy with Ivar,*" she replies. "*But I definitely felt something when I entered the castle. Something...unnatural.*"

"Great," I say sarcastically.

"*There's more, too,*" Shade says hesitantly.

My unease spikes. "More?"

Shade tucks her wings in tighter. "*When I found King Dalton, the physician was there again.*"

"Well, that's not a surprise, is it?" I say slowly.

"*The king really isn't well, Blake. Remember those welts we saw? It's worse. So much worse,*" Shade says. "*He looks like he's hardly left his bedchamber.*"

For a moment, I continue standing there, unable to move. I know Dad has been growing weaker, but I hadn't expected this. *No wonder the guards were relieved to see me if war is coming and the king has hardly left his rooms.*

"Fuck," I growl, and I storm through the castle toward the king's chambers.

My mates keep up, flanking me, and the guards patrolling the hallways straighten as I pass, relief shining in their eyes.

We reach Dad's bedchambers, and two massive demon guards stand outside his room. There was a time when I would have asked them nicely to let me through and given them a chance to act. Now, I keep striding toward them and say a single command. "Move."

The guards stiffen. "You know we can't do that, your highness. The king doesn't wish to be disturbed."

I'm not about to argue. *Huh. Too bad for them.* I'm

fully prepared to take on the guards myself, but Alaric and Nate move in front of me.

Nate grins at them. "You heard the princess."

The demons prepare to fight to stop us, but Nate and Alaric have them down in a few moves, unconscious on the floor.

"Well damn, why didn't you find your mates sooner? They're hella handy," Shade comments, whistling in my head.

Nate beams at me and Shade like he's a puppy who needs to be told he's a good boy.

I run my hand along his chest as I stride past and burst into the king's bedchamber.

King Dalton stands shirtless in front of a floor length mirror. He has his back to me, and black marks track across his skin, twisting and winding like it's a growing entity, trying to consume him.

I gasp. "Dad," the word falls from my mouth before I can stop it. I never call him that, but the sight of his back has my stomach churning.

He turns as we stop in the middle of the room, and Mason closes the door behind us.

"Ah daughter," he says wearily like me barging into his bedchamber is the most natural thing. "If you're here I suppose that means you've taken care of Ivar?"

I struggle to find my words, and Dante takes pity on me.

"Ivar has been neutralized, your majesty," Dante says, bowing his head.

All of my mates stand awkwardly behind me, and I hadn't thought how this would be strange for them. Too late now.

"What the fuck is that?" I blurt, pointing at Dad's chest because Ivar is old news. Now that he's turned, I can see how the marks spread over his chest, resembling the way bolts of electricity split off, crackling out through the sky during a lightning storm. The black marks reach up his throat toward his chin, and my throat feels tight just staring at it.

Walking over to a chair, Dad grabs his shirt and shrugs it on, doing up the buttons. "You know what it is."

"What? Witch's Burn?" I say, remembering the explanation he'd given me before my time in the Perstalian ruins. Many demons died after the great war with the witches, due to the exposure to the chemical weapons, but now I'm struggling to believe it. "I don't remember any of the tomes saying anything about the Witch's Burn sickness creating those black marks. Tell me the truth. I felt the power from the vault the moment I entered the castle. This is because of that power, isn't it?"

A slow breath rushes from Dad's nose, and he braces his hands on the chair like it's an effort to keep himself standing. His gaze runs over my body, noting the golden tattoos, then he turns his attention to my mates, assessing each of them like he's weighing up their worth. His lips twitch. "I am glad you've bonded with your mates, daughter. Now you may yet survive what's to come. I can only hope your training was enough."

"Training?" I think of all the things Dad's put me through since I was young. The countless challenges where I had to fight for my survival. "You're not making any sense. Why won't you answer my questions? A witch possessed Ivar and killed him. The witches are coming for whatever you took from them and hid in that vault." I pause, licking my dry lips. "Ivar said it's a sentient being trapped in there."

Dad flinches.

"We need to know what we're up against," I tell him. "Or the witches are going to come for it. If it's what's making you sick, let me deal with it."

Sadness clouds Dad's eyes. "You don't understand," he says. "I—"

The doors slam open and General Josek bursts into the room. "Your highness," the demon shouts, but his fierce expression calms when he sees me, changing to one of disdain. "Forgive me," he says to the king. "When I saw the guards down, I thought you were in peril."

"Actually, that's a good point," I say, holding up a finger and whirling on Dad. "Didn't I say to organize more protection because there's talk of an assassination."

"Ivar's spy has been captured and dealt with."

Okay, well that's good news. "But two guards?" I barrel on. "What were you thinking?"

Dad sighs. "Why are you here, General Josek? Has there been news?"

The general's expression becomes grave. "Nothing from the other realms, but there's movement in the city, and there's been at least two witch sightings not far from the castle. Both of the bitches got away before our soldiers could get to them, but I don't think it will be long now."

Dad straightens, letting go of the chair, and pain flashes on his face, though he does his best to hide it. He speaks to the general, but his gaze remains fixed on me. "Summon the war council, general. Something tells me we're about to have company."

CHAPTER
TWENTY-SEVEN

~ Princess Blake ~

We enter the war room after Dad, and Nate whistles as he scans the ancient maps and weaponry attached to the walls. His gaze fixes on a massive mace with wicked spikes around the head of the weapon. *"Reckon that would do some damage."*

"That was my grandmother's favorite," I reply via our mental connection. *"Touch it, and Dad will likely cut your hand off."*

"Yeesh, I was only admirin'" Nate says.

In the center of the room, a dozen demon generals and advisors stand rigidly around a large circular table. They slam their fists to their chests and bow their heads as King Dalton passes, and Dad takes his place at the other end of the table. I stand beside him, and my mates follow my lead. With five mates, the area is crowded, and we're all practically standing shoulder-to-shoulder.

Dante smiles at General Drazar who stands beside him. "Do me a favor and move over a touch will you?"

General Drazar's nostrils flare, and his tail flicks showing his displeasure. "What is the Coilan clan leader doing here? Shouldn't he be busy with his clan?"

"Or off burying his cock in someone, you mean," General Kaldoth laughs from across the table.

"Well, I do appreciate your concern, general. Indeed, I would much rather be pleasuring my bonded mate, the *princess*," Dante replies smoothly.

The generals pale, and all eyes are glued to me and my mates.

"Enjoying yourself?" I say in my head to Dante.

His dark chuckle sounds in my mind. *"Quite so."*

Alaric moves to Dante's side, squaring up his shoulders and shoving General Drazar over to give himself more room.

The general glares at my assassin, but he shuffles a little to the right, accommodating him.

"You expect us to believe the princess has bonded with a Drozac assassin and four others?" General Kaldoth spits from across the table, his gaze sweeping over my mates. "One being an archangel prince?"

"It's unnatural," says another general.

I expect Dad to call for silence, or you know, threaten to cut someone's tongue out, but when he doesn't react, I realize he's waiting for me.

"Shall I behead one of the pig-headed generals, my mate?" Mason asks me seriously.

"No, I've got this." In a matter of seconds, I'm behind General Kaldoth with a blade pressed to the general's throat. I let the knife cut in so blood streams down the general's throat. It's nothing he won't heal from, but the general's tail lashes the air, his eyes widening with fear. He tries to fight against me, but while I'd been strong before I bonded, now his attempt to free himself is pitiful. He soon realizes this, and his eyes bulge as he stills in my hold.

When he's silent, I speak, projecting my voice out to the room. "Speak ill of my mates again, and you won't be leaving this room alive."

The demons around the table watch me warily, and the growl that comes from Nate makes the walls rattle, the ancient weapons nearly toppling from their hooks.

"Nice touch," I send to my shifter.

"Knew you'd like that, gorgeous."

I resist the urge to roll my eyes. Releasing General Kaldoth, I retake my position by Dad's side.

Amusement dances in the king's eyes as he addresses the demons. "My daughter has indeed found her fated mates and bonded with these *five.* It is an unconventional matching, but one that's a testament to Princess Blake's power. The six of them may very well be the only reason the demons survive the upcoming war. No further ill comments will be tolerated."

No one dares to speak, but I see the dissonance amongst the demons from their hard stares and stiff postures. They had a hard time accepting a half-blood as their princess, but accepting five mates from different realms? That's a whole different challenge entirely. Still, no one says anything, and when they remain silent, Dad turns his attention to the 3D model of Seral city and the surrounding land spread on the table. Made from wood and carved stone, the intricate models rise above the table showing the winding stone streets and tall structures. My eyes skim over the largest clan houses, and the royal castle surrounded by thick stone.

Dad leans forward, bracing his hands on the table. "And if that's settled, let us discuss the most pressing matter at hand. General Josek, will you do the honors?"

The ancient general steps up from Dad's other side. "There have been two witch sightings not far from the castle in the past day. One was spotted a few streets away near Darston Alley, and another not far from the castle gates. The witches appeared to be scouting the area, but the moment they were detected, they escaped through portals before our soldiers could reach them. That brings the total witch sightings in the past week to twelve."

Total witch sightings?

Dad nods his head, and General Josek steps back. The king's gaze goes to me, and I stare down the generals. "We also recently discovered Ivar of the Fallon Blade clan was working with the witches in secret. The witches had supplied the demon leader with weaponry in exchange for information." I pause before adding, "We have reason to believe the witches may attack the castle and soon."

The room erupts as demons all start talking at once, shouting and theorizing.

"Why now?" General Drazar questions. For centuries, the witches have been silent, presumed all dead. "Why would they attack now?"

Dad meets my gaze and subtly shakes his head. *Okay, no talking about the power. Got it.*

"I believe the witches have been building their forces and planning this for some time. They want our power, and with the talk of my retirement and a power shift for the demons, they've clearly seized the opportunity and decided to move forward," Dad answers simply.

The chatter continues until someone shouts. "Do we have any intel on the size of their forces? Will you call on the allied realms?"

Dad's lips thin. "There's no telling how large their forces are, but they've seen sizable numbers in

Toralyn. And as of yet, none of the realms have replied to my call for aid."

"Why would they come?" another general snarls. "After you drugged and slaughtered a number of their alphas. We'll be fighting this war alone."

Fury ignites in Dad's eyes like an inferno set ablaze, and his massive throwing star is flying through the air a second later. The blade thuds as it buries into the wall on the opposite side of the room, the metal dripping with blood. The general's eyes fill with fear, and he looks down at the deep gash on his right arm. The wound is already healing, but instantly, the room quietens.

"This is not a council to question my decisions," the king seethes, his voice lethal and unforgiving. "You're lucky I need you during this time of war. The witches are coming, and unless we band together, Seral will fall after all these years. We're not here to scrutinize past actions, and I will not tolerate anyone questioning my authority. I am your king, and you will watch your tongue or die by my hand. Now, let us discuss how we can defend this city. The witches are here for our power, and right now this castle holds the largest power source in Seral."

I hold my breath, wondering if Dad's about to divulge the secret of the vault.

"There's a vault far beneath the ground that holds...the horns of our ancestors," Dad continues.

The air fizzles from me as disappointment wars with my frustration.

Dad keeps speaking. "Such power, harvested by the witches, would be devastating, and based on the pattern of witch sightings, it's safe to surmise that their goal is to obtain the contents of the vault and seize the royal castle. There's still no clear answer as to why the witches have attacked the angel realm, but I can only guess it was a ploy to distract the other realms and keep them out of the war with the demons. In any case, let's discuss preparations."

CHAPTER

TWENTY-EIGHT

~ Nate ~

"**W**e *need to know what's in there*," Blake says, her words a frustrated hiss as she spars with Mason, her sword clanging as it collides with his.

After the war council, the generals disbanded, each leaving to organize their soldiers. King Dalton dismissed Blake along with the generals, and she took us to one of the training rooms near the barracks within the castle walls.

I study the weaponry in the space, intrigued by the sheer amount of forged steel that's been strapped to the walls. I have to admit, King Dalton is quite the decorator. A sword with demon horns carved into the hilt and a single crimson jewel, remains on the wall in front of me. Before I'd met the princess, takin' that sword off the king's hands would have been a top priority. Now, I have no desire to steal it. For my entire life it was as if I'd been chasin' something. Always trying to find the most precious artifacts, the most coveted possessions. Now, I wonder if what I'd been searchin' for all along wasn't a 'thing.' It had always been...*her*.

I turn as Blake ducks and spins, sweeping Mason's legs out from under him, and maneuvering quickly until the tip of her blade is at his throat.

Mason grins. "Well done, my mate."

"I was hardly even using my power," She huffs. "You let me have that one."

The centaur's smile grows. "Let's save our strength for the battle."

My mate frowns, returning her sword to the rack against the wall. "I hate sitting here idly. At least, the generals are busy getting their soldiers in line."

"No one knows when the witches will attack," Dante says smoothly. "It could be days or weeks, yet."

"Or never, if they know what's good for them," Alaric growls.

Blake lets out a heavy sigh. "I just don't understand why Dad won't tell us what's in the vault. It's what the witches want. He expects us to blindly defend something when we don't even know what's in there."

"Could you not take us to the vault yourself, my mate?" Mason asks.

She shakes her head. "The vault has extra security. Only the king has access."

A cold knot forms in my stomach. I think of when I'd first visited the castle and attended the royal ball. I was only there for one reason, and that was the treasure in the vault. I don't let myself second-guess the next words out of my mouth.

"Years ago, I heard a rumor in Kanzepes," I say, my gaze colliding with Blake's.

Her body tenses as she takes in the expression on my face.

"It came from an intoxicated shifter I'd spoken to during one of my trips to the Bunny Burrows."

"Ah geez, do you have to remind her that you loved that place? Not smooth dude. Not smooth," Shade chirps, and I flinch at the hard look in Blake's eyes.

"I stayed at the Bunny Burrows," I hastily explain. "Not as a patron, but—"

"Wait, are you about to tell us you were a worker bunny?" Shade squawks interrupting me.

I shoot the bird an annoyed look. "*Not* as a worker bunny, or uh, worker jaguar, but it was a place to stay. Secretive. When you have as many enemies as I do, finding secure lodging starts to get tricky."

"All right," my mate says.

"That shifter," I go on. "He talked about knowing the demon king had a treasure in his possession.

Something he took from the witches during the war. A power so great, the demon king himself is afraid to use it."

"Well, that makes sense. We already know it must be powerful," Shade comments. *"Blake could feel it."*

"Information you still could have told us earlier," Dante points out dryly. "So why are you telling us this now, shifter?"

Their gazes bore into me, heat pounding against my skin.

"You were going to steal it, weren't you?" Blake says, reading my face. "Let me guess, it's why you were here for the ball?"

When I don't answer, the others curse.

"Wow, Nine Lives, and I thought I was an asshole," Prince Callan comments.

"You *were* an asshole," Dante confirms.

My heart thuds as I watch my mate carefully.

"And I'm guessing there's more to it than that?" she asks.

"Only that the shifter said, whomever gets their hands on the weapon won't only control the witches. They could control all the realms as well." I rub the back of my neck, and I give her a sheepish smile. "I would have told you earlier, but I guess I was afraid of what you'd think."

Blake doesn't look surprised, but there is a thread of disappointment in her gaze.

"I may have come here for the treasure," I add quickly. "But it's not why I returned. Whatever is within that vault is nothing to me now. You're my mate, and all I care about. But I had to tell you. The implications of the power in that vault might be the reason the king is so reluctant to talk about it."

I'm not sure what I expect my mate to do. Curse me? Fight me? She simply stands there, her brow creased. "And why did you want it?"

"The treasure?"

"Yes."

I hesitate before admitting, "Things are bad in the beast realm. You think the demons have problems, but in Kanzepes only the strong survive." I pause. "Or the most cunning."

She stares at me. "...Or the ones who have help from someone strong?" she guesses.

I shrug. "Someone's gotta look out for the little guys. A powerful weapon could change things. Even if it was only used for those in the beast realm."

Prince Callan crosses his arms. "Are you telling us, all those items you stole..."

"I knew others who needed them more," I reply with a mischievous grin.

"*Oh, thank god,*" Shade sighs. "*For a minute there, I thought I was going to have to hate you, barbs be damned.*"

"Please stop talking about his barbs," my mate groans, but she grins at me, the light returning to her eyes.

Striding forward, she whacks me on the chest.

Pain throbs beneath my breastbone at the hit, but I don't care.

"You're seriously lucky I like you," she tells me.

"Only like?" I tease, my heart racing as relief near cripples me. My hands slide to her hips, and I swear, I would be content to hold her like this forever.

She bites her lip, hesitating. "Let's not get ahead of ourselves, shifter." Her expression grows severe. "Keep things like that from me again, and next time I'll have your balls."

My hands slide to her ass, and I pull her tighter against me. "Please don't, because pleasurin' you is now my mission in life."

She chuckles, though I see the uncertainty in her eyes. "The beast realm. You'll have to tell me more about it sometime. All I know is what I've been taught. I didn't realize it was that bad."

"Another time, gorgeous. Let's focus on our witch problem for now. And I swear, no more secrets." I brush my lips against hers.

"Good," she rasps, and she claims my lips, her hands winding around my neck.

My cock hardens as I long to satisfy my mate. *My queen. My treasure.*

She moans as I deepen the kiss, and the others crowd closer, drawn to us.

The scent of her arousal permeates the air, the sweet honey and cinnamon scent growing stronger. I groan, my mouth watering. Fuck I love tasting her. Touching her. Making her scream...

Squeezing her ass, I grind against her, letting her feel just how badly I want her, but a piercing, wailing sound blares through the training room, and she jerks back. Her gaze sharpens as she tips her head up to where a speaker is fastened to one corner of the room.

"The alarm," Shade squeaks, panicked.

My mate's eyes darken, her desire replaced with a hard resolve. "The witches are here."

CHAPTER

TWENTY-NINE

~ Princess Blake ~

Morning light shines on us as we race to the armory. *Of course, the witches would attack during daylight hours when the demons are ordinarily heading to their beds.* Majority of the demon army is already positioned beyond the castle gates, but off-duty soldiers stream from the barracks inside the walls, rushing past us as we walk into the armory.

Inside the building is chaos, and General Josek is already there, fully dressed for battle. Spittle flies from his mouth as he barks orders to the soldiers, and they strap on their armor, grabbing their weapons. "Hurry up you maggots! Do you think the witches are going to wait before they start murdering your families? The witches are killing demons as we speak!"

The ancient general walks over the moment he spies me, his armor rattling, and his tail flicking from side to side. I've never liked the psychotic demon who was always too quick to resort to torture, but he stood by Dad's side during the last great war with the witches, and it's a comfort knowing he'll be fighting with us now.

"Your highness," the general says, his face as hard as stone as he stops in front of me and my mates. "I've never hidden the fact that I've always disliked you."

My mates tense like they're ready to put the demon in his place.

"Fuck listenin' to that," Nate comments, but I hold up a hand, making sure they don't do anything.

General Josek doesn't look the least bit concerned by their presence, though he must know I could have him slaughtered for simply speaking against me.

"You don't say," is all I respond to the demon general.

"I've never agreed with the choices your father made regarding you, including that stupid competition of his," General Josek says. "But none of that matters now."

My brows slam down. "What other choices?"

His gaze hardens like granite. "The time I feared has come, princess, and I believe your father may be right." He clears his throat. "That despite it all, you and your mates may be the only ones who can save us in the end."

"Nice to know there's no pressure," Dante drawls sarcastically in my head, but I'm too busy staring at the general to respond. From as early as I can remember General Josek has treated me with disdain, only interacting with me when forced to. For him to be saying this sends a shiver down my spine.

A strange spark of emotion penetrates the general's hard eyes, and his hand twitches. For a startling moment, I think he's going to reach for me, but he doesn't.

He clears his throat again. "Your father has left something for you in the back room," he says abruptly, and he turns, marching away from me and barking orders to his soldiers again.

"What was that all about?" Prince Callan asks, but I just wave them forward, leading them to the back.

My steps falter as we enter the small, adjoining room, and I spy what's in the center of the space. Held up by metal stands are six sets of armor, all of them in different sizes. Intricate swirls and marks are etched into the metal, and the light from the sky window above streams onto the polished silver, making the air sparkle.

Nate whistles aloud, and a slender demon who's fussing with one of the sets peers up.

"Princess," the male says as we walk over, and I recognize him as Dad's master armorer, Master Mathyl. The demon has the gift of being able to manipulate different metals to a small degree. I'd once asked if I could have the master create a set for me, but Dad had turned me down, saying I needed to learn to fight without the armor before I earned my metal plates.

"Are these..." I trail off, still unable to overcome my shock.

The demon peers at me proudly. "Hand crafted for you and your mates, your highness. Your father had me start working on them the moment he returned from Toralyn. Admittedly, I had to obtain help from a few of my assistants to get it done in such a short timeframe, but I hope you are happy with them none-the-less.

Stepping forward, I run my fingers over the breastplate of the smallest set of armor, and the wings that are intricately carved there.

"I would have expected the royal crest," I say to Master Mathyl.

"Ah yes, your father requested those to be added. You'll have to take that up with him," the master armorer replies.

The demon smiles at the others, indicating which sets of armor belong to each of them. "Given the specifications provided by the king, and the fact I had no accurate measurements for your mates, my assistants and I had to combine our gifts to create armor that will respond to the wearer."

"Meanin'?" Nate asks.

"The armor will adjust to your body," Master Mathyl explains. "I also consulted an armorer from the beast realm to make this happen."

Nate's brows lift. "So you're saying if I shift…"

"Then your armor will change to accommodate you," Master Mathyl replies, his eyes twinkling.

"Whoa, that's awesome," Shade squawks.

The corner of Prince Callan's lips kick up. "Now we won't have to see your naked ass every time you turn back."

"Wait, now I'm not sure how I feel about this," Shade amends, cawing with laughter in my head.

I circle the armor, still finding it hard to believe that Dad had these made for us, but there's no time to waste. I thank the master and get the armor down, dressing hastily as the war alarm continues to blare in our ears. Once we're strapped, we load ourselves up with weapons. The only thing left is my hair, and Mason steps forward, his fingers working quickly to create a long braid.

When he's done, he presses a kiss to my head. "There, my mate. Now you are ready."

My lips quirk into a smile. "How did you learn how to do that?"

"I have a sister, remember?" he replies with a grin.

"Gee you guys look badass," Shade comments,

flapping her wings from where she's perched on the top of one of the stands.

My mates are looking at me like they want to tear my armor off, and my body heats. Alaric hefts an ax, and I stare at my mates, my heart fluttering.

"We'd better go," I say, shouts still sounding in the main room of the armory.

Grabbing me, Dante pulls me to him, and he kisses me deeply. When he steps back, Prince Callan takes his place, followed by Nate. My shifter's hand snakes around me as he devours my mouth. "Time to be the life of the party, gorgeous," he says when he pulls his lips from mine.

Alaric is next, and his kiss is rough and demanding. Like he's making a promise that if I die, he'll follow me to the shadow realm. When he breaks away, he grips under my chin and rubs his thumb over my lips. "This isn't our final battle, enchantress. You make sure you stay alive. No matter the cost."

I nod once, mostly because I know that's what he needs.

Mason is the last to kiss me, and when he reluctantly pulls away, I swallow thickly.

"You don't have to come," I tell my centaur. "I know what happened the last time you were on a battlefield with the witches. I don't want to put you through that."

"The only thing I regret from that battle was that I wasn't strong enough to help my brethren," he replies, sadness touching his eyes before he gives me a determined smile. "This time will be different, my mate."

I give him a soft smile. "Let's hope so." Stepping back, I rest my hand on the hilt of my sword. "Shade, you stay out of reach of the action," I tell my crow friend. "Keep an eye on the area and be our eyes from the sky."

"You've got it," she chirps back.

I think of the rules Dad has taught me since I was young. *Rule number three of being a demon royal: Never surrender.*

Letting out a long breath, I roll my shoulders. "All right. Let's go kill some witches."

My boots slam to the ground outside the castle gates, and I let Dante down as Mason and Prince Callan land beside me, folding their wings. Alaric jumps from Mason's back, and Nate roars in his large cat form, leaping from the top of the castle walls to land near us. The ground shudders, and demon soldiers move around us, giving us space.

Ranks of demon soldiers advance forward as General Josek screams at them, his war helmet already splattered with blood, and the scene ahead of us is a mess of demons and witches.

Chemical weapons fly through the air, landing on demons and incinerating them with acid. A demon lifts his hand, sending out a wave of power, and three witches fall to the ground, clawing at their eyes.

"There are four large portals a few hundred yards from the castle walls, and witches keep pouring from them," Shade reports from high up in the air. *"Gods, Blake, there are so many witches."*

"And inside the castle walls?" I say to her, knowing full well there wasn't any action happening there only moments ago.

"Nothing yet," she replies. *"But the soldiers there are ready if any witches breach the walls."*

"Okay, good." One of my other crows sends me a mental image of Hawke, the leader from the Bloodsky clan, fighting alongside his demons as witches advance on their clan house. I hadn't wanted to involve my birds, but I needed their eyes, and all around the city, witches seem to be popping out of portals, attacking the clan houses, and targeting the biggest clans. No doubt, the witches have figured out that we're weaker if we're divided.

I curse because I'd been counting on the demon soldiers from the different clans banding together.

The generals from the war council have organized their troops around the castle walls, with General Kaldoth remaining inside the walls with his soldiers. A few hundred yards in front of us, a massive green portal burns in the middle of the street, the flames sizzling and licking the air as witches continue to stream from it.

My mates and I join the battle, cutting through the witches without mercy. Nate rips the head off another witch before tossing her body to the side, and Alaric dodges a spell aimed at him, ducking low, and cutting the witch's legs out from under her.

Prince Callan sends out a burst of wind power, blowing a dozen witches back. They crash into the surrounding buildings, but a few of the witches on the ground form up, chanting as they form a magical barrier before them, keeping his power at bay.

A witch hurtles a glowing orb at General Josek, and I grab the shield of a fallen soldier and throw it, deflecting the weapon before it comes into contact with the general's face. The ancient general nods his head at me and spins, cutting down three more witches in front of him.

Six witches form a line, aiming their chemical weapons, and an incubus demon sends out a burst of power. The witches lower their arms, shaking their heads as they fight against the demon's influence, and they start chanting something which allows them to regain control of themselves. Tossing their chemical weapons, the orbs smash against the castle wall, the acid burning small holes in the stone.

An arrow soars past my head, and Mason rears on his hind legs, charging a witch heading straight for me. The tattoos on my arms flare to life, and my mates and I regroup, working as a team and taking down witches.

When the last witch around us has fallen, the

ground is littered with bodies, and the demons cheer, lifting their weapons into the air.

I don't let myself celebrate. There are multiple portals around the city, and I leave General Josek and the demons, and my mates and I move to the next closest portal on the eastern side of the castle.

Dad is there, and sweat streams from him as he spins, spearing a witch and lifting her into the air before tossing her away.

I land beside him and throw him the sword of a fallen demon.

"Good of you to join us, daughter," the king says, catching the sword and driving it into a witch who lets out a high-pitched scream before crumpling to the ground.

"You shouldn't be here!" I shout above the noise of the battle. "Retreat inside the castle walls, my king."

Dad ignores me, charging another group of witches who advance. I beat him to them, and my mates and I dispatch them before Dad has a chance to act. I frown. Aside from the chemical weapons and a few smaller spells, the witches don't perform much magic. "I thought they'd be stronger," I yell.

"They've been cut off from the power of their ancients," Dad answers. "It's why they've wanted demon power for so long." I think of all I learned about King Celzar taking from the witches, and the incident with his love, Yenna, which started this all. A thread of sadness winds through me, but I don't have time for weakness. Not now while the witches are at our door.

Nate jumps into a pile of witches, swiping out with his paws, and blood drips from his maw as he makes quick work of them.

A witch hurtles an orb at my head, and Alaric catches it, smashing it back into the witch's chest. She cries as the acid burns through her cloak, eating into her flesh, and she falls to her knees before slamming face first to the ground.

More witches advance, and Alaric growls, his body growing in size. His plates of armor adapt to match his changing form, and the male grows so large his head reaches higher than the castle walls. He lumbers forward, striding to the portal and grabbing the witches as they exit the circle of flames.

The scent of burning flesh and smoke stings my nose, and the witches continue to fall. Blood sprays into my eyes as I take a witch's head, and I turn to see a witch advancing on Prince Callan.

"Look out!" My cry comes too late as a blade drives between Prince Callan's wings. Snarling, I grab out two knives and send them flying through the air. The witch falls with them buried in her throat.

"I am fine, mate," Prince Callan says, pulling out the sword.

"You're not fine," I hiss, rushing over to him, but I stare in surprise as his wound knits together, his body already starting to heal as fast as a demon's would.

"Looks like our bond also came with a few other upgrades," Prince Callan says with a twist of his lips. "That would normally take me hours to heal from."

I hold out my hand, hauling him to his feet, and I turn to the witch who's on the ground, blood trickling from her mouth.

"You think this is it, don't you half-breed?" the witch mocks, spitting out blood. I recognize her instantly as the witch who'd spoken to me through Ivar.

"You," I growl. "What are you talking about?"

She smiles, and coughs, struggling for air. "This is only the beginning," she says, and the light drains from her eyes, her head falling to the side.

Cheers erupt around me, and I lift my gaze to find the demons are yelling and shouting triumphantly.

The witches around us are all down, and no more are coming through the portal. My mates come closer to me, grinning, but I can't shake the feeling of unease pressing on my chest. *This is only the beginning.* The witch's words echo in my mind, and when a dead demon twitches at my feet, my heart stutters.

"Oh crap, Blake. The fallen demons!" Shade shrieks in my head. *"They're rising! Oh, the bodies!"* Her fear explodes through my senses, and suddenly a barrage of images from my crows around the city come to

me, of dead demons climbing to their feet, black marks covering their skin.

Two dead demons grab my wings from behind, sending pain shooting up my spine.

Dad cuts through one of the demons, and I twist as I go for the other. Before I can lash out with my blade, the demon is beheaded, and Dante comes into view. "You good, princess?"

"I could be better," I say, giving him a grim smile. My eyes scan over the scene around us. All the fallen demons are rising and attacking the demon army, and a new wave of witches starts emerging from the portal again, dodging around Alaric's massive form and sending a volley of chemical weapons his way. He stumbles back, avoiding the acid, and with the fallen demons on the witches' side, now we're grossly outnumbered.

I turn to Dad. "What is happening? The marks on the fallen demons. They look just like yours."

The king's eyes are so dark they're like black pools of night. "Come with me, daughter," he snarls.

My mates bolt toward me as the witches and undead demons advance on us. Alaric bounds over from the portal, grabbing me, Dad, and my mates, and carrying us over the castle walls in his giant form before setting us down. The moment our feet are on the ground, his body starts to shrink until he's in his smaller form, and Nate changes back as well.

"We need to get to the vault!" King Dalton yells

as the demon soldiers still outside the gates scream, overwhelmed by the forces they're now facing.

"We can't leave them!" I shout back.

The front gate sizzles, neon goo burning through the thick steel as witches send a volley of chemical weapons at it.

"If we don't get to the vault, we're all done," Dad says, his eyes colder than I've ever seen them.

"Don't need to fuckin' tell me again," Nate says to the king, and lifting me over his shoulder he races toward the castle. My mates and the king follow him, and General Kaldoth shouts after us.

Guilt twists in my gut, but I don't fight Nate.

"No, wait! Shade is out there!" I shout, panicked as the front doors of the castle close behind us, and Prince Callan and Mason bar the door.

"She's a tough bird," Alaric replies. "She'll be fine as long as she stays out of their reach."

"Shade," I send to her, but there's something blocking our connection. *Dammit.*

My heart pounds as I whirl toward Dad. *"Tell* us what's in the vault."

CHAPTER

THIRTY

~ Princess Blake ~

Dad growls, shaking his horned head as the black mark that's on his neck climbs up over his cheek. It almost reaches his eye before it stops. Sweat beads on the king's brow, and he breathes heavily as he leans forward, bracing his hands on his knees.

I take a step toward him. "Dad." The word slips from my lips, but he forces himself to stand straight, pain etched into his features.

"I'm fine," he croaks. "Follow me." He heads toward the corridor, and we move with him.

At the end of each corridor, the king presses his hand to a panel on his right, and a reinforced steel door slides out from the side of the wall, sealing shut.

"It won't keep them out forever," Dad mumbles, his eyes drawn down like he's struggling to keep them open.

He takes a step forward and stumbles. I'm there in an instant, draping one of his arms over my shoulder, and I'm surprised when Alaric takes Dad's other arm.

The assassin meets my gaze as I gape at him.

"We take care of...family," Alaric says, his voice low, and my heart aches.

Not too long ago, the assassin had been focused on his plan to make the king suffer, and now... My eyes get blurry with tears, but I simply nod and blink them away.

We help Dad along the corridor until we reach a tall black gargoyle made from black marble. Reaching forward, I touch the left clawed pinkie toe of the sculpture, and a secret door opens behind the statue.

Alaric moves behind me as we enter the narrow dark space, and I walk with Dad down a flight of steps, my mates on our heels. The air cools, growing damp as we follow the curving stairs.

When we reach the landing, Dad is quick to open the first vault door. Striding inside, we move past the first rows of demon horns that are secured in glass cases along the wall.

"Now, that's a trophy room," Nate muses as his

brows rise. "Looks like we had you all wrong, gorgeous. It's not heads or fingers that you wanted, it was horns."

I shoot an unimpressed look his way. "Don't get any ideas. These aren't trophies, they're..." My words trail off as I realize why I felt unsettled the moment we entered the vault.

"They're what, my mate?" Mason prompts.

Alaric has Dad's other arm again, and I let go of the king, my wings snapping out as I launch into the air, looking at one case with horns and then another. I press my hands to the glass, cursing.

"What's wrong?" Prince Callan asks, flying up beside me before following me to the floor.

Dad's gaze meets mine, and it's obvious he's picked up on the same thing I have.

"A demon's power is stored in their horns." I gesture to my hornless head. "Except me, I guess. In any case, after the witches started robbing our graves and killing our kind to get the power from our horns all those years ago, a new law was made. When a demon died a true death, their horns were to be brought to the castle and stored here to decrease the chances that a witch or any other being could easily gain access to that power."

Nate's brow furrows. "Makes sense."

"Yes," I say, peering around at the glass cases that stretch high into the air. "Except normally even when they're encased, the horns usually give off a buzzing energy. Now there's..."

"Nothing," King Dalton finishes for me.

"You think the witches have found a way to take the power already?" Alaric says, his gray eyes hard.

"Or something else has," I reply grimly. My gaze goes to the black door on the other end of the room, and I pull out my sword. Following my lead, my mates do the same.

Dad stares at the black door, his eyes distant and haunted. No, not just haunted. He looks...scared. For my entire life, Dad has been a consistent pillar of strength, and to see that look in his eyes sends a chill skittering down my spine. *Never show weakness.* It's the first rule Dad ever taught me. A mantra I've told myself countless times. A saying that became my whole personality. My whole damn life, really. And now...everything feels as though it's unraveling.

"We need to know what's in there," I tell him softly, my hand resting on Dad's broad shoulder. "Otherwise, we'll be going in blind."

The king's chest falls as he exhales a long, resigned breath. He mirrors my gesture, placing his hand on my other shoulder and giving it a gentle squeeze.

The room grows deathly silent, though my mates watch us carefully.

Dad turns his attention back to the door. "I always knew this moment would come, daughter, but I had hoped it would be under different circumstances. Even when the witches attacked, I had hoped we could defeat them before we faced this together. But it seems they're stronger than I anticipated, and this will all play out differently."

He moves from me and Alaric, and steps toward the black door. The moment he's within reach, a red laser light scans his face, and he whispers something under his breath. Two beeps sound, and a bland feminine voice comes from the panel beside the door. "Access granted." There's a popping sound, and a rush of stale air reaches us as the door unlocks and slides open.

My mates and I follow Dad as he walks into the room, and I assess the simple dome space we're standing in. An empty cushioned royal bed is positioned in the center of the room, and golden runes have been painted everywhere. The symbols repeat over and over, on the walls and on the floor, and some of the runes are smeared with blood.

"Witch runes," Alaric growls under his breath.

The temperature is a few degrees colder than in the main vault area, and I feel the tension emanating from my mates.

"Serafine? You're awake?" Dad lets out a surprised, choked whisper, and I snap my head up as the sound of that name crackles through me, familiarity making my head spin. *Serafine. Serafine.* I struggle to place it.

And then I see her. I inhale sharply.

Across the room, a female stands preternaturally still as she faces the wall. A long gossamer white gown hangs from her thin form, and her black hair is so long it trails to the floor. *It wasn't some beast or another kind of sentient being.*

At the sound of Dad's voice, she turns to face us, and my heart catches in my throat. *Sera. Serafine.* Dad rarely used her name, always calling her 'his love,' but a faint memory from when I was five surfaces to the forefront of my mind.

"Mom?" The whispered word is a foreign, strangled, surprised noise as it leaves my mouth. The female's black eyes flick to me, and I take in the curves of her face. A face that looks so similar to my own. Black runes cover her body, like tattoos carved into her skin, matching the symbols on the walls.

"How?" Dad says, and his voice cracks, sadness embedded into the word.

The female jerks her head to the side, the movement unnatural, and her gaze remains locked on me. "She woke us," the female says, and when she speaks, it's as if a thousand voices are talking at once. "She called to us."

I take a small step back. "What?"

"When you were with the deceiver," those voices answer, the word 'deceiver' echoing back at me.

"What deceiver?"

The female's head jerks again, and this time her attention goes to Dante.

My heart crashes against my ribcage. "Kai?" I rasp.

Dante's tail flicks, and he tightens his hold on his sword.

"Your magic called to us. It pulled us from that unwelcome slumber, and we felt him close to you—the demon in disguise. Serafine has never agreed with our plans, but she didn't protest when we suggested we protect you from him."

I struggle to breathe, thinking of when I'd been with the demon I'd thought was Kai. Only, it was really Dante in disguise thanks to Luna's illusion power. It was the first time my golden tattoos had appeared, and I'd thought I'd killed Kai.

"I didn't call for you. And h-he's not a deceiver," I stammer.

"The demon was lying to you," the voices reply matter-of-factly. "Just like that crow of yours. You are young and foolish. That bird is no more a crow than you are an angel. The only thing that has saved her, is the fact that we sensed no ill intent from your crow. Whatever she is, the curse placed on her is complex, and most of her memories have been locked away."

"What?" I feel sick, like my whole world is imploding. Like the world is burning around me, and I'm stuck somewhere unable to get out. "You mean, Shade? What curse?"

"Who placed it on her, we cannot say," the voices reply.

"What do you mean Blake isn't an angel?" Prince Callan says, his voice ice cold as he questions another part of what she's just revealed.

"Oh, you have kept it all from her, haven't you,

our mate?" The voices say, the female peering at where Dad has braced himself against the empty bed. More black marks cover his face.

"I'm not your mate," Dad growls, his voice laced with pain.

The female smiles. "Still in denial, are you demon king? Serafine belongs to us now, and by being bonded to her, so do you."

"Who are you?" I whisper, my heart feeling like it's being shredded. "What do you mean you have my mother?"

"Stay away from her," Dad rumbles. "You won't be able to trust a word from its mouth."

"Oh, we are your mother now. Daughter. Or sister. Whatever you wish to name us."

My stomach churns. "Sister?"

The female's lips curve. "Oh yes, you have no angel blood my darling. Only witch and demon blood in those pretty little veins of yours."

"What? Dad?" I turn my gaze to King Dalton, but the moment I see the look in his eyes, I know it's true. I stumble back a step, but Prince Callan is there, holding me.

A witch. I'm a witch? My head pounds, pain striking up within me. "No."

There's a flicker in the female's black eyes. A flash of gold before it's gone again. "Yes, child," the thousand voices reply at once. "Your entire existence has been a lie. Your father made you believe you were something you simply were not."

"But—" I struggle to breathe. "But why?"

Dad's gaze is pained. "Because your parents failed to accept what had already come to pass."

"What *are* you?" Alaric growls at the female.

"You may call us Reselle," the voices reply.

"The war with the witches had waged for centuries, and one day your mother, Serafine, came to Seral disguised as an angel," Dad blurts, speaking before Reselle can. "She intended to spy on me. To find out my secrets and report to her sisters."

My brows lower. "Her...sisters?"

"Yes. Your mother was... *is* a witch. But while she was here, she discovered we were fated mates," Dad goes on. "Eventually, she told me the truth about her, and we worked together to devise a way to try and stop the war and bring about peace. She explained about a winged race, whose leader had taken one of their anchors and stolen their power. About how another anchor had died since then and there was only one anchor left. That the witches were desperate, and their land was dying."

"Serafine betrayed the witches," Reselle snarls, her voice lashing out from across the room.

"She never betrayed them," King Dalton growls. "The witches betrayed themselves."

I stare at Dad sadly. "But your plan didn't work?"

The king's expression falls. "No. When she returned to her kind. To get them to see reason, they turned on her, calling her a traitor. We were bonded by then, and instead of taking her word, they believed the bond between us was fabricated by the demons. That I had corrupted her with my power, but that they could use it against us. The last anchor lay injured from the war, and they used her." Dad's eyes darken. "They used my Serafine. Conducted experiments on her, and manipulated the power of our bond to turn her into an artificial anchor, the first of her kind. But whatever they had done, she became not only an anchor able to access the magic of ancient past witches, but she also connected with a dark entity that had incredible power."

He glowers at Reselle. "By the time I fought my way to her, it was too late. Reselle was already fighting to take control of her mind."

My eyes burn, pain a searing lump in my throat. "Mom," I whisper, imagining the horrors she had endured.

"That dark entity was an unknown force. A creature from the far reaches of the shadow realm. A creature even the queen of the shadow realm herself would never dare touch. And through Serafine, it would have given the witches unimaginable dark magic," Dad continues.

"When that last big battle started, I thought it was over," Dad says solemnly. "But the witches hadn't realized one thing—she was pregnant with you."

My heart stutters, and I can't stop the tears that fall from my eyes. Prince Callan's hand squeezes my shoulder.

"She says you spoke to her. And just when I thought the witches would win the war, Serafine managed to fight back against the power within her. Using unbelievable strength, she cut off the witches' magic entirely, rendering them almost helpless. And with the allied realms fighting with us, it was enough for the demons to overwhelm the sisters and seize control."

Reselle sneers at us from across the room.

"She..." Dad's voice cracks. "She held onto that control for as long as she could, even after the war. Until you were born. And the moment you were in my arms, she begged me to lock her away. With the magic of the runes, we could keep Reselle contained in this room." His hand slips to his belt, and he pulls out a familiar-looking dagger. The one from the shadow realm. The one he'd had me steal from the shadow queen, Queen Krosia, some time ago. His hand trembles as he holds the enchanted blade, tears blurring his eyes. I think of how I'd had to use it to save my mates during our last test in the Perstalian ruins. Dad has always been testing me, always preparing me. And now I know why... I can't imagine what he must have done to get the blade back. If the creature, Reselle, is from the shadow realm, it stands to reason that this blade might also work on her.

Reselle smiles cruelly as she lets Dad finish his story.

"Why not kill her?" Alaric asks, and though his

words make me flinch, it's the same question I've been wondering.

His gaze slides to me. "Serafine was pregnant with Blake when they turned her into an anchor. The pair are tied, and when Serafine dies, it's likely that Blake will turn into the new witch anchor. We also worried that if we tried to kill Serafine, Reselle might be strong enough to jump through that connection into Blake, especially if she was still a child. But now...we have another option." He glances subtly at the blade when he says the last part.

Reselle's smile never leaves her face. "All thoughts Serafine still believes are true. But you both remain so naïve. You still don't even have a way to kill me, and now here I am. Your plan to keep us sleeping was admirable, but your daughter saw to it that we rose."

Dad's gaze flicks to the blade before meeting mine, and he subtly shakes his head. At first, I don't understand what he's trying to tell me, but then realization sets in. *"Reselle doesn't know about the power of the shadow blade Dad has,"* I tell my mates. *"She doesn't realize it's able to kill her."* I think of the marks over Dad's skin, wondering if it's all because she's connected to Serafine and in turn, Reselle. When the witches experimented on Mom, had Dad felt it through the bond? Has he been sharing her pain all these years?

I swallow hard, my throat dry. "Mom never left us," I say to Dad, more tears slipping down my face.

A tear drops down Dad's cheek. "All she wanted was to see you live, daughter. Your mother still had her disguise when you were conceived, and when you were born with wings we decided to pretend you were an angel. But now that you're ready. Now that you know the truth, I have to do my part." His grip tightens on the enchanted blade, and he darts forward, moving so fast it's a blur.

"No!" I start toward Dad, but I'm too slow.

Reselle lashes out with her power, a thick black coil streaming from her fingers, and she sends Dad flying back against the wall. His bones crack, and he falls hard to the floor. Gold flashes in Reselle's eyes but it's gone again in an instant.

Reselle's lips stretch wide, and laughter spills from her. The sound is a dark cackle that fills the small space, thousands of voices making the walls vibrate. "Even now we can feel Serafine's hope. Even as she claws her way through the darkness in her mind, trying to get to you."

"Let her go!" I snarl, anger searing me from the inside out.

"It's too late for that little half-breed," Reselle replies, still cackling, and the floor starts to rumble. "I'll be sure to send your mother your regards, but now, it's time to finish what the witches started. I'm nothing if not loyal to my subjects."

She sends a blast of power toward me, but Prince Callan grabs me and spins, and the black power flies past us, tearing a hole in the wall.

"The runes must have been created to keep Reselle in, but with the door open, the seal was broken," Alaric growls. "And with that hole, there's no trapping her."

I'm not sure how, but I start hearing the chanting in my head then. Even without seeing outside, I know what's happening.

"The witches are creating an enchantment," I say to the others. "They must know she's free and they're helping to bring the building down."

Nate curses. "The witches wanted us to come here."

The walls start to crumble around us, and Reselle smiles. "Goodbye, mate," she says to King Dalton.

A rock from the ceiling falls toward where Dad lays crumpled, but I'm there before it hits him, and I toss it to the side.

Still cackling the remaining walls start to fall, and Reselle sends an immense burst of power above her head. Her black magic rips a hole through the layers of dirt above us, tearing through the floors of the castle until we can see the sky high above us.

With a hideous shriek, Reselle smiles and shoots into the air, flying through the pathway she's created.

"We need to go!" Mason shouts, shifting form in an instant. Alaric and Dante climb onto his back, and Prince Callan flares out his wings grabbing hold of Nate. I tuck the enchanted blade into my belt and lift Dad, stretching out my wings. As everything starts crashing down around us, I launch from the ground, bursting up past the layers of dirt and through the castle. My mates are close behind me, and as debris rains around us, we dodge and swerve, avoiding the crumbling stone until we burst from the top of the castle and exit out into open air.

Reselle hovers in the sky high above us, tendrils of her black magic reaching into the clouds above and stretching in all directions. The clouds darken, turning the color of black smoke, and the ground trembles, houses falling around Seral city. We land on the roof of the castle, the building shaking beneath our feet.

THIRTY-ONE

~ Princess Blake ~

"**B**lake! *What the hell is going on?*" Shade's shrill squawk sounds in my ears as she flaps toward me. "*The demons down there have gone crazy, the witches are chanting like their lives depend on it, and I'm almost too scared to ask about your new floating friend who just busted out of the castle, quite literally.*"

"*Shade?*" I say.

"*Yes,*" she replies, flapping her wings and staring at me with beady eyes. "*Please tell me this isn't as bad as it looks.*"

I stare at my friend, and Reselle's words repeat in my head: *That bird is no more a crow than you are an angel.* Reselle claimed that she felt no ill intent from

Shade, but my mind is a mess of questions. The biggest one being: if Shade isn't a crow, then what— or who—is she? But I don't have time to try and figure it out now.

"That's my mother," I explain quickly, pointing to Reselle. *"It's a long story, but basically, she's been corrupted by some dark creature from the Shadow realm. Oh and I'm half witch, not angel, and if Mom dies, I might become the new and last remaining witch anchor."*

Shade is silent for a moment as she stares at me. *"Yep, I knew I shouldn't have asked."*

"If you can get me close to her, I can use the blade," Dad croaks, climbing from my arms to stand on his own. His body is mending quickly, though the black marks are still visible along his skin.

"How are you healing so fast?" Demons are the quickest at healing out of the different species in the realms, but Dad has been so weak lately, and he went down hard.

"Now that she's out of the vault, Reselle is growing stronger, and somehow, her magic is sustaining me through the bond," he answers.

"Okay, I'm still lost. Who the hell is Reselle?" Shade asks.

"The dark entity that has taken control of my mom's mind," I reply.

"Okay, this situation is messed up, but Blake, if that is your mom, can't you try and get through to her?"

"I don't know." The building shakes more

violently, and Mason's hand shoots out, steadying me. Around the castle gates, the witches have formed large circles, and they sway from side-to-side chanting at the top of their lungs. The demons are all chanting along as well.

"Are they all dead?" I ask Shade.

"No, when you went inside the castle, whatever magic reanimated the dead demon soldiers, it also possessed everyone else."

"It's Reselle," Dad says. "She's connected everyone to her. If we can stop her, it should sever the link she has with them."

Light flickers in the corner of my eye, and I turn my head as a large portal with silver fire opens up a couple of streets away. There's a war cry and archangel soldiers flow from the gateway. Prince Callan's brother, King Andal, is with them, along with a few legions of beast shifters that had been fighting in Toralyn, and a sizeable number of waterfolk from Norso. The only realm without soldiers in attendance is Rostof, realm of the giants.

They must have defeated the witches in Toralyn and come here.

"No, brother!" Prince Callan shouts, but we're too far away for King Andal to hear us.

The soldiers of the allied realms surge forward, attacking the outer circles of witches, and above us, Reselle lets out a high-pitched wail. Streams of black magic shoot through the air, striking the soldiers and we watch in horror as they all fall as one, climbing back to their feet with unnatural, jerky movements. Slowly, they form up, creating more circles and chanting with the others.

Bile rises up my throat, but I swallow it down.

Prince Callan's eyes burn with fury as he stares at his brother.

"We'll find a way to free them," I tell him.

"We have to get to Reselle, daughter. It's the only way," Dad tells me.

Reselle's laughter crackles through the sky, and I look up as she floats down, landing on the roof of the castle with us. "Are you all still alive? Serafine is putting up quite the fight in my head, but I'm not sure why." She opens her arms, taking a few steps on the shaking roof. "Look around you, Seral is ours. It belongs to the witches now, as do all of your friends."

Dad coughs and wipes at the black ooze which drips from his nose. He moves closer to me, and I know he's after the enchanted blade.

"We have to get her back," I tell him. "There must be a way."

Dad gives me a hard look. "Who Serafine was, who your *mother* was, no longer exists. This is the only way."

"*Blake!*" Shade's fearful cry sounds in my head, and I turn as Reselle sends a blast of power toward her. The dark magic slams into Shade, colliding with her small form. I go to run to her, but Nate grabs me, holding me back. I'm about to break free from his hold when Shade's body changes. My crow grows in size, her feathers shedding, replaced with smooth skin. Where she had wings, arms form, and I gape as my crow turns into a woman. A *human.*

Reselle pulls her power back, still cackling as the strange human lifts her head, and blinks at me. "Blake?" She says the words aloud, and her voice is soft. Startled, the girl lifts her hand, her fingertips brushing against her lips. "What? I-I, I'm not a crow." She peers down at her naked body, all smooth skin without a feather in sight. Her wide eyes are round with fright, and she stares at me.

"See, I told you this one was a deceiver as well," Reselle says to me. "Now you can see for yourself, child. I've managed to manipulate the curse so you can see her with your own eyes. The world may not be as you perceived it, but in time, I trust you will adjust to your new reality."

"W-what is she talking about?" the human girl says, unsteady on her feet. "Where are my wings?"

I open my mouth. I'm not sure what I plan to say, but Reselle speaks first. "But now that you've seen her, there's no point letting her live." Reselle sends out a burst of power and it slams into Shade, throwing her from the roof.

A scream tears from her throat, and I rush after her, my wings snapping out. Before I can move, Reselle smiles gleefully, sending power out that blocks my path.

"*Don't worry,*" Prince Callan says in my head, and

I notice his hand is out, power flowing from his palm. *"I caught her. She's on a balcony."*

"Thank you," I send to him, and I finally realize I don't have a choice. Spinning, I pull out the enchanted blade in one smooth motion and dart toward Reselle, but before I can drive the blade into her chest, Reselle smashes into me, and we fly through the air crashing into one of the castle towers. Stone rains around us, streams of magic flying past my head as we fight. I dodge and duck Reselle's power, lashing out with the jeweled blade, but I can't get close enough. Her power smacks into my chest, and I'm thrown back. My body skids as I crash back to the roof where Dad is. Prince Callan and Mason are in the air, their blades out as they go for Reselle, but she easily deflects their blows, cackling the entire time.

Reselle sets back on the roof, and she smiles. "I knew being Serafine's daughter that you would be lively, but I hadn't quite expected this much excitement," she says, her dark eyes sparkling.

The blade! Where's the blade? I stare around me as Reselle advances, and Alaric attacks, lunging at her. A roar leaves Nate's mouth as he shifts, his armor growing and shifting to accommodate his large form. The roof shudders at his weight, and when Alaric gets thrown back, Nate is there, his fanged mouth aiming for her head.

Reselle flicks her hand, and power blows Nate back. The giant cat slips over the side of the roof and my heart catches in my throat, but Nate's roar comes from not far away. He bounds back onto the roof, his claws digging in to the black tiles.

Around us, the chanting is so loud the voices pound in my ears.

"Ah, it's such a shame child," Reselle says, cracking her neck. "I had thought that I could teach you, and we would rule this land together. But if you're this insistent, I guess I'll just have to kill you."

Before I can dodge it, her power slams into me again, only this time, she's hit me with something different. Her power reaches into me, clawed talons tearing at my mind. A guttural scream rips from my throat as pain lances into me, my own power trying to fight against her. Trying, and failing... My mates shout out as well, the five of them frozen in place as her power keeps them from me.

Reselle gives me a wicked grin. "I guess I should have known. There's only space for one witch anchor now."

"No, Mom!" I wheeze.

There's a flash of gold in Reselle's eyes, and she snarls, clawing at her own head with her fingers. "Not now, witch!" Reselle growls, and the gold disappears, turning to black again.

My energy drains, and those claws scrabble more furiously against the barrier in my mind. Flapping sounds in my ears, and I look up, only to see the sky fill with birds. There are thousands of them, and they dive as they come toward us. I never sent out a call, but the birds race to my aid, filling my mind with all different images. Images of the sunset, of demons, of the city, of the dark clouds, of the birds perched on the roof with their friends. Their images are like a barrage of strength fortifying my mind against Reselle's influence.

When they near the roof, I yell, *"Don't!"* Screaming the command to them, desperate to make sure they stay away from Reselle. They reluctantly listen, but they circle the roof, forming a large blur of color as they fly around and around, creating a windy circle that tugs at my braid. The black of my crows mixing with the colors of the other birds in Seral.

Reselle's laughter grows louder. "Oh, can't you see child? Controlling birds is nothing. Not when you can control the minds of everyone else."

"Princess," Dante calls out, and I turn my head as the tinge of blue starts to disappear from his midnight blue eyes, Reselle's power burrowing into his mind.

No. No. Dammit!

I grit my teeth, trying to walk forward and break free from Reselle's power that's still blasting into me. But I'm too weak. She might not have my mind, but my body hardly moves an inch, and I feel drained.

"I see now," Dad's voice sounds across the rooftop, and my gaze slides to where he stands, hidden from Reselle behind a thick stone chimney.

The demon king holds the jeweled enchanted blade in his grip, but instead of staring at Reselle, he has the blade poised at his heart.

"What are you doing?" I shout at him, panic flooding me.

"I thought I'd have to drive this into her, but we're connected, even more so now that our bond has been corrupted. Reselle will feel the power of this blade, just as I will."

"No, you can't!" I rasp.

"Know daughter, that I couldn't be more prouder of the ruler you will be, and I am sure your mother feels the same. Remember, never surrender." And he pulls his hand back, pushing the blade into his heart.

"Noooo!" The scream that tears from me is unnatural, coming from a place so deep within me even my birds feel it, cawing like they feel my pain.

Reselle cries out as well, her dark eyes snapping wide. "What?" Her mouth gapes open as she grabs at her chest, looking for a weapon, though it's not there.

I can hardly speak, but I rush over to Dad, catching him before he falls. I hold him up, staring at the demon king as his breathing becomes more labored, and my mates form up around us protectively.

Tears well in my eyes. Dad pushed me to my limits, always putting me through strange challenges, but I see them for what they were now.

Trials to make me stronger. In his weird, messed up way, Dad has always cared.

The demon grabs the handle of the shadow blade and wrenches the weapon from his chest. "Here," he rasps, holding the dagger out to me. "While she's distracted."

Ignoring the weapon, I press my hand to the wound, trying to stop the blood leaking from his chest.

"It's not healing," I say, panicked. "Why isn't it healing?"

"Take it, Blake," Dad says insistently, still holding the blade. "This is the only thing that will rid us of Reselle. The realms need you now."

Tears streak down my cheeks. "But I need *you*."

His lips form a soft smile, his gaze going to my mates before returning to me. "No, daughter. All that you need will be here even after I'm gone."

"Blake," Dante's voice is gentle as he comes up behind me. "The king is right. This might be our only chance."

"We need to take the bitch down," Alaric growls.

"Let me do it, my mate," Mason says.

I shake my head. "No," I say, hardly able to get the word out. "It has to be me."

"Go, daughter," Dad says, and I blink back my tears as I finally take the blade from his hand. Dad leans against the chimney, and I release him, stepping out to face Reselle. My mates move with me, though they give me space.

Reselle is still grabbing at her chest, screaming, and I don't give myself a moment longer to think about what I'm going to do. I launch forward while her gaze is diverted, and I plunge the shadow blade into her heart.

Reselle jerks her head to the side, and her eyes darken as she grabs hold of me, but just when I think she's about to toss me from the roof, her eyes shoot wide with surprise. Her gaze flicks to where Mason is now holding Dad up, and then she peers at me before looking down at the blade. "Damn you," she says, those thousand voices crying out at once, and her head snaps back as she opens her mouth and lets out a pained wail that goes on and on, the air whipping around us.

"Blake!" Dante shouts, grabbing my arm, but I stay where I am.

Slowly, the sound grows weaker, and when it cuts off all together, my mom's head falls forward and she drops to her knees. I fall with her.

The air grows still, and my mates move close around us.

"Careful, gorgeous," Nate warns, but I already know Reselle is gone. I can feel the release of her power over the land.

Mom's chest rises and falls with ragged breaths, the blade still buried in her chest, but when she slowly opens her eyes they're a bright gold, the color so similar to that of my own eyes.

"My Blake, my daughter," she rasps, her hand

reaching up to my face, and the moment the words leave her lips, tears spill from my eyes.

Dad stumbles toward us with Mason's help, and he drops to his knees beside us, a harsh rattle sounding in his chest when he breathes.

"You did so well with her," Serafine says, smiling warmly as one of her hands goes to Dad, and he leans into her, his head resting against hers. "She's incredible."

I struggle to breathe, my chest feeling as though it's capsizing. Pain spreads from my heart like I'm the one who was stabbed with the blade.

"I've missed you, Sera," Dad says to Serafine, a tear tracking down his cheek as he presses a soft kiss to her lips. When he pulls back, she lifts her hand, brushing the tear away.

"You were always with me," she tells him. "And we did it. She's ready."

"No. No, No," I repeat the word over and over. "I'm not ready. I will *never* be ready."

"I loved you from the moment I knew you existed," Serafine tells me. *Mom.* Not Serafine. *Mom.* "Be kind to the witches. I have hope that without Reselle's influence, and with you as the new anchor, they will find a way to heal. They will need you now more than ever. And they will need a home. A real one. The witches were afraid, and without Reselle's influence, and with a renewed connection to their ancestors, I know they can be good again." She swallows, her throat bobbing. "Promise me."

I can hardly see through my tears. "I will. I promise."

"Don't be afraid of the power, my daughter," Mom tells me. "It will become a part of you. Normally there have been three anchors so they could balance each other and share the load of the power. You must rely on your mates. I can tell how much they love you."

Dad reaches for me, his hand cupping my cheek, and I lean into it. "Do not mourn us, daughter. I have waited for this moment. Finally, I can be with my mate. Rule well with your bonded, and one day, we will see you again in the shadow realm."

I nod, sniffling. "I'll find you." I don't know if that's possible. When we suffer a true death, our souls are said to roam the far reaches of the shadow realm. But I'll find a way. Someday. When my time comes.

My mates crowd around me, crouching down. Dante wraps his hand across my shoulders, and Prince Callan grabs my hand, pressing it to his lips as he kisses it.

Mom smiles at my mates before looking back at me, those golden eyes full of warmth, even as the bright color starts to fade. "We love you, daughter," Mom whispers. "More than anything." Her last words are barely audible from her lips, and Mom's eyes close as she holds onto dad, their foreheads touching as the blade remains buried in her chest, and the pair of them fall silent.

The world stills, and my birds stop flying. Hundreds of them land on the roof, settling around us, bowing their heads like they're paying their respects to the demon queen and his mate. Like they're there to support me. Others take to the sky, twirling and spinning as the dark clouds clear, streams of light washing over us.

I can't stop the tears that keep coming, but my mates are there. Holding me. Not speaking, but just... holding me, each of them with a hand on me. Like they're trying to remind me that I'm not alone.

The tattoos on my body glow brighter, until it feels as though the swirling marks are on fire. Instead of burning me, power flows into my body, golden sparks coming from Mom and landing on my skin. Like a part of her is coming to me.

I gasp, and a wind whips up around me and my mates, teasing our hair and pulling at our clothes. None of my mates let go of me. We all heard what Mom said. I squeeze my eyes shut and images flicker behind my eyelids, pictures appearing in my mind. Of a time when the witches lived in their land. Of the three anchors sending out the power to their sisters. The joy on their faces. The peace between their people. A peace Celzar shattered a long time ago. Yenna's face appears in my mind, and she smiles at me. Beside her, appears my Mom, and even Dad is there. I don't know where they are. Is that the shadow realm? All I know is that somehow, I'm connected to them. The power of the witch ancients implodes inside me, and there's no darkness. Golden streams of light dance in my vision, and I feel the connections to generations of witches. The pressure builds, light shining from my tattoos.

"*Let us in, our mate,*" Mason says in my head.

"*This burden wasn't meant for you alone,*" Alaric growls.

Prince Callan grabs my hand. "*We're here with you.*"

"*We need you, gorgeous. Let us help,*" Nate adds.

"*We've got you, princess,*" Dante says softly in my head. "*Always.*"

Lastly, Mom's words repeat in my mind: *Don't be afraid of the power, my daughter.* With another gasping breath, I let go, and some of the power overflows into my mates, golden light filling them as well. They all brace against the strain of it, but not once do they let go of me. Not once. The power pulses within us, and then it flows down, connecting with the minds of the witches across Seral.

The witches drop their weapons, and they start sobbing, the whispered words of loved ones on each of their lips as they see glimpses of family members lost long ago. For just a moment, in their minds they see the ones they've been so desperate to connect with, and while the images fade, the memories remain and so does the power.

Freed from Reselle's influence, the demons, archangels, water monsters, and shifters watch on in surprise as a different kind of magic flows from the witches' fingers. Beautiful flowers burst up from the ground, the sky fills with light, and the sisters laugh.

My mates and I pull back, smiling as we stare at one another, and I send out a burst of power, letting our soldiers see what the witches see. Glimpses of the witches' home that was destroyed when their magic was taken, just like Perstalia was destroyed. Of a time when the witches were content to keep to themselves.

"Blake!" Shade's voice comes to me from across the roof, and I rush over, peering down the side of the building. The human girl is a few feet up from a balcony, and she grips the edge of the building, her muscles straining as she tries to climb the rest of the way.

"Are you crazy?" I yell, reaching down and grabbing her hands. "What are you doing?"

She peers up at me with determined violet eyes. "I'm coming to kick some ass and save you. What do you think?"

"It's already over," I tell her, my lips twitching.

I pull her onto the roof, and she falls on top of me.

"What? I missed it?" Shade says. "I *always* miss the good bits."

Reaching around, I hug her tight, laughter bursting from me. She might not be the crow I knew her as, but I can feel this is my friend. My Shade.

My laughter soon turns to tears, and Shade holds me tighter. Her gaze finds my parents, and she lets out a pained noise. "Oh, Blake," she says, her fingers stroking through my hair as she holds me tight. "I'm so sorry."

We stay like that for a little while until my tears dry. "Uh Shade, your nipples are poking me."

Grinning, she wipes her own tears and peers down at her naked human body. "Yeah, weird huh?"

"You didn't know?" I ask her, even though that's what Reselle said. That Shade knows nothing about the curse placed on her.

She shakes her head. "No one is more startled than me. I have to say, though," she inspects her body, twisting from side-to-side. Not bad, right?"

I laugh. "Not bad at all. Though, we are going to have to figure you out."

She gives me a cheesy grin, though I see the inkling of fear and uncertainty in her eyes. "I'd like that," she says softly, and her smile lifts again. "Hey, who knows. Maybe I have mates out there, after all."

"Of course, one of your first thoughts would be about finding your mates," I chuckle.

"Hey, you can't have all the fun," she teases.

Prince Callan flicks his hand, and a moment later, a curtain flies over to us, carried by a gust of wind. My archangel smiles at me, and I grab the fabric from the air. "Here," I tell Shade, helping to wrap it around her like a toga. I've just finished tying a knot at her shoulder when cheering sounds from the ground.

My mates, Shade, and I step to the edge of the

roof, peering down at where the soldiers and witches are on the ground. Golden light still flies around me and my mates, and my heart squeezes as everyone falls to their knees before us. Witches. Demons. Even the archangels, beast shifters, and water monsters. They all show their respect, laying their weapons on the ground before them, and clenching their fists, slamming it to their chests.

I spot General Josek surrounded by demons, and I could be imagining it from this distance, but when he stares at me, all I feel is approval. And all I can think is that I finally feel...at home.

~ Queen Blake ~

One week later...

Dante adjusts the demon crown on my head, tucking a loose strand of hair behind my ear before he kisses me on the forehead and steps back. After the battle was over, things moved quickly. A grand funeral was held for my parents where they were buried in a brand-new gravesite with a large statue erected to honor them. Gone are the days of having to protect the demons' horns, and it feels right to have Dad's power flowing back into the land like it had in ancient times before the witches arrived.

The coronation followed that, and because

they're my bonded mates, Alaric, Dante, Callan, Mason, and Nate became kings of the demon realm, standing by my side.

They wait for me now, dressed in neatly pressed black suits with black ties, their matching golden crowns positioned on their heads.

"I don't get why we have to dress up for this," I grumble, smoothing my hands down the long black lace dress that hugs my body.

"Because you're a queen now," Shade says, bouncing over to me and adjusting one of the small violet roses that has been woven into my dark hair. She has fussed over me for the past two hours, and I'm seriously starting to grow suspicious of my friend. "You need to act the part," she adds. "Everyone will expect it."

Nate clears his throat. "Yeah. What she said."

I narrow my eyes at them. Now that I think of it. They've *all* been acting suspicious.

Mason comes forward, his hand sliding down the curve of my back. "This is a big day for my kind," he tells me. "It can't hurt to look good. Let Shade have her fun."

Shade beams at me, and while I'm still adjusting to her new face, it still feels like I've known her forever. "Okay, fine, but don't expect me to dress like this every day. I'm a *demon* queen, remember? No one is going to expect me to wear dresses all the time."

"Gotcha," Shade says.

She works on some final touches, and we exit the Coilan Clan house heading into the garden. With the castle under repair, we've been staying here for the past few days, and I don't mind one bit. The scent of apricots reaches my nose, and I move toward the closest fruit tree, reaching for an apricot.

Shade quickly diverts me. "Uh, no you don't, girl. I didn't just spend the last two hours getting you ready, only for you to get sticky apricot juice all over yourself. I don't care how tasty those suckers are."

"You know, I think I liked it better when you were a crow," I point out, dryly. "At least then, there was less chance of you dictating my eating habits."

"You'll thank me later," she says, patting my hand sympathetically.

We stop in the middle of the garden, and Mason reaches his hand out, the portal ring shining on his finger. A moment later, flames flicker to life, a portal opening up before us.

"Ready, my mate?" Mason asks, holding out his hand.

I bite my lip. "Are we sure about this? What if it doesn't work?"

"It'll work," Alaric growls.

Letting out a deep breath, I take Mason's hand, and we step into the portal.

When we emerge on the other side, sunlight washes over us, and we stride out, moving between piles of rubble that had once been the great city of Perstalia. We walk forward to where there's a massive gathering up ahead. The Perstalians are all here from The Haven, along with the witches, a huge portion of the demons, including General Josek, and delegations from Norso, Kanzepes, and Toralyn.

A row of Pecos birds line the path, their rainbow scales glittering in the light, and they bow their heads to me and my mates as we pass them. One of the birds nudges me with his beak, and I recognize Pask. *"Good to see you, little fleshling. Yes, yes, it is a very good day,"* he tells me.

"It's good to see you, too," I reply.

As I walk further, everyone notices us, and my heart pounds as thousands of gazes turn in our direction.

We stop in a space in the middle of the gathering that has clearly been left for us. Queen Nerelia tips her head to me, and not far from her, King Andal grins at his brother.

I take a deep breath and address the crowd. "Thank you all for coming," I say, spreading my arms wide. "For too long, this land has been empty. It's time we restore what was lost." The witches move closer, gathering behind me.

A witch named, Cadence, bows low as she approaches. "The sisters are ready, our queen."

"Good." Another breath hisses past my lips, and Shade gives me a reassuring smile. My mates come up behind me, and I close my eyes, letting the power flow out.

The magic of the witch ancients mixes with my

demon power, golden light streaming from us and spearing into the ground.

The witches begin chanting, swaying from side to side, adding more power into the land. The Perstalian's stamp their hooves, sending out their power as well, and the beast shifters howl and growl as the ground rumbles.

My magic strains as it struggles to push back all the damage that has come to the land of Perstalia. A large group of archangels with the power over air work to clear the sky, and beings from the land of Norso drop down, planting their hands on the ground as they summon water to the surface.

The earth shifts, and there's a deafening rumbling sound in my ears as the land reshapes itself before our eyes. A large river forms to the right of our group, and grass and bushes cover the land. Trees grow tall around us, some of them bursting with fruit.

The barren charred earth fills with life. Flowers sprout from the ground around us, and the air sweetens, no longer thick with a metallic acrid, scent.

When the ground stops shaking, and I know our work is done, I cut off the flow of magic, and Alaric is there, letting me sag against him.

The Pecos birds take flight, soaring into the clear skies, and the Perstalians join them, launching into the air.

When I look over, tears are streaming from

Queen Nerelia's eyes. She comes over and clasps my hands, a soft smile on her face. "I never thought such a thing could happen." Tears blur my own eyes, and I wrap my arms around her in a hug. She laughs in my hold, and then she moves back, hugging Mason while happy tears continue to stream down her cheeks.

Mason kisses his sister's hair. "Told you I'd be back," he tells her, and it makes her laugh harder.

The witches step away again as everyone celebrates, and Queen Nerelia wipes away her tears and walks over to them. Cadence and the witches bow their heads.

"Much has happened over the years," Cadence says, her voice sorrowful.

Her words make me reflect on all the pain that has been caused. I think of my mother, and the witches who used her to turn her into an anchor. Anger simmers inside me, but I let it pass. Those witches are long dead, just as Celzar is. Even the witch who had possessed Ivar's body was slain during the battle, and now all that's left are the broken souls who wish to heal without the influence of darkness.

Queen Nerelia steps closer to Cadence, and she reaches out, using a delicate finger to lift the witch's chin. "That it has. We have all suffered at the hands of others. Let this be our new beginning."

Cadence's gaze softens, but sadness fills her blue

eyes. "The witch realm is but ash. Not even magic could bring it back."

Since the battle, the witches have been mostly keeping to themselves in a camp on the outskirts of Seral City, but that's not a real home. "Then we'll give you somewhere else that you can make your own," I say. "There's a large area to the far west of Seral City. The land is uninhabited, and there's nothing there except for a few creatures who appear to be more than welcoming. Let's investigate and see if it's somewhere suited to the witches. Somewhere you can create your own new beginning." With my mates and I as the new witch anchors, we need to be in the same realm as the witches, but I'm fully aware we need to also be mindful of the demons having their own space.

Hope flickers in Cadence's eyes. "That would be...much appreciated," she says, dipping her head and stepping back.

Screeching sounds in my ears, and I look up, smiling as the Pecos birds continue to soar overhead.

"You'll still have your work cut out for you in rebuilding this place," I say to Queen Nerelia. "But we'll help out where we can."

"The land is fertile again, and the air is clean," she tells me, beaming. "It's all we need. It will be a joy creating something new."

She clasps my hands again before releasing me, and I spend the next while talking to the leaders and thanking them for making an appearance. When we've finished speaking with King Andal, Shade shepherds me away from him.

"Yes, yes, it's amazing you could come, and Queen Blake is amazing. We know," Shade says.

I bite my tongue to keep in my laughter as Shade steers me away from the archangel king. "What happened to 'looking the part'? I don't think being rude is a great look."

She waves her hand dismissively. "He understands."

"Understands what? Because you've been acting so weird."

"Just...trust me," Shade replies.

Frowning, I peer around. I'd been so distracted talking to King Andal that I hadn't noticed my mates were missing.

"Where are you guys?" I send through our mental connection, but there's no reply.

I whirl on Shade. "What is going on right now?"

Grinning, she simply keeps her lips zipped and steers me back to Queen Nerelia. A portal with green fire remains open beside her, and she winks at me, smiling, before Shade yanks me into the gateway.

THIRTY-THREE

~ Queen Blake ~

Shade and I exit the portal and step out into the forest near Seral City, and the familiar smells of the demon realm wash over me. Trees surround me on both sides, and violet and gold flowers are scattered across the ground, creating a clear path.

Up ahead, my mates stand where the flowers end. They're near the edge of a cliff, and they grin at my shocked expression. Violet flowers are pinned to their breast pockets, and to one side, one of Dad's oldest advisors stands patiently, his robes flapping in the breeze. Birds fill the trees, perched on the branches and on the ground, and they caw as they watch me with beady eyes.

"I—" My words fail me, and two crows fly toward me, dropping a beautiful bouquet of wildflowers. I catch it, and the birds fly off, joining the others.

Behind me, Queen Nerelia steps through the portal followed by King Andal.

"You knew about this?" I ask.

King Andal grins, and Queen Nerelia gives me a soft smile. "I can keep the portal open if you want a quick escape?"

Shade scowls at her. "Don't be silly." She links her arm in mine and starts walking me down the flower path.

Music starts up from somewhere in the trees, and I turn my head, surprised to find a trio of angels there singing a sweet tune. Luna and Noah stand not far from them, grinning stupidly at me.

My heart races, and I face forward, blinking dumbly at my guys.

"*I told you I didn't need this,*" I tell my mates. Marriage is a tradition we learned from the humans. For demons, bonding means more, but some still choose to get married and celebrate their union. My mates had asked me about whether it was something I wanted, but honestly, I'd never thought about it much. We had so many other things to worry about.

"*If you don't wish to go through with it, we don't have to,*" Prince Callan tells me.

"We only wish to make you happy, gorgeous," Nate adds.

"It was Shade's idea," Alaric chimes in.

I hold my friend tighter. "Thank you," I whisper to her.

Her eyes sparkle. "I might not remember hardly anything from my past, but I do remember the juiciest bits from a few romance novels. I always thought I must have remembered them from the human who kept me when I was a crow, but now I'm starting to think I must have been a book whore in another life. In any case, the wedding was always one of my favorite parts."

Sadness fills me when I stare at my friend. "Whatever had happened to you, whoever cursed you…I'm going to make them hurt."

She smiles. "Stop. Today isn't about me." She gestures with her head to the five males who are patiently waiting. "Enjoy this. I swear, I might have suggested it, but they've been acting like nervous boys since."

I laugh, my heart thudding ridiculously loud in my ears as we walk the rest of the way to them. When we're an arms-length from the guys, Shade lets go of my arm and stands to the side where Queen Nerelia and King Andal are now watching.

The guys all step up, and they stare at me with such emotion in their eyes that my throat bobs. Dante takes one hand while Nate holds the other, and the demon advisor steps forward.

"Skip to the last part," Nate tells him, winking at me.

"Yes, your highness," the advisor says. He clears his throat exaggeratedly. "Do you Queen Blake of Seral, the demon realm, take these five males to be your lawfully wedded husbands for the remainder of your days?"

I hesitate for only a second. Only a second to let me believe this is happening. To remind me that these are my mates, and we're bound for eternity. "Yes," I say, the word almost a whisper.

The advisor nods, and he turns to my guys. "And do you, the kings of Seral, Dante, Alaric, Nate, Callan, and Mason, take Queen Blake to be your lawfully wedded wife for the remainder of your days?"

"Fuck, you know we do," Nate shouts, and I laugh.

The others glare at the shifter.

"What? I just said what we were all thinkin'."

Mason shakes his head, and my mates all smile at me. "We do," the others say in unison, and Dante pulls me into his arms, planting a kiss on my lips. I breathe in his scent as he holds me possessively.

"All right, demon, my turn," Nate says, and Dante grins as he releases me, and Nate takes his place.

The shifter growls as he claims my mouth, and his lips are warm against mine.

Callan is next, and he holds me tight, pressing me right up against him. "You, Blake, are the air I breathe," he tells me, and the wind picks up around us, teasing my hair. When the archangel kisses me, his golden wings flare out, mimicking my black wings, and I melt against him.

It feels like an eternity until Callan releases me, and Mason steps close. "For so long, I was lost in the dark, my mate. You've brought light into my life, and I'll never let that light go out," he tells me. His kiss is gentle. A promise. Of the life we're going to have.

And then there's Alaric. The assassin is adjusting his tie awkwardly when I peer his way. Immediately, he drops his hands and steps toward me.

"Are you all right there?" I ask him.

He grabs me, his hands possessively going around my back. "I have you, Enchantress. I'm much more than all right." His kiss is punishing in the best way, and my heart is so full I wonder if it might burst.

Cheering and clapping sounds around us. The birds in the trees caw, some of them taking flight, circling overhead, and the music starts up again.

Dante takes my hand, holding me to him, and we stare out over the cliff to where Seral City is spread before us.

Shade steps up as well, along with Queen Nerelia, and King Andal. Luna and Noah move up on my other side.

"Did you ever think we'd be here?" I ask Shade as my fingers interlace with Dante's.

"What? Standing at your wedding in human

form? Or are you talking about the fact that the Perstalians are rebuilding their lives, and the witches have a future for the first time in a long while?"

My lips curve up.

"No," Shade says. "I don't think any of us imagined this."

"But we couldn't hope for more," Dante says, his tail wrapping around my leg, as my other mates press in closer.

"Here's to a brighter future," Queen Nerelia adds softly.

"As long as I have you all," I say, squeezing Shade's arm. "We'll face whatever comes our way."

A flicker of uncertainty touches Shade's eyes, but she smiles. "Bring it on."

WANT MORE?

Thank you so much for reading Tortured Royals! If you'd like to read an exclusive bonus scene that shows Blake in the future with her mates, sign up to Mia's newsletter via her website: **www.miahartson.com/gameofpsychossignup**

It's still surreal to me that I'm living my dream and publishing books that I love. Thank you for coming on this journey with me! If you enjoyed Blake's story, it would mean the world to me if you could leave a review on Amazon, Bookbub, or Goodreads. Reviews help indies so much, and I would be so grateful! xx

ALSO BY MIA HARTSON

HER CURSED PROTECTORS

Shadow Shifter (prequel)

The Blood of Monsters

The Cries of Monsters

The Curse of Monsters

The Wars of Monsters

Blurb for The Blood of Monsters:

Every decade, twelve young women from my island are gifted to the monsters.

This year, I'm in the line-up. But unlike the others, I want to be taken. Correction, I *need* to be taken—for my sister's sake. It's my fault she was chosen during the last offering, and I have to find out if she's alive.

I thought I was ready, but nothing could have prepared me for the four monsters who claim me. A vampire, wolf shifter, demon, and siren. They're terrifying, powerful, and infuriatingly arrogant...and now these alphas are fixated on me.

Turns out, finding my sister won't be as easy as I'd hoped. Now that I'm in their world, the monsters think I'll become one of them. I'm in their monster trials, and they're going to play with me until I turn.

These assholes think it'll be easy to break me, but they

picked the wrong girl. Because I'm already a monster. They just don't know it yet.

*This is a fun reverse harem fantasy novel for audiences aged 18 years and older. **Language warning **Slow burn romance **Multiple POV*

Acknowledgments

First and foremost, I want to thank my readers! You are the reason I'm living my dream of being an author, and I'm so grateful to every single one of you who has picked up my books and continued to read until the end of the series. My main goal when I sit down to write is to give readers an escape for a while, and I hope I've managed to do that.

To my ARC readers, including the team from the Books and Bitches Book Club. You guys rock. For an indie author, getting reviews is critical to the success of a book, and I'm so thankful you took the time to read my books and post reviews. You are amazing and so appreciated!

To my husband and alpha reader, Chris. Thank you for listening to me ramble about this story, for reading all the drafts, and for giving me feedback that always helps to make the story better. I love you. To my girls for always supporting me and believing in Mommy and her books. I might dream up these different worlds, but real life will always be better because of you. I love you so much.

To my beta readers, Clare and Jessica. Thank you for helping to pick out those annoying typos, and for being my cheerleaders for these books.

About the Author

Mia Hartson is a fantasy and paranormal romance author who enjoys writing about strong heroines who aren't afraid to get their hands dirty (or bloody), and hunky, misunderstood heroes who would do anything to protect their girl.

Mia lives in Adelaide with her husband, two girls, and her fur baby. When she's not writing, she's devouring another book, binging the latest fantasy TV series, or going on adventures with her family.

For more information about Mia Hartson, her books, and upcoming releases visit:

Website: www.miahartson.com
Newsletter:
www.miahartson.com/gameofpsychossignup
Facebook page:
www.facebook.com/AuthorMiaHartson
Facebook reader group (Mia's Mischievious Monsters):
www.facebook.com/groups/miahartsonsmischie-vousmonsters

www.ingramcontent.com/pod-product-compliance
Lightning Source LLC
Chambersburg PA
CBHW050854210726
48290CB00004B/1230